Times Like This

ONE MILFORD PUBLISHING

ISBN: 978-1-6847-0118-6 (sc)
ISBN: 978-1-6847-0117-9 (e)

Lulu Publishing Services rev. date: 04/12/2019

Contents

Photograph by Ryan Gosselin

✳✳✳

Walk in her Genes

"Her work has caused rumbles in the science community," the reporter continued, "Miss. Arnold, how do you respond to the claims of the potential your discovery has made for the future of science and medication?"

"I say there is still a lot to learn. Any contribution to the field is greatly appreciated, whether you are just a donor or even a researcher yourself, we must work together to solve humanity's greatest problems, and genetics is a growing frontier that can answer many of our greatest questions. And what I say to those who praise my work, I say you can make it happen too..."

Chloe turned off the television. It was right about time for a Thursday morning meeting, Chloe, reading over her notes and thinking she spotted a valuable trend her colleagues would not see, was struggling to figure out how to communicate the new knowledge. Already deep into the semester, Chloe continually found it harder and harder to mentally prepare herself to commune with her research team.

Light barely crept through the blinds, competing with a lone, scented candle on her workspace that inadequately lit her dorm leaving facetious shadows that meagerly resembled the confidence she once had during her undergraduate program in France. She fumbled around, attempting to remember what she needed. Awe damn! What time is it? Chloe thought, remembering her watch. Reaching for the shelf, her eyes stop at a title, *Encyclopedia of Human Sociological Structure, Volume 3: History's Greatest Civilizations*, I need to finish that before I start reading about modern social structure, Chloe thought to herself. Chloe looked over to her desk one more time as she tied her hair up. Shoving materials into her bag, Chloe's wrist cramped from sorting through dozens of papers. Nonetheless, she wrapped herself into a thick coat and made her way to the meeting.

Chloe walked the whole way to the building where the biology department held seminars, attended lectures, and conducted research. Upon entering this gem of American architecture, thoughts flooded Chloe's head. Thoughts about the lectures she attended there, how her experiences were similar and different to the expectations she built on her first visit that warm summer day, split Chloe. The hollow halls, once cooled by the summer breezes rushing through open doors, echoed with squeaks created by the melting snow between her shoes and the marble staircase. The second floor, less grand than the first, acted as a taproot to the many branches of lecture space. When lecture hall 22-B was on Chloe's right, she made her way inside. No surprise to her, none of her classmates were there. The peace of an empty seminar room soothed her like a calm before the storm. It was a small effort, but anything to avoid the unnecessary attention she was used to. Eventually, her peers filed in, followed by a professor.

Chloe felt awkward whenever she was around Professor Sophoman. Chloe never understood his stance on formality. He wore a suit the first day of class. Every other day he wore plaid or athletic clothing, regardless of the belly it revealed. A thick mustache shielded his new students from his upper lip. She noted the way he stood: very proud, despite average height. He looked as if he would love to prove someone wrong like he was a knight in shining armor, believing too greatly in his role of defending the stance of scientific advancement. After debriefing them on the semantics of their program, he began that first day with a basic lesson on evolutionary and genetic influences on cellular systems to set them in the direction of their research.

"Can any of you remember how the HindIII sequence effects the intracellular communication system?" Sophoman asked rhetorically.

Chloe raised her hand.

Segwaying into his next thought, "This affects the production of luciferase..." Professor Sophoman continued on, marinating the students with his piece of mind.

As the months carried on, his behavior continued, as Chloe came to understand his spiny exterior.

"Lets go gentlemen, you know the drill." Professor Sophoman began the discussion with his shoulders presented proud and his chest pointed toward the class.

Chloe followed as the men at the table gathered their notes, their findings, every bit of new information from the past week and spread them out along the table.

"Can we all agree sample D-22 should probably be cut out of our data?"

"There is nothing there."

Nods slowly emerged followed by grumbles of agreeance. Chloe became uneasy.

"I don't actually think that sample we cultured is bad. We can use Chi-squared to figure that there may be an external factor causing the fungus to act this way," Chloe suggested with voice frailty. Some of her colleagues leaned forward and avoided eye contact. One man was pinching the front of his face.

Sensing high stress levels in the room and attempting to break the awkwardness, Chloe asked, "What is wrong?"

"Obviously there is som..." An angered peer muffled himself. Now cool and collected, he responded with condescendence, "the external factor is poor culturing, we can't analyze every sample for confounding investigation, this is our faults, we don't need *you* proving that mathematically."

Professor Sophoman interrupted, "Okay... okay, Alex. We are trying to work together here, Chloe is doing *her* best."

Alex rolled back in his chair and the dozen and a half students around him responded as if it were them being attacked. Avoiding eye contact, he couldn't help himself but to smile. As for the rest of the crowd, they looked to their professor in this moment as if he were the last person to teach them anything. Chloe knew she was onto something, but couldn't help feeling anything but embarrassment.

Rightful against him as it may, how dare he speak like that! Chloe thought, looking at her professor with contempt, she fought her urge to speak on others' issues. Frustrated as they were, they all patiently awaited his next direction.

When the conversation came around to her again, she became selective in letting them know about everything she has done so far. She knew they wouldn't be open to the level of work required to answer a question they think has no answer if it comes out of her mouth. Besides, for every allegation against them, she had at least ten questions to answer. Chloe knew a forfeit was the only way to temper their relationship, but it has already so far gone. The conflict within consumed her.

"What have *you* found this week?"

Chloe choked on her words.

"Chloe?"

Unsure of herself, it was now impossible for her to fall back on the previous confidence of her findings, "I haven't noticed anything particularly noticeable," Chloe started, shaken. "These cells are very good at accepting our gene edits. My samples reassure our previous conclusions that I can replicate the DNA we put into it…"

A soft voice broke her concentration, "At least she knows something she might be good for…"

Some harsh chuckles broke out, dividing the room.

Ignoring this, Chloe tried to lie about her data, "I think Brandon's point falls short where… where…"

Predictable as a robot, someone from the crowd spoke sharply, "Where does Brandon's point fall? That he can do more, faster?"

Laughter and rebuttal broke out simultaneously as the room became more chaotic. Professor Sophoman was too busy, poorly concealing his own take on the matter to control the class properly. When it finally became easier for Chloe to think, Professor Sophoman regained ability to take back control when his boredom of the situation peaked, "Okay, it is clear everyone is eager to get back to their studies. I think we have discussed as much as would suffice for one normal week. If you need me this anytime before next Thursday, you know how you can find me. Dismissed."

✳✳✳

After the meeting, Chloe realized how hungry she was while wanting to find time to relax. Let me see if Olivia or Candice is nearby, she thought to herself. A text was sent and she made her way to the dining hall, hoping to loosen up.

When she arrived, she recognized the overwhelming nature of her visits to relieve her hunger. Chloe looked across the warm room for something to catch her appetite. A man stood next to her, towering, with several pieces of pizza and a grilled ham sandwich. Chloe helped herself to some caesar salad as she wondered to herself how do they eat so much? An old lady with a warm smile behind the salad bar reached unnecessarily to help her grab it.

"No. That is okay. I got it." Chloe said, trying to diffuse the awkwardness.

"Oh okay dear, what a pretty accent you have!"

Sheepish, Chloe felt guilted into responding, "Oh, why thank you…" She trailed off as she walked away, avoiding unwanted conversation. She grabbed a few other food items and the respective condiments before finding a place to sit.

Chloe observed the free space that was the dining hall eating area. She did not immediately recognize anyone there so she found an empty table and waited for her friends.

As she waited, she spotted another girl with odd colored hair. This was a style she saw often here in the US. The first time she came across something like it, she thought the style was very odd. Her initial thoughts of 'what will everyone think of her,' months later, turned into, 'they create a false standard I can't live up to, why do they do this to themselves, and to me? There is no way our evolution should allow this!'

Upon Chloe's integrity grappling with her fear of societal expectations, Olivia interrupted her corrupted thought, "Hey girl!" She chimed in with that same bubbly tone she normally did. When the girls first met, her soft attitude was very comforting for Chloe, despite their language barrier.

"Oh my! Look at those tortures!" Chloe had once said in excitement the first week upon meeting the girls.

Of course, by the direction of her attention, they knew what she meant, "You mean the turtles," Candice replied with an awkward humor.

"Ah, yes, turtles," Chloe laughingly replied.

Unintentionally interrupting Candice's next thought, Olivia asked, "Do you know what torture means?"

"Um, yes, I know what that means… it's like, actually no, I have no idea," Chloe laughed at herself.

As the weeks progressed, and the semester's challenges grew tougher, Chloe learned to appreciate friends like Olivia and Candice. Although, the playful teasing has switched material, by now, her English was good enough for her to truly think she made no mistakes.

Regardless, Chloe was happy to see her, "Hi, how are you?"

"Clearly better than you," she replied lightly, "you *still* put mayo in your ketchup; you weirdo. You live in America now sweetie, you shouldn't create these foreign mixtures!"

"What can I say, I am a weirdo!" They let out a humbling and reassuring laugh together.

When Chloe was full and had forgotten her classmates as much as she could, she knew it was time to leave. Upon reaching her dorm, Chloe grabbed a notebook and a pen. She began mapping out everything she would need to develop her research. She felt disgusted, misleading her peers, as vile as they were, she knew it can not be in vein. In quickly realizing she would be wasting her time in her room, she headed to the research facility. All that walking gave her time to think. All that thinking make her nervous. As thoughts consumed her mind, she wondered how long it would take-would she have the time-maybe she wasn't as smart as them after all. Finally, upon arrival she can distract herself to ease the anxiety.

With a full stomach and eager to start again, Chloe started her regular routine: tie hair, throw on apron, strap on goggles and gloves, gather materials. Working on the samples, she knew she could do much more than what her peers wanted to work on. Even knowing it was just more than a statistics calculation that led to her questioning, she needed to make more to take a closer look. Using a stem culture, she replicated her samples dozens of times.

"Hey Chloe." Richard walked into the lab.

Chloe, thinking frantically about an explanation, forgot how to respond properly.

"Richard, hello," an awkward pause got her back on her feet, "How are you?"

"Very well, thank you," he began gathering materials and then looking through hers. Suspicious of her labels, "what are you doing?" he questioned.

She quickly attempted to diffuse the situation, "I am looking for trends in gamete production of waste samples to figure out if a certain cross link prevents the growth patterns we want."

"Why would you do that?" as if the preposition was absurd, "there are so many possibilities to sift through, it seems like a massive waste of time. It would be much more efficient to look for favorable traits in the samples we already selected to continue researching," he looked over at the papers sprawled out across the workstation. "This is so much data. How long have you been here?"

"Since lunch," said Chloe, unrevealing.

"When was that exactly?" questioned Richard, without retort.

"Since 11:30." Chloe revealed, scrambling to collect everything from sight. And putting her samples with the rest of her personal lab equipment, "So, anyway, I'll see you later Rich."

The clashing of her shoes stopped when she realized something that would put her in a predicament. Remembering she forgot to hide the sample that was in the microscope, Chloe thought, if she went back to hide it, he would think something was up, wouldn't he? But if she didn't, he would see it. Her only hope was that he wouldn't know what he saw in the microscope. She turned back to peek her head into the lab just in case. No Richard. Hiding the last piece and swiftly exiting, she made her way to her Thursday chemistry lecture.

*** ***

Oh man, I hope this can be relatively painless, Chloe thought to herself. She crept passed the sentinels of campus freedom, hoping not to stir attention. Vulgar signs glorifying female power, bashing newly elected politicians, and highlighting pressing social matters served equally as inspiration, intimidation, and comic relief depending on the level headed viewer.

"Hi there… Where are you going?" a voice rattled Chloe's attention. Chloe fired back in defense, "Class."

"Oh, it's a shame you didn't come to help us." the protester exclaimed disappointment.

A mere pointing of her finger was followed by weak explanation, "I need to go to that building."

"Go to class then," the protestor rolled her eyes.

The condescendence of her tone was hard for Chloe to let go. What does she even know about me, Chloe questioned. The basis of human confidence was frail when faced with such out casting behavior. Unaccepted my women, unaccepted by men, who would accept her? Remaining undeterred, Chloe recognized the most important thing was to preserve her strength in order to force herself to accomplish the goals she'd previously set.

The cold air was making it hard enough to keep her eyes from welling with tears. The bombardment of guilt from more radical women made it hard for Chloe to think straight. Dismantled by the commotion, she realized the only thing she could do was keep her head down. Sacrificing embarrassment, she walked as fast as she could through the people in her way.

Chloe, finally able to work her way past the square, to the lecture hall, in which they blocked the pathway, was overwhelmed by what had just happened; too overwhelmed to pay attention to her feet. "Ah, la vache!" she squeezed out while catching herself above the fifth step. I hope nobody saw that, she thought, looking around. Confused by the whole matter, she thought to herself, wow, it had been a while since hearing herself speak French.

***

D-22-0.33ii she read off the label. This one would be dyed blue, Chloe thought, peering into the microscope. The chromosome structure aligned the 5' of a dihydrofolate reductase promoter gene with 3' of a terminase production gene during metaphase II. Her eyebrows shot up as she realized what was happening. Letting out a happy sigh, she smiled, realizing the mutation she was looking for made the cell produce the terminase in place of the reductase.

A voice cut through the excitement of her work, "Hello, Chloe. Some of the guys said you would be working in here this week and I wanted to see what progress you have made."

Without warrant, Professor Sophoman entered the lab hastily. Chloe grew uneasy knowing she would have to disclose herself, "I am analyzing the samples, trying to figure out the best means of artificial gene replication."

"What is this nonsense?" Professor Sophoman asked scornfully, "We said yesterday we were wasting our time looking at these samples. Please don't spend any more time doing this; our time in the lab is very expensive."

Unsure of what to say, Chloe felt useless defending herself, "I am sorry, Professor Sophoman. I will stop this immediately," she lied to his face.

"What is this obsession?" he fired.

"How do you mean?" she replied.

Defending himself, Professor Sophoman answered, "If you respected our work as much as I do, you would understand our limitations. Unlike the French, Americans get angry when you waste their money!"

"I'm sorry, professor, but I really thought this would help," Chloe rebutted.

"Okay, Chloe. Please move on," he directed.

Without giving up, Chloe said, "Look at this, the cross link I suspected is self-terminating. This means if we fix it at this site we can still use this sample for its superb ability to replicate the genes we want."

"Hm." The professor then looked puzzled, "what part of 'no' don't you understand?"

Knowing well that he perfectly understood what she just said, and that he did not want to compromise his authority, Chloe attempted illusion, and without explanation, walked out of the room with a straight face.

"Chloe?" the professor seemed to lose himself, "Where are you going? Are you sick?"

What do you know, Chloe thought.

***

Rummaging through her closet, Chloe found a thick cardigan, thinking to herself, who says warm can't be fashionable!

"Are you ready yet?" Candice and Olivia impatiently sprawled across the former home of many of Chloe's most important possessions.

Chloe teased her friends, "What? Believe me, my rug is *above* your standards!"

"Go to hell," Olivia defended her upbringing, "where are we going again?"

With sarcasm, Chloe ignored her question, "Well, I don't know where *you and Candice* are going, but apparently I'm going to hell."

Laughing at them for the fools they were, and at herself for not knowing what to say, Candice finally intervened, "Guys, we are going to Rocks."

"Yes Olivia, do you know how to have fun?" Chloe asked with sarcasm again, "who knows? Maybe you'll meet a nice man there?"

While on their way, Chloe found a good moment to point out, "A benefit of staying on campus is that most things are within walking distance," hiding the slight unwanted nervousness she was experiencing as the neon sign reading "Rocky Rocker" enlarged itself.

"Yes and I'm sure it's not because you can't afford an apartment," Olivia slipped in, "I bet you really wanted a short walking distance when mom and dad offered to pay for a dorm!"

"You're a jerk, you know that?" Chloe shrugged off with laughter.

Before paying to enter, the music already shook their chests.

"Oh my god, I love this song!" Candice spoke up.

Suspicious, Chloe thought to herself, there is no way she knows this song! Nonetheless it didn't matter. Fog and bright lights limited the view of a long-haired 24 year old that didn't look like he saw the sun very often that stood in front of a large machine. An audio engineer, Chloe thought to herself, she couldn't do that if she tried.

Within seconds, Chloe had no idea where she was or where her companions had run off to. The music that had once seemed exciting and fun now seemed draining and repetitive. Rolling her eyes, she thought to make more use of her time and made a quick exit.

***

Groggy, Chloe rolled off her bed, finding herself on the floor. Nothing a cup of coffee and a cold water face wash could not fix.

Chloe's backpack was long overdue for a reorganization, nonetheless, she grabbed her sandbag full of notes and scurried to the computer lab, dropping her coffee mug in the sink. To her unsurprise, numerous missed calls and text messages were left untouched on her phone following the disclosure of her return home to her friends the night before. The walk to the computer lab gave her the time she needed to keep ignoring them.

Finding the proteins she observed in the lab on a database is easy. Modelling the DNA is not. Luckily, Chloe had no plans that day.

***

"Hi, how can I help you?" the cafe clerk asked.

Describing her favorite coffee from home, Chloe replied, "Yes, hello, um… I will have a hazelnut coffee with milk, please."

Chloe was sitting with her notes and her computer, sipping her coffee, when none other than Professor Sophoman walked in. Of course, I would find him here, Chloe thought to herself.

"Professor!" Chloe jumped up, vying for his attention.

To her success, he responded, "Hello Chloe, how's it going? You do not look so well."

"Professor, I have constructed a plasmid on our program that will split the terminase promoter gene. This means we can use the samples we already constructed for their intended purpose," Chloe broke down as precisely as possible, looking to him for approval.

The professor leaned in, intrigued. "Huh," the Professor added, looking at the 3D model on her screen, "Does it work?"

She continued, "I can model the reaction in these steps, and look, there was a mutation causing an extra magnesium atom in the polymerase

11

to redirect the DNA replication." Chloe described her victory plans, "I need a few days for testing, but I think it should work."

"I will tell you this *will* save a lot of time, however, this is not what I had in mind for our lab training," the professor rebutted, "however, this is good work. Let me know if you need help and we will tell everyone else on Thursday."

That was the coldest day of the winter. Unbeknownst to Chloe, a long sleeve covered by a university hoodie would not be enough to contain her body heat. Eyes watering and fingers freezing, Chloe struggled to keep herself up as the wind cut into her skin. Nobody was out enjoying the day, rather everyone outside was racing to their next destination.

***

Along the Horizon

She gazed upon the window, wondering of the unknown and what the future would have in store for her. Sasha glanced back at her family and smelled the crispy chicken being pulled out of the oven. Coming out of her daze, she strolled to the kitchen table and sat down.

"Lola," her father started, "have you decided where you're going to stay once you get to Madurez?"

"Dad, we've been over this. I'm going to move in with my boyfriend since he'll already have lived there for a year," her sister responded with an eye roll.

Sasha sunk into her seat and stuffed her face with some mashed potatoes. She wondered when her parents would ask her about her plans for the island, or at least mention it. Madurez was the island that every 18 year old had to travel to, and for some reason, only her village did it. Legend had it, a man swam to the island in hopes of finding new land and instead found all the answers to life. Sasha didn't believe a word of it, but the man's tale of being reborn had become a tradition nevertheless. Except now, kids were swimming six miles to gain the recognition of being an adult. None of them knew what was on the island, it was frowned upon to actually give any information to anyone under 18. Kids had to figure out for themselves, that's how they matured. So they focused on the one thing they could prepare for, the swimming portion.

"Sasha," her mother called. She perked her head above the table and gazed upon her mother with hopeful eyes.

"Did you finish your homework?" her mother asked concerned.

"No," Sasha answered with a sigh.

Pushing herself away from the table, she sulked to her room. *If I was rich I wouldn't have to worry about my future*, Sasha thought. *I could just buy a boat and sail to the island without having to swim all the way. It's just a stupid rite of passage, one that they should've gotten rid of a long time ago.*

She stared at her ceiling as she wondered what her life would be. *Why can't I just practice? So many people start from such a young age, so it's a breeze for them. What is wrong with me? It's like I'm telling my body to move, and it won't listen to me. If I could just get off my bed...*

Sasha groaned loudly as she grabbed her pillow. She screamed as loud as she possibly could, pouring all her worries and fears into it. As her throat grew sore and her voice went hoarse, she lightly laid back on her bed.

Sasha suddenly heard a pounding on her door. *That's expected, I mean I did just scream bloody murder.*

"Sasha! Are you alright?" Her mother asked worried. She cracked her door open and sat at the foot of her bed.

"Sasha, what's wrong?" Her mom scooted closer to her and stroked her head. She laid her head on her mom's lap and felt her anxiety slowly start to dissipate. Although her mind felt like it was spiraling out of control, the nurturing touch of her mother's hand helped her realize that she wasn't completely on her own.

Staring up at her big, brown eyes, Sasha continued her silence. *She couldn't understand.*

"I know your father and sister can be ignorant and hard to handle, but don't forget that I'm here too. I'm always on your side, no matter what." She placed a kiss on the top of her head and pointed at her backpack.

"Now do your homework."

***

"Mami! Papi! Do you know what today is?" Lola demanded, practically bouncing off the walls.

"Hmm," her father said with a smirk, "I haven't the slightest idea."

While her sister and father went back and forth, joking about the significance of today, Sasha tried to conceal the knots forming in her stomach. It was Día de Creciendo, the day Lola had to swim to Madurez.

The day was spent gathering the supplies they had packed the days leading up and shoving them into their truck. While her parents were scattered throughout the house, her sister was trying on her new bathing suit that she bought with her own earnings. She beamed as she strutted around the house, wearing her symbol of responsibility. She passed Sasha's room and paused. She turned back and swaggered into the room.

"What do you think of my new swimsuit?" Lola asked expectantly.

Sasha picked her head up from her book and glared at her sister's expensive purchase. *Of course she's going to brag about her new suit,* she gripped to herself. Forcing a grin, she held two thumbs up.

Lola approved of her reaction and swiftly went back to modeling her outfit. Sasha groaned loudly as her sister left her door opened.

Soon it was time to head to the coast. Sasha's mom had packed her a ham sandwich for the ride, but she doubted she'd be able to eat at all today. Throughout the ride, she had watched her sister's demeanor change drastically. She cracked her knuckles and twirled her hair, which might have seemed normal to the regular eye, but when her foot started tapping nonstop on the car floor, Sasha knew something was wrong.

Sasha leaned in closely to her sister and whispered, "Is everything okay?" Lola faced her and quickly transformed her frown into a smile.

"Of course! Why wouldn't it be?" Lola responded calmly.

Squinting her eyes at her sister, Sasha was met with nothing but a brick wall. *So what if she doesn't want to tell me how she's really feeling,* Sasha told herself. *Her problems are not my responsibility.*

And with that, they continued on their way in complete silence.

***

They arrived at the coast and both girls were herded out of the car by their parents. A breeze swept through the tall stalks of grass. The leaves from the hollow trees seemed to whisper cautious tales of the future. As the simmering sun beamed down, Lola's burst of courage rapidly drained.

"Come on guys, we don't want to be late for your own ceremony," her mother said as she grabbed bags full of God-knows-what in both hands and started speed walking.

"It's not just *my* ceremony, Mami," Lola complained, "it's everyone's in my grade."

Her mother rolled her eyes as she continued to race to the edge of the cliff where people had gathered. As they neared the crowd, Lola turned to Sasha with her eyes wide with fear. She could tell her sister was trying to say something, but her body wouldn't let her. Sasha placed her hands on top of Lola's, and noticed that she wouldn't stop shaking. Surprisingly, her sister didn't pull away.

"Sasha, I'm scared," Lola admitted timidly.

Sasha stood, shocked at those words that she never imagined her sister would say. They stared at each other for what seemed like forever. In that moment, she could sense that every fear she had about Madurez, her sister had too. Lola must have been pretending to be excited about the island. When in reality, she was probably dreading it more than Sasha was. Maybe they were more alike than they cared to admit.

"Swimmers, take your mark!" the announcer's voice boomed through the mic.

Sasha blinked and the moment was gone. Back was Lola's smile and perky attitude. Giving her sister a brief hug, Lola headed off into the crowd.

Sasha saw her sister step onto the edge and crouch into a diving pose. She couldn't tell if it was because it was so cold in the morning or her nerves, but her whole body started to shiver. She could hardly contain her teeth from chattering out of her mouth.

What if she doesn't make it? I know she's one of the most annoying people I've ever met, but I still love her. I mean, it wouldn't be that terrible if maybe she did get some cramps, just to knock her off her little pedestal, but I don't want her to die. It had been years since anyone had actually died during the ceremony. I don't want my sister to be that rare statistic.

The sharp blow of the whistle brought Sasha back to reality. She watched in horror as her sister dived into the water. As she saw Lola's whole body disappear into the water, Sasha felt her heart shatter. It probably would be years until she saw her sister again.

***

It had been 11 months since Lola left for Madurez. Life had gone on as normal, even though Sasha could see her parents always lingering at pictures of her sister. Even the house seemed to miss her. Dust piled up in corners of the room, dirty laundry was left to rot on the basement floor, and although she couldn't be certain, Sasha could swear that the lights didn't shine nearly as bright as before. Ignoring her worries, she strolled down the stairs to the kitchen to find a pile of plates awaiting her. *Ugh.* She rolled up her sleeves and thought of a moment last summer, when she had no responsibilities, when her sister was still there.

It was in the middle of July when a slam of the dishwasher echoed throughout the house. Footsteps pounded on the stairs leading up to her room. Suddenly, her door was violently ripped open by Lola. Her rampage didn't stop there, she gripped Sasha's covers with both hands and yanked the fabric off the bed, exposing a frightened Sasha.

"Lola? What're you doing?" Sasha asked half asleep.

"You didn't do the dishes like I asked," Lola stated bluntly. Baffled, Sasha tried to understand the situation in front of her.

"...Okay?" They stared at each other, Lola's glare becoming more apparent.

"I specifically asked you to do the dishes when you came home. I had to go to training right after school and all you did was take a nap." Rolling her eyes, Sasha tried to zone out of the conversation.

"Hey! Look at me. You do nothing in this house while I do everything. If you want me to continue driving you to school, then you better help out," Lola said matter-of-factly.

Feeling her blood boil, Sasha snatched the end of her covers and jerked it towards herself. Lola was taken by surprise, but quickly regained her grip. The sheet became a competition. Nails dug into the fabric, pulling threads apart. The once comfy, fluffy blanket, was now turned into a pawn in their sibling rivalry. And just like their relationship, both sides were tearing apart from each other, barely hanging on.

"Get out of my room!" Sasha shrieked, letting all of her hate take control of her body.

She felt her hands burn, her nails going through the covers, digging into her palms. Her jaw tightened and her teeth grinded as she imagined chucking the blanket to the floor and grabbing tufts of Lola's hair and just pulling. As she was about to initiate her plan, their mother flew into the room.

"Are you serious?!" Their mother demanded as she yanked the fabric away from them. They abruptly stopped, acting as though they had no idea what had happened.

"Come on, you aren't kids anymore. How long is this going to go on for before you learn to get along? You know, when I'm gone, you guys are only going to have each other. So please, for me, stop fighting." Lola shifted back and forth on her heels while their mother sighed and sullenly walked out of the room.

The girls glanced at each other. Lola gingerly picked the covers off of the ground and gently laid it on her sister's bed. Sasha went to the kitchen and silently began cleaning the unwashed dishes that laid before her. As she started her chores, she heard footsteps stop behind her.

"Hey, Sasha? Do you want to go shopping with me tomorrow?" Lola questioned nervously.

Sasha carefully placed the plate in the sink and turned off the water.

"Yeah," she answered without turning around. Hearing the footsteps disappear, she couldn't help but feel a grin appear on her face.

As the memory of that day faded away, Sasha felt a tear slowly fall down her cheek. Brushing her cheek with the back of her hand, she picked up another dirty dish and tried to clean her thoughts away.

***

Sasha woke up late in the afternoon, as she usually did, to her alarm clock. Without opening her eyes, she smacked it until the noise stopped. After a few minutes of rest, she finally got out of bed. She grabbed her phone and looked at the time. As soon as she realized what day it was, she raced to the bathroom, immediately kneeled over the toilet, and released the contents of her stomach. Once she was done, she started splashing her face with water. Staring at herself in the grimy mirror, she watched her flushed face slowly return to normal. She took a deep breath and tried to concentrate on anything but her future.

"Why didn't anyone wake me up sooner?!" Sasha shrieked.

She rushed to get dressed into her swimsuit that was almost tearing apart at the seams. It had been exactly two years since Lola's Día de Creciendo and now it was hers. She quickly put her hair into a messy ponytail and brushed her teeth. She ran out the front door only to find her parents' pulling into the driveway.

"Where were you guys?" Sasha questioned as she threw open the car door to get in.

Her eyes widened at the sight of her sister in the backseat.

"W-what are you doing here?" Sasha stuttered. She could barely believe her eyes.

"Hey, Sash" Lola greeted her. "I missed you."

Sasha jumped into the car and wrapped her arms around her sister. Tears welled in her eyes as her breathing became heavy.

"I'm here for your big day," Lola said.

Sasha tore away from her sister and tried to slow down the thoughts that were flying through her mind. *What was the island like? How did you get here? Are you and your boyfriend still together? Are you happy?* She had so much to say, and yet nothing came out.

"I bet you're wondering how I got here," Lola answered for her. Sasha just nodded and buckled in her seatbelt. Lola chuckled.

"I was able to pay for a boat ride here with the help of the people I met on Madurez," she explained.

At the sound of that name, Sasha grew nauseous. In all of the excitement, she had forgotten what she had to do today. She began biting her lip and bouncing her leg up and down. Lola glanced at Sasha's leg and put her hand on her knee.

"Hey, I know it's scary. I also know you're a terrible swimmer-" She started.

"I've gotten better since you left," Sasha interjected.

"Okay, sure. But this isn't a race. You can go at your own pace. Stop worrying about everyone else and just focus on yourself for once," Lola told her with a genuine smile.

21

Sasha glanced at her sister with gratitude. She stared at the stranger that was her sister. Maybe the island wasn't so bad after all.

"What made you so wise all the sudden?" Sasha inquired. Lola let out an unexpected chuckle, one Sasha had not heard in a while.

"I mean, I think I've always been this wise. But learning to take care of myself and not worry about everyone else probably brought out that wisdom," Lola stated thoughtfully after taking a second to think. Suddenly, Lola glanced down at her own wrist and began to untie her beaded bracelet.

"W-what are you doing?" Sasha asked as she took a moment to appreciate the simplistic beauty of the homemade jewelry.

"I made this bracelet with material I found on the island. I wore it just because I thought it showed off my natural ability to accessorize, but I think it means much more. You can think of it as hope. It could be fear of the unknown. Or it could be a lousy piece of seashells connected by some strings of bamboo. But whatever it means to you, I just hope it brings you to me," Lola said with a hint of a tear slowly making itself more apparent.

As her heartbeat slowed and her body temperature made its way back to normal, Sasha reached out and felt the weight of the jewelry drop into her palm. She rolled the seashells between her fingers and heard the rattle as she inspected the intricate design. *It must've taken her hours to find the right shells. They all go together, in perfect harmony. And she's willing to just hand this over to me?*

Sasha furrowed her brows and felt the wetness form in her eyes. Her sister tied the bracelet around her wrist while she watched in admiration. Trying to think of words to say, Sasha couldn't find any that fit her emotions. All she could muster was, "Thank you." Lola nodded with a smile and returned her attention to their parents.

Gazing at the window longingly, Sasha watched the trees zoom past her, just a blur of dull green as she awaited her fate.

✳✳✳

Sasha stared at the body of water in front of her. Uncertainty lied ahead of her. A blur of land that determined her future.

"On your mark," the announcer started.

She wiped her sweaty hands on her bathing suit.

"Get set," the announcer chanted.

Turning her head to gaze at her friends, she realized they all had fancy bathing suits with brand new caps and goggles. All she had was her sister's hand-me-downs. She saw her friends all glaring at the rich kids in their glamorous boats. They were holding contests on who they would take on their boat with them, indulging in the power they possessed. Sighing, she watched underprivileged kids desperately beg for a ride and perform humiliating tasks in order to please them. *They must have convinced themselves that they were incapable of doing it on their own and that their only chance was getting an advantage.*

"Go!" the announcer screamed into the microphone.

Sasha barely had time to calculate what was happening. She didn't prepare a perfect dive like the others, and she certainly didn't jump in right away. She didn't even hear what the announcer said.

She felt a powerful hand on her back push her off the cliff, propelling her into the cold, unforgiving water. Feeling a rush of adrenaline coursing through her veins, she swam up to the surface to see her sister peering over the edge. *Of course she would push me in,* Sasha thought. *She's still my sister.*

She suddenly felt her instincts take control. Her legs started kicking and her arms propelled her forward. The salt water burned her eyes, but she persevered. She could see a glimpse of the island in the horizon and could hear the words her sister said to her in the car still ringing in her head. So she paddled on, with conviction, to start her new journey. Glancing at the other swimmers around her, she immediately sped up. But as she saw the look of terror in their eyes, she realized it wasn't a competition. They weren't racing to see who was better or more mature, they were all just swimming, together, to get to a better place.

Ivy

"atch out! You are going to step on her leg!" Peyton yelled. Carter nearly fell trying to avoid stepping on Ivy.

"I'm so sorry P," Carter replied in remorse.

"It's okay, just be careful," Peyton said.

Peyton and Carter continued playing, using their extravagant imaginations. Today they were pirates and Ivy was the ship. They spent hours searching for the 'buried treasure.' It was different every day. One day Peyton was Rapunzel letting down her hair, the next day they were astronauts boarding their spaceship. Ivy was always a big part of their games. She may have been a tree but she was just as real to Peyton as Carter was.

The car had been wrapped around the guard rail, like wrapping paper encloses a present. Tangled metal seemed to intermingle with the steel rail as smoke hissed from the hood, signaling the accident. That was how the firefighters first saw the car, approaching it cautiously, worried that the interwoven metals might have somehow punctured an oil tank or a gas line to the engine; thinking the worst-that the car would ignite. It was only later that the family realized that would have been the least of their problems.

Peyton was five years old when her little sister passed away. It was a freak accident, the family of four had been on their way home from their grandparents' house. On a snowy night, like that one, it was about a 45 minute drive. Mr. Brant, the girl's dad, drove the big suburban with caution, knowing the conditions were treacherous, even with new tires on the four wheel drive beast. He could barely see the road ahead, as the snow reflected off of his headlights. The next few seconds were a blur. He remembered losing control of the car and despite trying, it slid and spun uncontrollably slamming head on into the guardrail. All four of the Brants flung forward, stopped only by their seatbelts and the airbags that deployed from the dashboard. When the truck came to a stop, both parents turned around to check on the girls, who were crying hysterically. As the mom calmed the girls, Mr. Brant called 911 to report the accident as he knew, based on the smoke spewing from the front of the car, it would likely be undriveable.

After a thorough check by the EMTs and a precautionary visit to the emergency room, the family was released, miraculously with nothing other than a few scrapes and bruises. That night, the whole family went to sleep in some sort of shock, thankful to be alive. The next morning was eerie. Usually Ivy would wake the family, screaming with excitement, ready for pancakes-the ones their mom would make, special, with sprinkles and real maple syrup. In just one night, two year old Ivy went from running around the house full of energy, to laying in bed listless. Her parents were worried the doctors missed something-that they saw no noticeable injuries, but maybe something was wrong they couldn't see. They took her back to the hospital that morning. Hours passed as doctors ran in and out, taking blood samples, running CT scans and performing every other test they could think of. Finally the head neurologist came into the room with results. Ivy was suffering from a blood clot on the surface of her brain. More specifically, an acute subdural hematoma, resulting from the impact of the accident. The doctor explained how she needed to be rushed into surgery as soon as possible to relieve the pressure. Her parents immediately consented to the procedure, and minutes later, Ivy was taken to the OR. Anxiously waiting, Ivy's parents were calling family members while Peyton was sitting- starring, waiting, knowing nothing but her sister was hurt.

A few hours passed and the same doctor that had delivered the news that Ivy needed surgery approached the family. His face was filled with dread, like he was about to say something he didn't want to, or though it seemed. Ivy's parents rushed to the doctor meeting him halfway, asking questions frantically,

"How is she?"

"Is she ok," and "when can we see our baby…"

The doctor didn't answer the parents immediately, instead he offered them their answers through silence. After a few seconds, as reality sunk in, they abruptly halted their questions.

"Mr. and Mrs. Brant, I am so sorry," the doctor said. "We did everything we could, but we were too late," he finished, "Ivy passed away in surgery…"

Ivy's mother fell to her knees, hands over her face sobbing uncontrollably as her father knelt down to comfort his wife as if comfort was even possible. Being five years old, Peyton didn't understand the situation much. She watched as her parents grieved and felt unsure of what to do. Seeing her parents so visibly shaken was enough to make her cry. At that moment, the family of four turned into a family of three, they sat in the hospital waiting room, mourning. Though Peyton was only five years old and didn't understand much, she knew she wouldn't get to see her baby sister anymore and that she would be in the sky with Nana and Pop.

***

It had been five years since Ivy passed away. Peyton was just about to turn the big double digits, ten years old. Bursting with excitement as her parents asked her to make a "birthday wish list" which would include all the gifts ten year old P wanted for her birthday. She filled her list with everything a girl could dream of, Barbie dolls, slime, a new ipod touch, clothes from Hollister, Justice, and so much more. The list seemed to go on without an end, listing anything and everything that Peyton could think of. The excitement she showed at finally being a 'big girl' however, was brought to an abrupt halt by the last wish she put at the bottom of her list. There, at the very bottom, scribbled in her messy handwriting were the words, "My Ivy." Reading the list, P's parents felt helpless. They knew they could buy her all the slime in the world, but nothing could bring back her baby sister.

On May 23rd, Peyton woke up with the biggest smile on her face. She was finally ten years old. So excited to see what her parents had planned for her big day, she rushed downstairs. The downstairs was filled with the smell of her favorite food: pancakes with sprinkles and maple syrup. Her parents had decorated the house with banners, baby photos, and pink- lots and lots of pink. As soon as she reached the last step, her parents began singing.

"Happy birthday to you, happy birthday to you, happy birthday dear Peyton happy birthday to you!" her face lit up as she blew out the ten candles that covered her pancake.

After a delicious breakfast, P began to open her presents. Soon enough, the living room was filled with wrapping paper, all kinds of slime, clothes from all her favorite stores, and a Barbie dream house. The wish list was right in front of her, everything she had wanted, until she noticed one thing missing. Her mother recognized the disappointment on her face, and having anticipated this she handed her a pair of bright pink gardening gloves.

"Your last present's outside; follow me!" Peyton's mom cheered out.

Peyton looked at her quizzically as her mom's hands flew into the air and a smile she'd missed so much finally shown on her mom's face. Bounding after her, the two made their way outside. Peyton had no idea what it was but she followed her mom. In her backyard she found her dad digging a hole in the corner of their backyard. Squinting at her dad with a perplexed look, trying to make out the hole being dug in the ground she started speaking.

"What's that for?"

"It's for this," her mom walked over holding a baby tree. The tree had a tag on it, "To: Peyton From: Mom and Dad".

"What is it?" She asked.

P's mom put down the tree and held her daughter's hand.

"It's an oak tree, we are going to plant it here in memory of your sister and how strong she was." Peyton's eyes lit up as she smiled so wide, that the missing front teeth she'd had fall out two week earlier shown. Her father let out a small chuckle.

Suddenly a few tears began to roll down her face. Not knowing why she was crying and not wanting to disappoint her parents, she wiped them away, though they kept coming.

"Oh, come here sweetie, it's okay!" her mom opened her arms preparing for a long, heartwarming embrace.

Peyton hugged her mom as she replied.

"Mom, they're happy tears!!"

"I love it," Peyton said, touching the tree. Gliding her finger from the bottom all the way to the top of the tree, touching every bump and crevice, Peyton glanced at her parents waiting for someone to break the silence.

"I really miss her…" Peyton said softly still examining the tree.

"Us too," Her dad replied. Peyton was old enough to know her parents couldn't bring her sister back, but for a moment she liked to think *what if…*

After a year, the tree began to grow. There were new branches full of leaves, and it was almost as tall as Peyton. Day after day, Peyton was in her backyard playing around the tree, talking to it, even having picnics next to it. She interacted with the tree as if it was her little sister, Ivy. Every day after school, P would sit outside next to the tree either doing homework, or just chatting. During storms, Peyton always checks on Ivy, making sure her branches are not falling off. During snowstorms, Peyton makes sure to remove big piles of snow from the branches to prevent them from breaking off and if she spots animals climbing around it she chases them away. Often times, Peyton would invite her friend Carter over to play in the backyard with her. He didn't quite understand why she loved the tree so much, until one day, when he stepped on a low hanging branch. Peyton was very upset, she had to explain to him that her little sister had passed away and the tree was in memory of her. He didn't get why a tree took the place of her sister, but he also didn't want to question her. From then on Ivy played a big role in all their games. Some days she'd be their home base for tag, others she'd be their car, or boat. It was a new game every day.

Peyton talked to Ivy even as she got older. When high school began her dad had placed a bench underneath the tree, this way Peyton could sit and chat all she wanted. During her junior year of high school, also known as the most stressful year for all high school students, P did a lot of venting to Ivy. Most days after school she would come home and march straight to the backyard before saying anything to her parents. She would talk to Ivy about the girls who would pick on her, or the boys she thought were cute, all the new things she learned in school, like geometry, and Spanish. Whatever was on her mind, she would share with Ivy. During her senior year, in December, a nor'easter hit hard. Usually Peyton would be shoveling the snow off of Ivy, making sure she didn't fall over due to all the extra weight. This storm was different though. P was at a friend's house studying for a very important exam. Hours of studying had passed and the snow had piled up, her friend's mom suggested that Peyton should sleep in the guest room for the night and go home in the morning as the roads were impassable. That night, P went to bed very anxious, not only about the exam but also about Ivy. Beginning to pray, Peyton put her hands together and closed her eyes, *Dear God please protect my Ivy.*

P rose to the sound of her alarm the next morning. Looking at her phone, she saw that her mom had just texted *I'm on my way.* During the ride home, P noticed as they drove, that the storm had uprooted many trees. As soon as they got home, she trekked through the icy, deep snow that covered everything visible. Walking in the backyard, P was relieved to find Ivy was still upright, though covered in loads of snow. She grabbed a shovel and began to brush off the snow.

"What a relief, thank God you're okay Ives, I was worried," Peyton said to the tree.

A few days passed and Peyton took her exam and passed with a 80%. The snow had finally begun to melt, but Peyton's parents noticed the tree was leaning. Upon further inspection, they found that the weight of the ice and snow from the harsh nor'easter had cracked the oak's trunk. With the tree now almost twice as tall as Peyton, and its proximity to the power lines going to the house, her parents decided it was necessary to cut it down. When P was at school her parents hired workers to cut the tree down. Peyton strutted in her house ready to begin her normal after school routine. Today she was excited to tell Ivy all about the 80 she received on her exam. She walked across the living room to the backslider, she began to open it then stopped as her dad said,

"Peyton sweetie, come sit down, we need to talk to you," her dad said softly as her mom moved over a little making space for her.

P walked over to the couch and sat down in between her parents. Thoughts began to race in her mind as she wondered what her parents wanted. The look that he father had on his face showed that something was off; something was wrong, but what could it have been?

"Yesterday your father and I found a crack in the tree..." her mother said sadly, looking down at the carpet.

"What? I just brushed the snow off her the other day, is she ok?" Peyton ran to the backdoor before her parents could finish.

"Where is she!?" Peyton screamed, she felt her world fall apart around her, "you cut her down?!?!" she began to cry, "Why would you do that?"

Her parents rushed to her, trying to comfort her but it was no use.

"Baby we had to, she would've fallen on the power lines" her mom said as tears started to fall down her face.

"No," Peyton said breaking away from the tight hug between her father and mother, "you gave up on her, just like you did when she was two." Peyton cried and stomped down the hallway to her room, her heart was broken and the one outlet she had to feel better was no longer and option.

Shutting the door with more force than Peyton knew she had, the house felt silent. Her parents were at a loss of what to do. Assuming it was better to give P time to calm down, her mother and father stayed in the kitchen, speaking in quiet whispers.

Peyton woke up the next morning to a familiar smell, maple syrup. Her mom was making her favorite, pancakes with sprinkles and maple syrup. Still upset, she walked into the kitchen to find her mom cooking up a storm and her dad sitting at the counter scribbling in numbers on a piece of paper, most likely playing sudoku. There was a plate filled with pancakes for her. Heat rose from the plate of pancakes it was obvious that they were fresh off the griddle. She sat down and next to her plate was a little gift box with a card. On the front of the envelope that held the card it said, "To: P From: Mom & Dad". A tear ran down her face before she even opened the card. Still feeling terrible about all she had said to her parents the night before, she opened the card and it read,

Our beautiful baby, we know how much the tree meant to you, we would never want to hurt you. Your baby sister loved you, and she is always with you. Love, Mom & Dad. She untied the bow that held the box shut, inside she found a necklace. Not just any ordinary necklace, it was a special one. The necklace was a sterling silver locket. On the front of the locket engraved was a name, "Ivy Brant". On the inside there was a tiny branch from the tree and engraved on the other side it said, "In My Heart Forever". Tears poured down her face as her parents joined her in embrace.

"I love you guys," P cried.

"We love you baby," her parents replied.

＊＊＊

Table for One

"**D**anny! Get down here, dinner is ready," my mom yells up to me.

It's September and I haven't come down for dinner since March. Lately I have been locked in my room and only come out to go to school. Being alone is the best. Letting myself think, without anyone judging me. Getting up to go to "family" dinner doesn't interest me. I find it hard to enjoy my time, when I am surrounded by darkness. I hate it here. The reason I stay is because the memories live here. So many memories live in this house. The darkness may follow me, but little reminders of happiness keep me here. My mom keeps screaming for me to come down for dinner. When she hears no response, she decides to come upstairs and bother me. I hear her loud footsteps, almost thinking it was my dad. Hearing her voice made me realize that it will never be him.

She shouts, "Danny c'mon! We haven't had a family dinner in months."

Family dinner? How do you have a family dinner without your whole family? My mom just tries talking about feelings and all that boring stuff anyways. If my dad was here though, we would talk about sports and he would sneak chocolate doughnuts after dinner. That is all just a fantasy, because my mom doesn't want me to be happy, obviously. She just doesn't get it. She doesn't want to see him. She got a new boyfriend and it's just not fair to dad. He still loves her, he tells me all the time how much he wants to come home. I recently started to see my dad more often. My mom doesn't know, but sometimes, at night when she would go to bed, I would sneak out to see him. It made him so happy. I can tell he wants to come home and be with the family. He means a lot to me.

When I was younger, I would stand on the couch and wait for my dad. It would feel like hours, and no matter what, we would never start dinner until dad came home. We were best friends. Everything I wanted to do, my dad was right there next to me. When the blue truck would pull into the driveway, my heart would drop and my tiny legs would sprint to the door. He was only at work, but to me, it felt like we were apart for so long. My dad taught me how to do everything. He taught me how to play baseball, how to do my math homework, and he even started to teach me how to drive. These past months have been hard. Lying to my mom is not easy. She called me crazy when I told her I saw my dad. She says he's dead to her, and that hurts me more than anything else. He is such a big part of my life, and I have to hide it from my mother.

Time passes by really slowly. The leaves are starting to change and so am I. I left my room three times this week and my mom is ecstatic.

"I'm hanging out with Brian from school today." I say quickly, so she doesn't ask too many questions.

"Danny, you know if you met a girl you don't have to be so sneaky about it, I would love to meet her." My mom says with a huge smile on her face.

Correcting her is no use, I just don't want her to think it's my dad. The less she knows about what I do the better. Her thinking that I met a girl is the best thing right now.

Without answering, I quickly grab my yellow jacket and my keys. Rushing out of the house to get away from my mom is an everyday thing. My one goal is to get out the door without answering too many questions. Today went well, she didn't really ask where I was going, so that means she doesn't suspect anything about my dad.

The blue truck in the driveway lifts my mood and brings me back to a perfect time. Every time I see the truck, it brings me right back to all the memories with dad. Walking down the steps of my house, my eyes fall on my dad walking down the street. My day just got ten times better.

"Hey dad! Wanna come to the diner with me?" I say with a huge smile on my face.

"Sure! I would love to," He says as he walks closer to me. It's weird to be the one to drive now. I remember when he was teaching me how to drive in this exact blue truck.

While my dad passed me the keys, my mom gave nervous wave from the porch. My dad gave my mom a kiss and we jumped in the truck.

"I just don't feel ready. I've only driven two times." I say with a quiver in my mouth.

"Danny, the highway is not much different from what you are used to. Just faster," He buckles his seatbelt making sure it's tight.

With my palms getting sweaty against the leather of the wheel, it was almost as if my dad could sense the tension in my body. As my right hand went to the key, I felt my heart racing faster straight to my fingertips, as I turned the car on. Placing a hand on my shoulder, my dad spoke in a soft voice.

"There is nothing to worry about, I wouldn't put you in this situation if I didn't think you were ready," my dad reassured me.

My dad had that way about him that made everyone comfortable. If my mom was the one teaching me to drive, we would never get out of the driveway.

Now, driving is like breathing; I barely even think about it. It's funny to think back at how gittetery I was. Getting into the truck with my dad shows how much has changed since then.

We both hopped into the truck. Remembering some of our old rituals, I grab my phone and play some of our classic favorites. There are so many songs that we use to sing together in this car. Looking over at my dad singing is truly amazing. In the rear view mirror, I catch a glimpse of my dad, the smile on his face is out of this world, I guess it's contagious. Now I'm further away from sadness and nothingness. I wouldn't want to share these memories with anyone else. Too bad the diner is so close to the house, because I don't want this moment to end.

"It's been so long since we have been here. I am so excited to have our traditional Sunday breakfast again," My dad says while I turn down the music.

I think to myself, can this get any better?

"Table for two please," I proclaim to the host. Maybe she remembers me and my dad from when we would come here every day.

"Okay, right this way," the host says, giving me a menu.

"Thank you!" My dad says while sitting down in the booth.

"What are you going to order?" I ask.

"The same thing I've ordered for years. Chocolate chip pancakes," my dad answers as if I should have known.

"Remember when we would go to this diner every single Sunday?" I question, a big smile on my face.

"Yes, Danny, but things are different now and you know your mom would be so upset if she found out you were talking to me," my dad mumbles. I try to ignore what he said.

"I want you to come home. Mom misses you and it's just not the same without you," I beg. My heart begins to fill with sadness. We have this conversation every day.

"I can't Danny. You just have to accept that I can't come home," my dad raises his voice.

As my eyes begin to tear up from sadness, I noticed some of the waitresses staring at me. Yeah it's not every day you see someone crying at the diner, but at least stop staring at me. They don't get how hard it is to not know when you're going to see the person you love next.

"Are you ok, do you need anything?" The waitress asks.

"I'm fine, I'll have an orange juice." I answer, my face turning bright red from embarrassment.

"And I will have a coffee with milk and sugar." My dad replies.

We sit in awkward silence until our drinks arrive.

"One orange juice for you and I'll be back over to get your order in a few minutes." The waitress says.

"Wait! You forgot my dad's coffee!" I raise my voice so she can hear me.

"Oh, sorry I'll bring it over," she announces. She looked at me like I was asking her something out of this world. Her eyebrows began to frown as her eyes squinted. Why is she doing this? I wonder if there is something on my face.

"The service here is awful," I say while rolling my eyes.

It's been silent for a few minutes now. He is probably upset about the argument we just had. I notice he seems upset. He doesn't seem as happy as he usually is. Whenever we fight, he gets really upset, and so do I. It's almost selfish to fight, because we aren't enjoying the minimal time we have together.

"I'm sorry about before, let's have a good breakfast together." I suggest.

"Listen Danny, I love spending time with you, but you are gonna have to realize that not everyone is going to understand our relationship," my dad claims. His head keeps looking back and forth like he is scared or nervous.

"I just wish things could simple like before. Now I have to lie to see you. And people act differently around me. I wish things were less complicated," I reply. As my heart begins to race, I feel myself about to cry.

The waitress brings over my dad's coffee and asks me again, "Are you okay?"

"Yes, I'm completely okay," arms crossed against my chest, as I say with an attitude.

Glancing across at the other booth, I see an old man looking at us. I raise an eyebrow in his direction, unsure of why he's looking at us with such a perplexed expression across his face. Why can't people just mind their own business? All we're trying to do here is enjoy time together- why can't people understand that?

"Well, are you ready to order?" The waitress asks with that same confused look she was making earlier.

"Yes, I will have waffles and my father will have chocolate chip pancakes," I say, hoping she would get it right this time.

"Okay and for the chocolate chip pancakes, would you like that to-go?" She adds.

I look at her for a moment and think to myself 'wow is this women crazy, she must be blind.' I decide to let it go because I think there might have been something wrong with her. Why would he want them to go? He is sitting right there.

I answer after contemplating what I should say, "No, he will take them now."

After the waitress walks away, she starts whispering to her

co-workers. They are all in a circle and one by one they all look over at my dad and I. It's not clear to me what they are saying, but their faces pretty much give it away. The frowned eyebrows and the slanted heads make me believe they are talking about me. I can't believe they are doing this. How rude can these people get- my dad and I love this place so much; we always used to come here.

"Don't say anything, we should probably leave soon, you don't want your mother finding out you're with me," my dad whispers, noticing my frustration

"I'm just going to tell her, last time I told her it wasn't that bad. I didn't see you for a week, that's it," I say with confidence.

My dad's eyes widen. "No Danny! You can't do that. She won't let me see you anymore and this time for good. It's not fair, you're all I have. We have to keep this a secret or you won't see me ever again," my dad says with a stern voice, but not loud enough for others to hear.

"I can't keep lying to her. I'm pretty sure she heard me talking to you the other day in my room. I care about the both of you and maybe she will understand this time," I add.

"If you tell her then we will be torn apart and you don't want that, do you Danny?" My dad says as he begins to tear up.

"No that's not what I want dad, I just think she will understand this time," I assure him.

"Well before you do that remember the consequences," he states.

"Okay."

Finally the waitress comes back with our food, in one hand my waffles and the other my dad's chocolate chip pancakes. Finally she got the order right.

"Here you go sir, I hope you enjoy," the waitress interrupts.

"Thank you!" I cheer because I was so hungry.

As a child, my dad and I would come me here on the weekends. We would hop in the blue truck and he would play music loud and we would dance. We didn't know the words but we still had fun. After we got our food we would go and get mom groceries for dinner throughout the week. She loved when we would come home with groceries and my dad would always sneak chocolate doughnuts even though she didn't let us eat it. As I got older, my dad and I would still go out for Sunday breakfast, but then my mom stopped letting me see him. Ever since then, she doesn't like me talking about my father or talking to him. My dad says he misses us and being home. Every time I tell my mom, she makes me go to therapy and I don't see my dad for a bit. Just a month or two ago this happened. I remember it was summer time and my dad was really upset about my mom. He knew that he wasn't allowed in the house but I needed to let him stay at night because he was all alone. I would sneak him through the window once my mom fell asleep. Staying up all night, talking to your best friend, isn't so bad. He would only come at night and it was harmless. Then one night, my mom heard me talking to him and she was not happy. At first, she was confused. She didn't understand what was happening; she probably doesn't understand now either. The next day she decided to "help me."

"Danny, come down stairs," my mom shouted up to me.

The smell of pancakes and bacon filled the air, just like how dad would make it. Did my wish come true? Is my dad back home?

"Coming!"

I tumbled down the stairs as fast as I could. Bolting down the stairs I see my mom- only my mom. Did I really think my dad was going to be down there? I should have known.

"Danny I want to take you to see my friend Dr. Taylor today. He is just going to talk to you about your dad because I know you have been having a hard time lately," my mom said while putting a plate of my favorite foods in front of me.

"I'm not having a hard time, I see dad all the time; he is great, he misses us," I say while munching on my pancakes.

"I just want you to be able to talk to someone that might be able to help you," my mom says as she unloads the groceries. She takes chocolate doughnuts out of the grocery bag, but she never buys chocolate doughnuts. She must really want me to go see this guy.

"Okay fine I'll go," I reply just to make her happy.

After breakfast we go to Dr. Taylor. His office looked like a jail cell, but I knew this would make my mom happy.

"Hi Danny, how are you?" Dr. Taylor asks as he pulls out a chair for me.

"I'm good, just don't know why I'm here."

41

"I just want to talk a little about your Dad and how your relationship is with him," he mentions.

"Okay, well my dad and I are great. We have lots of fun together and I try to spend a lot of time with him. But, I do feel bad for him, because he misses my mom and I," I tell him while looking around his office.

After this, I don't remember much; he seemed to do a lot of the talking. I left his office and after that, I didn't really see my dad much. As each day came and went, my loneliness grew more and more. Nothing but sadness filled my days. Boring conversations with my mom were endless. Feelings and emotions were my mom's favorite topic, it was almost like she wanted to torture me. School wasn't even an escape from my house. Friends became just people in my classes. I had nobody to talk to. Nothing was motivating me to do any studying or homework, so my grades fell down with me. I can't believe my dad would abandon me like this. He just decides when he can come in and out of my life. That's ridiculous. He knows how much I need him, I have told him many times. If he doesn't come visit me tonight, I am going to be mad at him.

While laying in my bed at 2am, I hear a light knock on my window. Scared out of my mind, I pulled my covers over my head and made myself believe that it was the wind. After what felt like forever, I got up the courage to poke my head over the covers. It was way better than the wind, it was my dad. Why was he here? Why did he come back all of a sudden? He hopped through the window and gave me a hug.

"Why haven't you come to see me?" I looked down in distress.

"You have to know that it's not my choice. All that matters is that I can see you now," he said while giving me a hug.

"Don't do it again, it's the worst feeling," I walked over to turn my lights on.

"Danny, if you want to keep seeing me, you need to keep this a secret, or else your mom will find out and take you back to Dr. Taylor, and he didn't help you at all," my dad whispered to me so my mom wouldn't hear.

Footsteps from the hallway outside of my room grew louder and louder. No way was I screwing this up. My mom wouldn't know he was here. My light switch was all the way across my room, but I managed to get there in time.

"Danny, what are you talking about, are you okay?" My mom whispers.

If she thinks I am sleeping then she would think she was dreaming. My eyes glued shut and all that's going through my mind is, don't open the door. I start to panic, where is dad? She can open the door any second and she could see him. Then, the footsteps sound further away. She left. When I turn my lights on, my dad is nowhere to be found. I'm not sure how he did it, but he left just in time.

Since then, sneaking around is an everyday occurrence and lying is a normal for me. It's hard to hide such happiness from my mother. She loves to see me happy, but I haven't showed happiness in months. My happiness comes from my dad, so I have to hide my happiness too. Isn't that ridiculous?

Looking over at my dad with his chocolate chip pancakes brings back so many memories. He seems to be happy now. But how can he be? He is separated from his family and he can only see me occasionally. My dad's plate is completely devoured and so is mine; they have the best breakfast here.

"Are you ready for the check?" the waitress asks, this time with no uncomfortable looks.

"Yes we are, thank you," I respond.

"Would you like anything packed up to bring home?" She asks while giving me the check.

While glancing at our licked-clean plates I answer, "No, I think we are good," while shaking my head and drawing my eyebrows together.

Standing up to go pay the check, I notice my dad is gone. Kind of weird that he didn't say goodbye, but I will see him tomorrow. I hop back into my blue truck and decide to go home.

Driving in silence is sometimes better than music. It stinks that after being with my dad all day I have to return to my sad dark house. Before getting into the house, I have to make sure to pretend to be sad so my mom won't be suspicious. To do this, my strategy is thinking about really sad moments. Like when I didn't see my dad or when my dog died. Anything to get me out of a happy mood works.

Right before walking into my house, I wipe the smile right off my face and slouch a little bit. My mom is sitting on the couch and it seems like she is thinking about something. She has a glass of wine and she looks at me like I'm doing something wrong. Like most nights, my plan is to go up to my room without talking to her. While she is looking at me, I take a step up the stairs. She is being weird right now, so my best bet is to dart up the stairs. Before my foot meets the second step she calls me.

"Danny, come here!" My mom yells.

Slowly making my way towards her, my heart begins to beat. We haven't really talked in a while, so I am not sure what will happen. Being scared to talk to your own mom is a bad feeling.

"Danny, I want to talk to you and I need you to know that I am not mad at you." My mom says with a nurturing tone. There is no way she knows about dad. She's probably still mad about family dinner.

I sit down on the couch and she gives me a hug. She knows how much I hate hugs.

"Danny do you know what is real and what is fake?" She questions.

I don't answer, I don't know how to. What does she mean?

"Yes, I know what is real and fake. I'm not stupid," I say while throwing my hands away from hers.

"Danny, I'm not calling you stupid. I just don't think you know what is real and what is just in your imagination," my mom says while putting her arm around me. I push her arm off. I don't need her comfort. She thinks I'm crazy, she has always thought I was crazy.

"Do you remember what Dr. Taylor told you?" My mom asks.

"No, all I remember is how bad he made my life," I say with a stern voice.

"No Danny, he helped you. I know it's hard to see now, but maybe we should go back and talk to him." My mom rubs my back like that is going to make me want to go.

"The answer is no. The only reason I went in the first place was to make you happy, little did I know it would make me feel so empty," I reply while running up to my room before she can talk more.

"Danny get over here; you are not doing this to me again. You make this way harder than it has to be for me. To see you talking to your dad, when you know what happened hurts me. I can't move on from the situation. This has happened too many times Danny. I can't be a good mom because my heart is breaking. I just want to help you," my mom raises her voice, but she is still very calm.

My mom does this often. She realizes I'm happy and she gets jealous. She wants me and my dad apart and I won't let it happen again. Why should she decide who I can talk to? She can't have control over my relationship with my dad. He's the one bit of happiness I have left. Waking up in the morning, knowing I can talk to my dad, is the highlight of my day.

"You can't do this to me mother, you can't take me away from him, not again. Just because you don't talk to him doesn't mean that I can't be happy," I say with a nervous quiver in my voice. I don't normally stand up to my mom. She has been through a lot too.

"You are putting pain on yourself and you just can't see it. I am going to get you help and you will be able to see what's real and everything will go back to normal," my mom demands. It's almost like she thinks not seeing my dad will help me.

Hearing this hurts me. She thinks I'm insane. Is it really that big of a crime that I have a relationship with my father? Talking to my dad is the only thing that will help right now. And if my mom makes me see Dr. Taylor, then I need to at least say goodbye.

"Mom I am sorry but you are insane and you aren't treating me fair. Dad is my best friend and you know I can't live without him," I say bravely.

"Danny. I let this go too far. You will come with me into the car or I will have Dr. Taylor come here himself," she demands.

I need to think about this. There is no way I can go with her. Absolutely no way I will go through that pain again. No way. I need a plan and I need it fast.

"I'll come with you… let me go get a few things from my room," I say, hoping she will let me.

"Ok, hurry." She says while she looked at me with a worried face.

This is my chance. Leaving my dad without saying goodbye isn't a choice. While sprinting up the stairs and into my room, my brain is about to explode. All my necessities are being stuffed into a tiny drawstring. I am scrambling around my room looking for paper. A note will be the only thing I leave my mom, that's my only option. If she knows that I am safe, maybe she won't come looking for me.

Dear mom,

I know you want the best for me, but stopping me from seeing dad will kill me. I am safe and I will always be safe with dad.

Love you,
Danny

While throwing the note on my bed, I hear my mom coming up the stairs. Now is my moment. The window. The window is my only way out. Am I really about to do this. I throw my bag out the window and look down. My plan is to jump, but it's so high off the ground. It's either a twisted ankle or never seeing my dad again. My stomach starts to turn. Loud thumping is coming up the stairs. Putting one foot up on the ledge my heart drops once again. No chickening out now, there is no way. 1...2...3... Next thing I knew, my entire body is being thrown out the window. I can't believe I just did that. My eyes open and there I am, on the ground in the middle of a bush. I can't tell if my adrenaline is kicking in or the bush saved my fall, but I don't have any major injuries. Realizing that in just moments my mom is going to notice that I am gone, gives me motivation to grab my bag and run as fast as I can. As a child I could never imagine running away. Everything anyone could want was in my house. A loving family is all I needed. Six hours without my dad was hard as a child, there was no way I could run away. Being torn between parents is one of the hardest things to go through and that's why I am running away.

Halfway down the block, I realize that it would be a million times easier to get in my car. The nerves of my mom catching me build up. The only way this plan will be successful is if I have my car. Luckily there are no screams or crazy ladies running around so maybe she hasn't noticed yet. It is hard to turn my key because my hands are so clammy. I need to go somewhere my mom won't look for me. The only thing around me for a few miles is houses and random neighborhoods.

Gas stations and fast food is basically all I see, until I see the diner- the diner my dad and I love. I get a table in the back and order chocolate chip pancakes. Headlights are shining through the windows. Could that be my mom? Did she already find me? Very quickly, I crawl under the table and put my hood on. What would I do if she found me? I have no clue. My world would fall apart. That dark and lonely place isn't a place for me, not again. It was the worst feeling, like someone took a piece of me away. All the emotions built up and I started losing friends at school. Hiding from the world was the only way I would feel better. No one to tell me how to feel.

It's hard to hear over my heart beating so loud, but I hear the door to the diner open. My mom is nowhere to be seen when I peak my head over the table. I need to relax. Sitting back up in the booth and there he is. My dad. It's almost like he knew I needed him. We have that kind of connection.

"Dad! I really need to talk to you and I need your help," I pant. I look around to make sure no one can hear me.

"I'm here. What's wrong?" He reassures me.

"It's mom. She found out I was talking to you and she was going to take me to Dr. Taylor. So I ran away," I mumble so nobody hears.

"How long ago did this happen? We need to get out of here!" He looks around frantically making sure no one is around. He runs his hands through his hair in distress and grabs me out of the booth.

"Just now. I was hoping I can stay with you for a while," I ask.

"Yeah let's get out of here quickly before she comes looking for you," he declares while he signals me to leave.

We walk fast out off the diner and he gives the waitress $20 for my food.

"Hey excuse me sir, you can't leave without paying," the waitress yells.

"My dad just paid," I say as I walk out and jump into the car.

When we get in the car we see the waitress come outside and she starts screaming.

"Dad, why is she yelling," I start to run to keep up with him.

"Don't worry about it, get in the car," he says, opening the door.

There is no plan about where we are going, anywhere but here is okay with me. Not much is going through my head. Besides relief. I got away from my mom and I am happy with my dad. After about 15 minutes of driving, I wonder what the plan is. Butterflies fill my stomach, I can't tell if they are nervous butterflies or excited butterflies. Maybe a bit of both. This all happened so quick. Am I doing the right thing? Then I remember how I felt alone with my mom.

"Where are we going?" I ask my dad.

"I was thinking we can drive as far as we can and then we can find a place to stay. I just want to get you far so your mother doesn't find you with me. I know what she was going to do and you don't know how happy I am that you came to me. We will be okay," he says while rubbing my shoulder.

Finally being with my dad brings me peace. Not too long ago we were going on long drives in this exact blue truck. We have been driving for about forty-five minutes. This time no music or talking, strictly driving. For some reason I don't feel like I usually do when I'm with my dad. It's nice to not have my mom nagging in my ear though. We are in the middle of nowhere, but it feels so good to be free. Complete silence fills the car. I look over at my dad and he is fidgeting with his hands. As I go to put the radio on my gas light goes on. No time to spare, so I quickly get off the highway. For some reason I recognize this town. I just don't know how. The houses seem familiar and luckily there is a gas station down the road. While getting out of the car to pump gas, I start to think about my mom. She must be so hurt and she must feel so sad. What she did wasn't fair to me, but I don't want her to be alone. My eyes begin to water. One single tear turns into many. My dad seems too distracted with his own emotions to help me with mine. Also bringing up mom would just put a damper on the rest of the car ride. Headlights blind me, but I can't stop thinking about my mom. I sit down next to the gas pump and bury my head in my legs. How am I now putting this pain on my mother? Losing someone you love is an awful feeling and that's how my mom is feeling.

"Danny?" someone says. My eyes are blurry and foggy from the tears, so I can't see who it is.

"Danny, is that you?" My eyes start to clear, and it is my uncle. A lot is going through my head now, I have no clue what I just got myself into. He definitely sees my dad, and he is definitely going to tell my mom.

"Uncle Tommy?" I say with a confused tone, rubbing my eyes.

"What are you doing this far from home?" He asks.

I see him looking into my car. This isn't good at all.

"Oh, just a little road trip," I say while blocking his vision of my dad in the passenger seat. I guess if I act like no one is in the passenger seat then maybe he will think no one is.

"Danny why are you this far from home all by yourself?" He moves closer to me.

I quickly get up and wipe my tears. I can't let him see my dad.

"Things at my house aren't going great, so I decided to take a drive," I'm not even focused on my mom anymore, I just need to keep him away from seeing in my car.

"How bout you come to my house, it's really late and I know your mom wouldn't want you out. I'll call her and let her know you are okay." His concerned voice reminds me of my mom.

My heart is beating, he cannot call my mom. She will kill me.

"It's okay, you don't need to call her, I was just heading back," I start walking away so he will stop talking to me.

Am I in the clear? How didn't he see my dad? I don't want to make anymore contact with him. The more he knows the more he will tell my mom.

"How have you and your mom been after your father passing away?" My uncle asks.

I stand there in silence for a few minutes. What does he mean by "father passing away?" Something about the way he looks at me is similar to Dr. Taylor. The narrow eyes, the quizzical look, all calculating me as if I was a problem that needed solving.

I got in the car and sat in the driver's seat as my mind raced back to the day I was in Dr. Taylor's office.

"Can you tell me about the day your dad taught you how to drive Danny?" Dr. Taylor asked.

"I just remember driving around town. I was nervous and he was talking me through it," I had told him. My hands had been sweaty, clammy almost. But Dr. Taylor had looked calm as could be. And his eyes, his eyes looked at me so-

"Danny! We need to get out of here," my dad whispers, pulling me from my thoughts, back to the truck. "Tell him we're going to eat and lets go." He throws me the keys.

Dr. Taylor seemed like he had the answers to help me. I remember thinking why my mom wanted me to see him? Why did it matter what happened the day my dad taught me to drive?

My mind is so empty and the only thing I can think of is Dr. Taylor. The way he looked at me. Why did he look at me like that? Did he feel bad for me? Why does he seem so interested in this day?

"Do you remember anything else from that day?" Dr. Taylor asked.

"Why can't I remember anything else. I don't remember getting off the highway or getting home." My head began to ache in frustration as the days began to blur together.

My dad isn't on my mind much right now. I don't want to answer my dad. Looking back to my uncle, I saw him still looking quizzically at me. I don't feel as safe and secure as I usually do with him.

"Danny, are you alright?" He reached his hand into the window, placing it on my shoulder. His touch brought me back to reality.

"Why don't I drive you home," he suggests with concerned eyes.

The look on my Uncle's eyes was similar to Dr. Taylor's. Almost like they know something that I don't. I felt safe with Dr. Taylor, he wasn't judging me. Maybe it's just because he is a therapist and that's why I feel so safe with him. But the way he looked at me made me feel as if I should know something about that day. What was I missing? I am trying to remember. An ache in my head arises.

"Danny, the day you and your dad were driving together, he died," Dr. Taylor walked around his desk to get closer to me. He placed his hand on my shoulder as if we were family.

My mind began to clear. We got in the car that morning. The nerves were taking over my body, but my dad was there to calm me down. As we started backing out he gave me a rundown of what to keep in mind while driving. The roads were mostly clear and I was just in neighborhoods until I felt comfortable going on the main road. I decided to put on the radio to listen to music. Music usually calms me down, even though adults think it's "distracting."

"Lets try the main road now," he says while turning down the music.

"Alright," while putting my right blinker on.

Driving wasn't that hard. I was doing it. My nerves began to dwindle as I realized how easy it was. Looking over at my dad and seeing a big smile on his face, made me feel good. He was proud of me. He loved teaching me, and I loved being taught. While on our way to an empty parking lot to practice parking, I looked over at him and it wasn't the same. His hands were on his chest and he has sweat dripping down his forehead. His face began to get red.

"Danny, bring me to the hospital," while holding his chest tightly.

I remember not knowing what to do. I didn't know what was happening. That day was always a blur to me, but I thought it was just a normal day. My mind was clear but everything was still foggy. Why can I still see him? All I want to do is talk to him. My eyes fill with tears and nothing seems real. I know he is in the passenger seat, I know we were in the diner a few hours ago. He is here I know it. Why would Dr. Taylor say that? I don't know what to believe.

"Dad?" my eyes begin to blur from the tears.

When I hear no response, I look over to the passenger seat of my blue truck. Instead of seeing my dad, like I was hoping, I see an empty old seat.

Fight or Flight

n abrupt *ding* of the "fasten seatbelts" sign resonated throughout the cabin as passengers awoke on American Airlines flight 271. Some sprouted up immediately while others remained uninterrupted in their slumber. I had been awake for nearly four hours, halfway en route to our destination. My seat had to be the most uncomfortable on the whole aircraft, riddled with rips of fabric, probably from the last person who couldn't catch some Z's. I spent most of my time in that fuzzy blue seat gazing out at the ever-changing horizon of clouds looking for answers as to how I ended up in a flying hunk of metal through the atmosphere that Tuesday morning.

The Uber arrived at my door just as I finished brushing my teeth. I had been cleaning up the mess I had made from the night before. In a courageous attempt, I frantically threw all of my belongings into a bag and headed towards the idle vehicle. I began out the door, baggage in hand and was greeted by a friendly customer service agent. We conversed on the ride to the airport about what he noticed driving all different types of people around, just to never see them again. I guess we were kind of similar in that sense. I viewed the world from the corner, while he was forced to establish quick relationships with complete strangers. It's not that I didn't like seeing people or making conversation, I had just never been the best at it and it was much easier to shy away from the things I wasn't good at.

Going to the airport was a bit of a struggle for me. The whole trip was unplanned and kind of sporadic from the very beginning. First off, the alarm on my very reliant phone decided to sleep a little longer than expected, which led to a more eventful morning. Granted the usual time to wake up was five, and I had hibernated until six, but stuff still had to get done before I left. A hot shower followed by a quick change in clothes to something a bit more presentable than my pajamas. After clothing myself in a hurry, I fled to the kitchen where the first cup of the day was to be brewed. Coffee in the morning was essential. There was no good way to operate and manage everything on my plate without the daily dosage of caffeine. The early rise came as no other, just a part of my routine. Today I would learn how to fly.

Airplanes had always been a method of transportation I was not willing take. Between the possibility of human error and the chance of inclement weather rattling the aircraft, planes were ultimately not my forte. Something about putting humans where they shouldn't be always confused me. It didn't make sense to increase your chance of death for the satisfaction of a new experience. For example, if I were to try and climb the face of Mount Everest, it would not be in my best interest because although the odds of death when ascending are roughly one in sixty-one, once you get to the top, your chance of death while descending drops to one in twenty-seven. Granted, flying is technically the safest mode of transportation, but the whole process of packing, going through customs where masses of people congregate, with the addition of taking off and landing, sounded like a recipe for disaster that could easily be avoided.

The idea of risking something with minimal potential reward simply didn't resonate with me. My life was normal and consistent, which I was much more comfortable with anyways. It gave me a sense of stability and control which I often needed. The urge to be in control and have a grip on what was going on had always been a problem for me.

I often fled away into my thoughts and believed I still had a decent grip on the emotions going through the somewhat adolescent body of mine. I was aware of what emotions I had and why they occurred. I had a talent for that. Being so quiet in the back of the classroom, you begin to recognize the littlest of details of who's crushing on who and the ones in the class who don't want to speak, even though they have much more to communicate than the emptiness of silence. I often felt the pain of others, seeking my best to comfort those who needed it, but rarely looked at myself in the mirror. It's never easy to identify what you're doing wrong, only when you critically think about it for a little too long and realize the moment in time is superficial. The moments in time where your actions were hesitant and the outcome was unknown puzzled me. Curiosity always led me in a direction that I honestly, couldn't always control, not because of my own doing, but because I was the only who craved the answer. Risk taking was never the objective, but a mere consequence of conquering my fears. The plane was no different.

The ride to the airport was long and awkward. I didn't feel comfortable in the back of that black sedan. The way the engine rattled as the driver swerved between lanes was painfully sharp. The windows, a bit too tinted. The seats for heck sake acted as some sort of pantry where the crumbs and remnants of the passengers last meal laid in place. I was uncomfortable to say the least but the driver and I maintained conversation before arriving at the terminal. He had asked if I had ever flown before with which I responded a questionable, "Yeah, of course." The driver's brow raised in confusion and insisted on helping me get the luggage out of the trunk. My body slipped out of the vehicle and onto the sidewalk. I turned around and headed for the caboose where the driver's arms extended carrying my backpack and fat chest of clothes.

Sports and clubs, like any extra-curricular activity, were of no particular interest to me. I would have rather stayed at home and fantasized about reality or read articles on the origin of space and time. When you get bored with all the people around you and bored of the illegitimate challenges each day presents, getting lost in your thoughts in your own little world becomes a whole lot easier. Straying away from much social contact was actually quite easy.

With all the technology at my fingertips I could get things done efficiently and in a timely manner when online. I had liked the idea that I could tap into an online profile and put on this persona that I could be whoever I wanted to. It's not that it wasn't me, it was just easier to speak about myself when a picture wasn't attached. Disclosing personal information like that to an unknown amount of people sketched me out. It was a lot easier to put some time and energy into a well thought out persona and just run with it than set up a personal identification account that others could possibly use against you. Although, I had the ability to be whoever I wanted to be online, there was a disconnection between reality and the life I wanted to live. School was one of the main proprietors in the situation of people not generally believing what is said online.

There were often times when I felt alone and unnecessary in the community until I took it upon myself to make a change. The thing is, you really have to make an effort to care about what your life is like and dedicate yourself to succeeding. I would constantly contemplate about how the school system was rigged in a sense. Rigged towards the kids who didn't have all the necessary materials to succeed. Most people might consider the economic factors that apply to a successful education, but coming from a middle-class family did not pose an economic challenge in the attendance at school. Functioning in that type of environment was difficult for me and quite frankly an institution was never a good fit.

I would think about things like how I dealt with my loneliness or my hatred towards people who were egotistical and how the situation I was put in did not allow me to succeed to my full potential. However, putting the blame on others only worked to a certain extent. There hits a point when you lose hope and lose interest, but it's just a test. A test that represents who you really are as a person and whether or not you're seasoned enough to get through the adversity. It's true, no good lesson comes without sacrifice because you must understand what more than one perspective is to really get a grip on life.

I often found that the way people act towards you is usually in the perspective that they are looking for something in return. They can often let you down or waste your time so the necessity for them is not that necessary. People tend to do what's best for themselves whether it's fitting in with a group to minimize discomfort or actually understanding their position and trying to succeed. Personally, I did not like to succumb to the norm and as a result I had very little friends. I often envied those that were able to communicate with others well and talk about how they felt. I craved attention like most children did, but didn't always receive it. Over time, this resulted in me putting this preconceived notion into my head that I couldn't have friends because they wouldn't want to associate with me. I had been truly jealous of the fact that they had something I didn't which led to dislike and anger.

The fact of the matter is that sometimes it is easier to just get up and get away from the situation to move on. One must attempt to combat the adversity in their lives whilst upholding their character and being seen as independent. The unfortunate truth is that making split-decisions can be seen as spontaneous or sporadic. One's decision to choose a different life at first might seem crazy or even insane for those who couldn't possibly understand. A vision to live happily and without worry were ironically daunting to me.

Up until that point, the flight had been awkward; stuck in the middle seat between the two strangers. Luckily, they were still sleeping even after the rumbling of the turbines. A family in the front row attempted to calm down their child as it belted out a high pitched scream.

It was at that point when the life was wrenched out of the plastic armrests as I tried to grab something that wasn't shaking. *What's happening? Where are we? When are we landing? Who's operating the pla-.* The captain interrupted. "It seems as though we have hit some turbulence approaching our landing in the city, do not be alarmed." *Oh great!,* I thought to myself. I had gained all this courage to finally bring myself somewhere completely out of comfort zone and now this? It was as if I was stuck in a World War II plane being rocked by the conditions, loud noises for all to hear.

I questioned how I could possibly be the only one in my row who had been awakened by the rattling of the jet engines. The two twin turbines ripped through the sky and the clouds began to make way. A streamline of sunlight flashed the interior of the cabin as my eyes squinted into the warm ball of light. A sense of relief flooded my body and the seats of the plane suddenly regained their consciousness. *"I will make it.",* I murmured to myself. *"I can do this."*

Almost eighteen years had passed before I had taken my first steps. Never before had I been in an airport. Never before had I stood in front of a gate and quivered with fear, not knowing what was on the other side. Never before had I taken those steps, never before had I continued to move forward.

Freedom Found

There it was. The Famous Haunted Castle of Wethersfield. Okay, that wasn't actually its name and it wasn't exactly haunted. It was just an abandoned castle; but there I was, staring up at its towers.

Honestly, I can't tell you how I got there. Well I drove, but I mean mentally. Two days ago my vow still stood never return to this place, it was just too creepy for my taste.

I had broken that vow.

The steps were green, the concrete devoured after years of uninterrupted growth. The doors towered over me. Even though I was eighteen and stood at a short 5'1", I felt even smaller. The castle was old and made of stone so that it didn't deteriorate over time. The width of the yard was about as wide as the castle itself, the neighbor's tall bushes brushing against its left side. Sunlight broke through the clouds and shed beams onto the towers. The dirt had little grass on it and the small gardens that circled the house were sinking back into the earth. An iron black fence enclosed the yard and clearly wasn't doing its job, the land practically spilling out onto the sidewalk.

Dominating the neighborhood, it looked out over the hazy sepia-toned Lakeview street. A crow screeched behind me in the old crabapple tree as it swooped down to eat the last fruit of the season.

I clutched the brass key in my hand. I was too afraid that a hole would develop if my pocket held it and it would be lost forever. I had walked around the entire property and not one door could be opened.

My feet were planted where they started this castle journey; the front door. It was boarded up and for a good five minutes my eyes bore a hole straight through it. There was no way it was going to open. What a waste of time.

Graffiti on the door read *demo* for *demolition*. Tacked on the door was a piece of paper, not the flimsy printer kind—government issued. The few lines printed on the paper screamed what the graffiti made me suspicious of: my time was running out, in a short month or so this place would be more rubble than it currently appeared. Unfortunately, my grandma never told me I wouldn't be able enter this place. Actually, she didn't really tell me anything.

She was a 92-year-old woman when she passed two days ago and I loved her with all my heart. She grew up in Calabria, Italy and lived in poverty. Coming to the United States when she was just 21, she made a new life for herself in the trade of sewing. She worked hard, becoming the only tailor in our town, and, if I may say, the best. Her mind was the epitome of wonder and dreams, moving here even though it terrified her. She taught me to be hopeful and never settle for anything less than my best.

I couldn't imagine living life without her. As someone who has struggled with anxiety all her life, my grandma would listen to my problems every day after school and reassure me. Even just a few months ago I came home from a long day of school and immediately delved into a conversation about my experience walking through the halls between classes.

"I don't know where to look when I'm walking. Do I look at the ceiling? At the floor? Ugh. You know," I ramble on, "this is not a normal thing to think about. People just walk. No one thinks about where they're looking. What is wrong with me. Ugh. Alright. I'm done. Never mind." My feet hit the floor as I slid off the handmade comforter on my grandma's bed.

Before reaching the end of the long hall to the kitchen my grandma spoke, "You're right. What is wrong with you?"

I spun and faced her with a half-smile, "Alright, I get it. You're joking. Stop."

"No, truly. There is something wrong with you. You're trying to decide whether to look at the ceiling or the floor." She paused for a long while. "But you know what? I did the same thing and still do it now at 92, so I guess I'm not normal either."

I laughed. My grandma always knew how to remind me I wasn't alone.

"Looking straight ahead when you walk like most people doesn't help you reach your destination faster than looking at the ceiling or the floor," she continued, "but it is more boring you know. I'd rather take the fun road to somewhere than the boring road to the same place," her eyes squinted as she smiled.

The next day, as I walked through the halls, I scanned the floor as I put one foot in front of the other trying to reach my next class as fast as I could. My eyes went on a journey as they traced the blue and red tiles against the white background, searching for a pattern. My grandma was right; it was more fun this way.

Now as I stood, feet planted on the cold earth, I was reminded of the fact that the key in my hand was from her. The castle before me was her former home given to her by my great great grandmother.

***

I went home to my room after giving up finding any possible entrance to the castle. My mind lacked any ideas that could aid me in my search. I didn't even care about the key or what it went to, at the time I was on the "quest" for my grandma.

She used to live with us before her passing, my mom refused to put her in a home saying how "she had too much pride for that". My grandma lied there in bed just two days ago, breathing slowly. She seemed so peaceful. My feet took me toward the doorway, I didn't want to see her last breath.

My grandma spoke, "Clara! Wait...wait." As if loud footsteps would hurt her health, I quietly tiptoed over to her.

"In my dresser draw," she made an opening motion, "on the left side...a key, take it. Go to my old house. I love you-alw-" she struggled to get the last word out, but she didn't have to, I knew what she would say.

There I was, feet digging into the shag carpet, not sure of how to handle the emotions that would come next. It wasn't like one of those dramatic soap opera moments but it felt that way. The sobbing came slowly until my back became parallel with the wall, as I pulled my knees to my chest.

The sobbing was quiet but my mom knew I was crying from down the hall. I don't know how but she always knew stuff like that. She came in holding back tears, already knowing the scene that awaited her. Her arm around me, she attempted to make me feel better, telling me how my grandma loved me dearly. Then like the flip of a switch my emotions went from sad to angry. Angry that my grandma was gone, angry at the world for taking her. My mom's arm flew against the wall as I sprung up and made my way down the hall to my room. The door slammed signifying a conclusion to that day: my body would take residence in my closet so I could grieve alone.

**

My bedroom walls dissipated; the haze of memories were done washing over me. I grabbed the key after venturing out of my closet that same night. I just figured my grandma must have wanted me to have it, those were her last words after all.

Five days passed. A week. Four — an entire month. My visits to the castle in an attempt to find a way in had become futile and as a result, my searches became less frequent.

About a month later, and before I could even register where I was headed, my car found its way to the castle once again. My eyes bore a hole in the main door as my heart beat faster. Was I reading it wrong? The demolition date had yet to be set.

Until today.

Demolition would begin tomorrow morning. There would be no more chances. This was it. I had to find a way in and quick.

**

Sitting in the cafeteria at school the key subject was about to resurface.

"So, what's up in Clara's life lately?" my friend Chris's eyes searched for an answer from across the table. He was always interested in everyone's lives, constantly digging for a story. My palms became sweaty. The center of attention was the last place I wanted to be. What could I say to that? My grandma was still gone. I was depressed. Period. Riveting story.

"Yesterday I stole a pumpkin off my neighbor's porch," I had to make something up.

Chris was wide-eyed, "Wait, really?"

"No," I said flatly. My hairline grew sweaty as my friend's eyes bore into my soul. *Okay. Think. Think. What do I say? Break the tension. Time has passed. Now more time. Now more. Say something!* Dizziness overcame me as I attempted to calm down, pinching my skin to numb the pain of the awkward silence.

"O...kay...anyone else?" Chris finally spoke, his eyes searched for any response from the table, but no one spoke up. I was sitting next to Susan who was sitting next to Anthony who was sitting across from Chris. There were eight seats.

The key was burning a hole in my mind and, more literally, in my backpack. I placed it inside this morning hoping to ask my friends for help. The moment was awkward and their lips remained still. What a perfect time to ask.

"Guys I have a question." My voice shook as my mind ran through all the things they were about to think of me. *"A key. That's stupid.", "This sounds like a children's book.",* or *"She's been gone for a month, move on."* Instead, the three of them perked up. Finally, something to talk about.

I pushed aside the things they might have said and trudged on, "So you know how my grandma passed away about a month ago." Their eyes grew heavy as I was overcome by waves of pity. "She gave me a key," I continued a little reluctant. "I don't know what it goes to but she used to live in that castle on Lakeview Ave and she indicated that it opens something there. I went over about a month ago and kept searching and sear —," Chris interrupted before I could continue.

"What?! *The* castle. *The* Famous Haunted Castle of Wethersfield?!

63

Uh, yeah, I'm in. Let's do it," he was bubbling with excitement. Like I said, always chasing a good story.

Susan chimed in, "I'm not as enthusiastic as this guy over here," she motioned at him with a smirk, "but it sounds like a real adventure. I'm in too." Anthony was the last to get on board, he was reluctant but decided it would be better to join in than miss out.

I was elated. The plan was then discussed. We would meet on the castle steps at 8:00 p.m that night. That way, the neighbors wouldn't see us trespassing if we actually found a way in. Even though it used to be my grandma's home someone bought the land from her and technically we weren't allowed inside. I had never felt that way before: a willingness to take a risk.

***

"Shhh! Be quiet!" I was scolding Chris for singing the Batman theme song while getting out of his car, "You're defeating the purpose of meeting here at *night*."

"Alright, alright, loosen up a little this is probably the only fun adventure you've been on in... your entire life?" his eyes were joking but his mouth was telling the truth.

Once Anthony and Susan arrived I showed them around the property. If you can believe it, it was creepier at night. The windows and white curtains were tinted such a vibrant yellow from the sun's gaze that even we could see it from where we stood on the sloped ground.

Something brushed against my leg. My mouth made a screaming noise but it was so faint someone three feet away wouldn't be able to hear it. I turned around running right into one of those bushes encircling the house.

"Whoa, whoa, whoa!" Chris' voice came from down below. He was lying on the ground with a blade of grass.

"I told him not to do it," Susan insisted.

I was fuming. "Jerk," my eyes squinted as my words came through gritted teeth.

"Like I said, loosen up," he reminded me.

My wrist watch must have been showing me the wrong time. Nine o'clock already? We had been walking around for an entire hour and had accomplished nothing.

Just as my thoughts started free falling into a black hole of lost hope Anthony shouted out, "Found something!"

Judging by his voice he was around the back of the property, probably where the old swing set was. I remember swinging on that same swing set high above the castle at just five years old. There was one day in the depths of summer when it went so high that I flew off the swing. My pupils saw the ground coming closer and closer as I glided through the air for what felt like an eternity. Then, before my mind could register what was going on, the ground disappeared. All I could see was my grandma. She caught me before the earth could, just like she was always there to catch me when I fell. That same year, she put the castle up for sale. She was 79 at the time and my grandpa was dying of lung cancer. It was just her living there and she couldn't keep up with the place anymore. Thirteen years later the glossy red paint on the swing set was long gone and a new color was painted on. The color of brown rust and shame. If a ghost appeared swinging on that swing I wouldn't be surprised.

When we reached Anthony he was pointing to the grass.

Chris was annoyed, "Alright buddy. We've been looking for an entire hour and this is all you've got?!"

"No, Chris. That's not it. Look." Anthony was pointing just above the grass. There, a small button was placed in the tiny bit of stone before the ground.

I was beside myself. "But there's no door on this side. What's it going to do?"

"Look," Susan seemed just as annoyed as Chris, walking away from us toward the swings to sit down, "if we don't try we'll never know. So. Try."

My knees bent as I peered at the button. It was nothing special, red, and as small as a quarter. Beads of sweat formed on my face. *Watch. I press this and the castle blows up.* Without thinking my finger met the cold red.

"Alright!" Anthony screamed a little too loud for comfort. I've never seen him like that, genuine excitement leaving traces across his face.

Silence cloaked the property. Nothing. Not even a squeak. From over at the swings Susan was stirring. My body stayed put, captivated by my unmoving surroundings. Something would happen. I knew. I hoped. My anxiety was kicking in now, stronger than ever.

This was stupid. There they were. The thoughts had found their way in. *I should be doing my homework. Were we trespassing? Yes. Oh my god. We were trespassing. But it's my grandma's old property. What am I thinking the police won't care. We'll be arrested. We'll never see daylight again. And I dragged my friends out here. They don't care. They'll never let me live it down,* my head was going to combust.

The train of my thoughts was stopped in its tracks before it could derail any further. "Step away from the wall!" Susan was frantic.

My eyes found the slit in the wall that was growing bigger and bigger with each passing second. Anthony tripped on his feet as he crawled over to the swings. Chris, always the adventurer, had a face as white as the ghost that was probably watching this all from the swings.

The wall was the door. *Of course. The door isn't the door. It's the wall.*

Dust flew out like snow. Okay, not that much, but it was disgusting and there was a lot of it.

"Me first!" Chris' face had turned back to its normal color.

I was a little more hesitant, "No! Wait, wait. Hold on. Wait," my attempt at trying to have everyone go in together was futile as Chris was already running toward the opening. It had been boarded up for thirteen years, who knows what was in there.

Susan ran off the swing set and Anthony had composed himself as their feet were running toward us.

"Now. Let's do this." My voice was shaking; I didn't sound too convincing. My anxiety remained in the yard as we took a step inside.

***

Imagine the *Titanic.* That's the best way to describe the furniture. It was old. Really old. In any event it used to be pretty, I remembered some of it from when I was younger. A music box started playing *Twinkle, Twinkle Little Star* and my head whipped around toward the door. *Okay. Goodbye. This was fun.*

"Geez Clara it's me!" Susan found a whole shelf full of old trinkets and toys from when my grandma was young. Even though she moved out it was her decision to only take a handful of things with her. Most of it was left here and the guy that bought the land clearly hadn't made a visit. She said, and I quote, "What do I have to care about material things at my age?" I could see where she was coming from, material things won't make you happy your whole life.

Footsteps sounded upstairs, shaking dust from the ceiling. I looked around. No Chris. It must have been him. Anthony was in the kitchen near the front of the castle and I was still in the doorway. *Alright get it together. Find what this key opens and get out.*

I walked through the house, the walls where pictures of our family used to hang were bare; tiny holes the only reminder that they once existed. We searched until my watch read four. *What?! Four in the morning? Mom's going to kill me. What can I say, it's a castle. It's enormous and it wasn't going to take us a minute to comb through.* We looked through drawers and closets, under papers and beds. But then a thought came to me. The basement. *Oh great. Of course. The basement: land of creepy and home to the swing ghost.* My friends were scoping the attic, or so they said. I think they just wanted to look through the tiny windows in the towers, survey the street from up high.

My anxiety had found the entrance to the castle and was searching around for me.

"I'll save you the trouble. Here I am!" my voice angrily projected aloud.

No. It was not going to go down like this. We have been up all night. I want to go home. No more waiting for my friends. I'm doing this myself.

My hand grasped the gold colored handle. Cold rushed up my arm, the temperature in here turned anything made of metal into ice. The hinges creaked as I opened the door slowly and then fast, like ripping off a Band-Aid. The thoughts started to enter my head. *Will the steps even hold m—. No! Stop! No! I'm not afraid of this old, stupid basement.*

My hand felt the cold wall, the chipped paint pricked me. Finding the light switch I flicked it on. There was something staring up at me from the bottom of the stairs. It was quite honestly my worst nightmare. What was that? Taking a few steps, each stair sounded like a hundred dead bodies grieving in a graveyard. Yes. That bad. When had anyone last entered this place?

There were twelve steps and I was on the seventh. The thing staring me right in the face. I took another step and could make out what was engraved on the wooden box that looked up at me.

To: Clara Love: Grandma
May You Find Your Way to Freedom

I had reached the end of the stairs and my hands grasped the box. There it was. A keyhole. My backpack left my shoulder as the key made its second reappearance after a long while. It shook as I trembled.

My back faced the box. I couldn't do this. Maybe she just wanted me to learn some philosophical lesson: *it's not what's inside the box that counts, it's the journey to find the box!* Alright, I was just making an excuse, but I genuinely didn't want to find what was in there.

No. I'm doing this. Now. My feet pivoted on the cold concrete, hands gripping the box so hard my knuckles turned white. *Stop being a coward just open it for God's sake.* I inserted the key into the dark box twisting as hard as I could; considerable rust had formed on the inside of the lock. It opened with a few faint creaks and squeaks. The smell of the old warped wood floated into the air. There, inside, was a neatly folded piece of paper. My shaking hands gained possession of it before I could blink, eyes already scanning the page like skipping to the end of a long story. Only four lines long. It read:

My dearest Clara,

If you're reading this I have moved on from this world. It was time for me to go — I simply had completed this adventure we call life. It seems you were the last person I needed to help on my journey. You see, you don't need me anymore. You don't need me to catch you when you fall. You did this all on your own. You.

I love you-always,
Grandma

A tear forced its way onto the page as my eyes caught the light coming through the small basement window. Footsteps surfaced upstairs; it was time to go.

"Clara! You good?" Chris was peering down from the top of the stairs.

"Yes," I replied with a smile. "Yes I am."

Within the Streets of Philly

The cold crisp air blew past with a freezing cold breeze. It was dry in Philadelphia which caused the man's nose to turn red, shivering for warmth. The rags he called blankets, barely provided any comfort or heat to the numbness that started to spread throughout his arms and legs. The clicking of men's boots seemed to creep up closer from the left of the sidewalk. A man in a gray suit started to approach, his top hat slanted down, covering his face. His jacket was long and black, the fabric was worn as if it was an expensive wool. Before the suit passed by, the helpless man called out "spare change" holding out a recycled tin can. The man looked down for a split second before darting his eyes back up into the direction of his path. The familiar feeling of despair overcame the old man; he remembered what he did to put him where he was.

"Brian!" A voice screeched, splitting the sounds on the street apart.

"Jane!" he said, beginning to sprint towards her. It was hard to shove through the crowd of people, both frantic and excited to reunite. Running up to her, Brian smiled as Jane leapt at him into a strong embrace. Brian's dark green uniform started to blend into the crowd of other soldiers with their families.

"I couldn't wait to see you," Jane said cheerfully as tears of joy streamed down her face.

"I missed you so much, Jane." He cried out with relief. Brian had just returned from Munich after helping to defeat the Germans with the U.S. Army. The war, being finally over, Brian was just happy to be home. Looking forward to a warm meal and a blanket that actually kept him warm, he couldn't wait to head home with Jane. The two both left as fast as they could, eager to start their new lives together. They were so overwhelmed by the new feeling of being limitless, feeling like the world stopped spinning for them. Brian and Jane knew that was only the beginning of a new start for them- that they would have a full lifetime together to experience the ups and downs.

***

The cold air started to freeze his soul. Brian, unsure of how much longer he could sit outside, was pulled from his trance by a man, who was walking towards him. It was the only person he'd seen in the past two hours. He seemed busy with whatever he was doing. Walking closer, it was clear who this man was, he had always turned down Brian for spare change before. Brian just sat back and looked forward, struggling with whether staying out in the cold for another few hours would yield any results.

"Hey sir, I was wondering, if, uh, I could buy you a sandwich?" the slim suited man said. Brian's eyes darted right up.

"Yes, please, thank you sir," Brian said gratefully, following the man through the frozen streets. The two stumbled into an old, rusty sandwich shop. Brian stayed close to the man, waiting to take his order as he felt his empty stomach start to grumble.

"I'm sorry I ignored you those times I passed by on the street, I just uh-." he paused. "I'm Chris."

"I've gotten used to it; the name's Brian," he replied, glancing back at the man, as if it were nothing.

"I just thought I could do some good for someone today. Thought you might need some help," Chris blurted out.

"No thanks, just a sandwich is fine," Brian said back to the man. He looked back at him, his smile slowly fading. Being as proud as he was, he couldn't admit to the man that he needed his help.

"So if you don't mind my asking, w-what happen?" Chris asked with concern in his voice. Brian paused, remembering his troubled past, what left him where he was. Brian grunted and awkwardly looked down.

"Well, c'mon I'm buying you a sandwich, I just want to know where you're from."

Memories swarmed in Brian's head, "I'm from here, South side."

"Well, why are you living on the street?"

It was a gulp he couldn't swallow, feeling the tension rise in his head. "I uh, had an addiction," blood rushing to his face, "I used all my money after the war."

"You're a veteran?" Chris was puzzled. "But shouldn't you have a shelter or help from the government?"

Brian felt the tension rise in his chest. "Yeah, but I um… did some time in a cell." Chris sat back, a face full of concern as his eyes became glued to the ground.

"Oh," were the only words he could make out to break the silence. "Was it, ya know, something small or big?" Chris asked, concerned by his question.

"A big screw up," Brian replied, his eye never moving from the floor.

***

"Can you stop drinking for once, Brian!" Brian was glued down to the coach with his head spinning around, unaware of what was in his surroundings, crowded by Jane's high pitched scream.

"Quiet!" He shouted out with a slur before taking another sip of his half-full beer can. Brian could barely hear Jane yelling about him in the next room.

"And until you can stop being such a drunk, get the hell out!" Jane shouted back.

Brian's attention was caught and he found the strength to get up. Filled with adrenaline and rage, he darted up, trying to find his steps as he walked towards the door, yelling words he couldn't even understand; he couldn't comprehend his own thoughts. He felt a large push from behind in the back from Jane, kicking him head first into the neighbor's door across the hall from his apartment.

"And stay out!" The door slammed after Jane finished her speech while she cried, Brian barely heard ten seconds of her speech as he was physically forced out, too drunk to even stand.

**

Chris didn't talk much after Brian brought up his jail time, it seemed like he scared him off.

"Hey I'll see you around, grab you a coffee sometime," Chris said, collecting the check and starting to move out.

"Ok sure, thanks" Brian said with confusion. It had been awhile since someone was so kind to him, it made him feel a warmth, a feeling of happiness. He walked out of the shop with a smile and trailed through the cold. "Why does he care to be so nice to me? He said he'll get me some more food too?"

It was times like this that made Brian regret the choices he made, the people he trusted. Unable to accept the fact that someone was doing a kind act. Karla came to mind, thinking of trust. It was hard to think of the person who ruined his life, the trust and love he had for her, the bond he thought they created. The feeling of trust being destroyed was worse than Brian watching some of his army friends die in combat. He got back to his spot, a curb on the side of the building, his begging spot as the alley behind him as what he called home, a tent behind the dumpster. The thought of being homeless was something Brian thought he would never encounter.

Waking up to the smell of rotten eggs and garbage was a daily for Brian. The stray cats meowing like crazy from hunger wasn't exactly a good morning bird chirp he used to hear in jungle of the war. Though it was better than being awakened by an officer banging a flashlight on metal, shining a light into his face, screaming to get up. The cold Chicago air was dry and thick, it made everyone miserable, Brian had to live in it. The cold began to grow on him during the season. The morning routine was to go sit at the corner and pray to god that someone would leave him some change. Once he had grabbed his seat and got comfortable, he felt happier than usual, with no reason Brian just knew he hadn't felt this way in awhile. Soon enough, Chris wandered around the corner with two cups of coffee, one in each hand.

"Morning, Brian," he shouted, starting to approach closer.

"Hey, uh, Chris" Brian said awkwardly, surprised to see him so soon.

"I brought you up on that coffee" as he began to sit down. "I wasn't sure how you take it so I grabbed a cream and sugar for you." Said Chris as he began to take a seat on the cement curb. "How's your morning been?" He asked, sipping the coffee as he tried to avoid the hot steam seeping from the lid.

"Kinda crappy, cold as hell out here." Brian mumbled out.

"Yeah, I would image," Chris sighed and looked down. "So hey I was wondering, well, only because it kept bothering me to know but uh, how did you get here? If you don't mind my asking." Chris asked, hopeful in his tone.

Why should I trust this guy? He could be just like Karla, Brian thought to himself. An urge told him to speak up, to let his story be old so at least someone could hear it before he goes.

"I used to drink a lot. My wife, Jane kicked me out because of it. I shouldn't have been thrown out but I guess she had good reason. I was in World War 2, I saw horrible, unforgettable things, but Jane throwing me out was worse than then bullet I took to the shoulder." Brian took a sip of his coffee to warm him from the cold. Chris seemed interested in the story as his eyes grew wide and inventive. Brian began to dig through his memories. "I was fine but they evacuated me out eventually and took me home. I wish I still had my purple heart, Jane probably kept it somewhere or sold it by now. I began to live on the streets because Jane wouldn't talk to me or give me any chance back, I had no one to turn to besides living under the freeway with the other homeless."

"Um sorry, but how couldn't you get a job, you're a veteran." Chris interrupted.

"Well I tried working small jobs but uh… I couldn't control the booze." Brian sniffled, trying to forget the past. "I had to start moving some bags for some people to give me some money. It still wasn't enough for a house. I stayed on the streets for about 3 weeks until I met this woman down under the freeway, Karla, she was new and was just too good to be true. I started to move my area closer to hers as we started to become closer. She was striking, her hair was dirty blonde, long and slick. Her eyes were evergreen, they were hypnotizing." Brian then sipped his coffee, preparing for the big secret he would reveal. He began to second guess if he was worth the time.

"Did you like her? Karla?" Chris said with a slurp of his coffee.

"Karla, she was crazy, craziest woman I've ever met. A manipulator is the only way I could describe her. She ruined my life, the main reason I'm here. Karla and I started to become closer with each other, She was my short time girlfriend."

"Well, what happen?" Chris said, eager to hear.

"Karla was tired of living under the freeway and so was I quite frankly. My money wasn't enough to give us a plane ticket or a home. I was desperate and thought of robbing someplace quick. She was all in the second I said the words. She brought up the idea of robbing a bank, we would steal a car, drive to the bank, get the money, and head for Canada. She made it seem so simple and that it would be a quick flash and run, no one would get hurt." Chris looked rather interested than scared, he had a peculiar frown on his face. Brian decided to continue on, open with him now, he just wanted to know him and his past. "I thought of the booze and how my life could be completely different, I'd have money and have no fear of losing alcohol, I was just hooked." Brian took a deep breath to clear his throat.

"So how did you get a gun? Didn't you not have any money?" Chris repositioned his seating.

"No, I didn't, that's why I never should have gotten in that damn car with Karla. We were supposed to meet up sometime in the afternoon that day to go steal a car. Before I know it, Karla comes in an older suv and tells me to get in. I had no idea how she got the car, I was just ready to go. It was when she handed me the gun, I was asking questions. She said she stole the gun from her friend's boyfriend and told me not to worry about it. I just assumed she had it under control when really, she was pushing me into it."

"Why did she want you to put yourself in that position, even herself for that matter," Chris brought in, interrupting his line of thought.

"Well I thought it was because she wanted to get away with me so bad and I wanted that too and I just looked past it. So she parked a street behind the bank and handed me the gun. She said "Be quick,

I'll be waiting right here, good luck." I should've never listened, I just wanted the booze and a new beginning. I thought I loved her" The cool air interrupted his story as Chris began to get up to his feet.

"Hey let's walk somewhere, it's cold out here."

"Yeah alright." Brian said, starting to get up to his balance. The two started to walk the streets, people passing by with shops left to right.

"So you were at the bank," Chris said in effort to start up Brian's story again.

"I got out of the car and she handed me the gun, it was a glock 45, I remember holding it and flashing back to the war. It made an uncomfortable presence overcome me; I was scared. I could shoot of course, if I had to, but I don't kill for fun. I was trained to kill for protection and the safety of our country, I haven't held one in at least twenty something years, since the incident. It felt so familiar when I shoved the glock into my waistband and started to jog up into the bank. Opening the door felt like I was going against a group a Germans in a shootout. I yanked open the door and threw my shirt over my face and I ripped out the gun, I unlocked the safety and shot two rounds into the air. "Give me the money! I want it all now!" I yelled. The bank lady nearly passed out and started pulling bricks of cash out. Surprisingly, there was no one in the bank besides the woman but she was taking forever to get all the money. "Give it all! Hurry up!" I yelled to her. I felt horrible for putting her in that position, but the money was driving me; I didn't have much time. I started to freak out and I just snagged the cash off of the counter when I heard sirens in the distance. I started to sprint from the store, putting the glock back into my pants and ran with the cash in my hands. At least $20k-the most money I'd ever seen, let alone held. I started to run to the street behind the bank where the car was. Police pulled up the street behind me as I took the corner to meet Karla.

"Hold that thought," Chris said quickly. "There's a restaurant a few blocks from here, we'll get some lunch?" Brian wasn't going to turn down a paid meal.

"Yeah, sure, um, thank you, Chris." Brian said thankfully. It was odd to Brian that Chris was okay with talking to him. After telling him so much he was surprised he didn't think he was a horrible person.

"As I was saying. I ran to Karla with the car and two police cars were speeding up behind me. When I reached the street. My heart sank. Karla wasn't there, the car was gone. I was screwed and I knew it, my adrenaline just told me to run but I couldn't out run the cars. I was swarmed by police as I was brought down to the ground, police everywhere pointing guns at me. I nearly blacked out when the last thing I saw was looking up and seeing Karla above me, shouting out my rights as she arrested me."

Chris brought Brian into a restaurant called "The Ole Diner" Brian had never been but was up for anything to eat. Once seated, Brian immediately brought up his story again. "So now you know how I was put behind the city's bars," Brian said, smirking because it felt good to talk to someone about it.

"Well she was an undercover, she set you up into this robbery." Chris said with shock in his voice.

"Yeah... She uh... She ruined me." Brian looked down to flip through the menu when Chris said, "So... How was it in jail?" he sounded like he wasn't sure if he should ask or not.

"Well it wasn't too bad. I did just under ten years, kept to myself and just kept thinking of getting out. The withdrawals were horrible, I could never go back to my old ways, it put me in the worst position. The second I got out of jail, I headed to the streets to find a place to sleep, pretty much where I'm out now." Brian closed the menu and looked up, taking a deep breath, weight lifted off his chest. "Well, that's my life story, hope I didn't give you too bad of an impression." Brian said with a small chuckle.

"Well, you've been through a lot, see it seems like you're not much of a bad person, though your decisions have put you where you are." Chris explained. "I think of it as a way to live a good life, no bad guy ever gets away. Karma is karma, you will always get what's coming for you." Chris paused and looked up with a grin.

"I can see what you mean" Brian let out a sarcastic laugh.

"I realized by just walking by you and not giving you the time of day to know you or your story. You seem like a nice person Brian, and you served our country, I'm sorry you ended up where you are, it's just how the energy you put into the universe works." Chris said sitting back in relief, he just given a huge lesson to Brian; an eye opener. They two caught a glare of the waitress approaching them, sitting in silence at the table as they awaited to place their orders.

"Hi, may I take your order for drinks?" broke the silence.

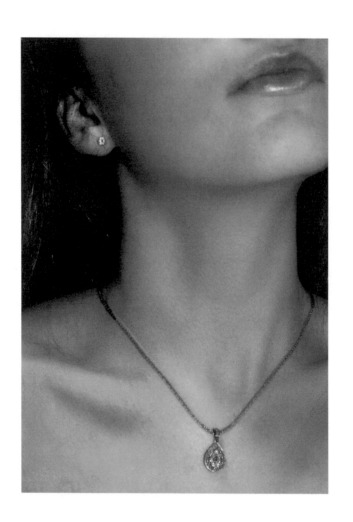

Diamond in the Rough

"I got you something." He pulled out a black velvet box. Alice blushed.

"Oh, you didn't have to." The box made its way across the dinner table and into Alice's hands. Alice thumbed the box over in her fingers before opening it, the soft black velvet felt expensive. Alice was conservative with her money, but she didn't mind a lavish gift every once in a while. Opening it, she smiled.

"It's beautiful! I love it." She took me out and placed me around her neck, where I would stay for the next forty years.

I was gifted to Alice Hollingsworth by Bernard in 1978.

"I hope you love it." Bernard told her. Her smile warmed me up and brought me to life. I knew we'd be a perfect match. Alice and Bernard were happy then. They had just gotten married at the church they went to every Sunday morning. They bought a beautiful big house in Southampton. Since that day, I've lived upon Alice's chest, seeing everything she sees, and I wouldn't want to experience life with any other person. She may not have the most exciting life, spending her days in the city typing away on a computer, but she treated me well and I could not be more grateful. Shortly after Bernard gave me to Alice, two babies came along, both in the same day. Their names are William and Juliet. They sure did bring some light into Alice's boring life. I was lucky enough to watch them grow up. Juliet has been eyeing me since the day she turned eleven.

It's been different lately. I haven't seen Bernard in what feels like

years, and the twins for even longer. I think that's why Alice has been
so sad lately. I used to see Bernard and the twins every morning, every
night, and everyday Alice didn't work. William and Juliet grew up and
went away for school.

***

"Bye mom," we were standing outside the building Juliet would live
in for the next year. "I promise I'll come home in a few weeks. Don't
miss me too much." She told her mom as she hugged her goodbye.

"Okay, sweetie!" Alice responded, filled with happiness, squeezing
Juliet tighter. Rain was falling, and I was muffled into Alice's coat,
wishing I could see what she could.

I wish I had gotten to see Juliet's face for the last time. She had come
home, but it wasn't exactly 'soon.' The seasons had changed twice before
Juliet ended up coming back home from Cornell; that's where she went
to school. William, on the other hand, never came back. Sometimes, I
would hear Alice talking to William, but I never saw him. Tears often
flowed down Alice's face, reaching me, which made me sad as well. He
even went to school close to where Alice works, I could tell because I go
into the city almost everyday. Alice would get frustrated when William
agreed to come stay with Bernard, but not her. I understand how she
feels because I just want to see him myself. I don't know where Bernard
went, certainly not to school, he was too old. I knew Alice just missed
her son but I don't know why he didn't miss her back.

William often stayed with Bernard. And maybe Juliet did too, but
I wouldn't know that. I just wished that William would have chosen
Alice because he is more fun than Juliet. Juliet only brags about how she
does in school, and Alice pretends she cares, but I know she just misses
William. He was the real pride and joy in her life, she loved watching
him play hockey every weekend.

***

Alice took me off so she could shower, like every night. I sat in her
room hanging with all the other necklaces; the ones she never wore. I

had been dozing off when Alice turned the lights back on and grabbed me. That was weird. Alice had never put me back on at night before. I was so confused when I looked at the clock and saw it read 7:00. Why was I returning to my day time spot? Alice looked into the mirror, and she looked stunning; the most beautiful I had ever seen her. I knew she wanted to impress somebody, and I knew it was Bernard. She hopped into her car and drove off. After about twenty minutes of being in the car and watching the sunset, we arrived at a restaurant.

"Welcome to Antonello's, party of one?" A guy with a strange accent asked.

"Actually I'm meeting someone." Alice responded with a smile.

Alice sat down in a booth, across from a handsome man. His hair was as silver and the fork sitting on the table in front of him. He looked deep into Alice's eyes with his own.

"You look lovely, Alice." He told her. She blushed.

"Good evening and welcome to Antonello's, can I start you with a drink?"

"Actually I think we're all set to order, I'll have the steak, and Penne Alla Vodka for the lady," Ron told the waitress, grinning.

"Sure thing I'll put that right in for you." The waiter told them, a fake smile plastered across his face.

"You remembered!" Alice chanted as her face lit up.

"How could I forget? Every Friday night back at Columbia." Ron responded. I didn't know how he knew what she liked. Bernard could not even remember Alice's order, but then again they did not go out together a lot. We sat at the table for a very long time. Alice seemed so happy. With Bernard, she was never that happy. He was always serious, I thought Alice was too. But not with this new guy. She laughed, and he laughed with her. I felt a sense of relief; she was finally smiling again.

✳✳✳

Alice continued to see this new man for weeks to come. I found out a lot about him, his name was Ron and he had a son. I remember him running up to Alice to introduce himself the day we went to a football game. At first, it aggravated me a bit that she was interested in another boy besides her own son, but I came to the realization that I was happy her void had been filled, William or not. Ron was a good guy who made Alice happy, and that was all that mattered to me. After they saw each other consistently for a few months, I had a sense Ron was right for Alice. I'd never seen her so vibrant. Like every Thursday, Ron tapped on the door. Hearing the knocking, Alice quickly finished putting on her makeup and made her way down the stairs, being overly cautious of hitting every step with the new shoes she'd put on-probably to ensure she wouldn't trip. Walking quickly to the door, I could feel her chest grow warm, as it always did right before she'd see Ron, quickly accompanied by a redder face. Opening the door, Ron asked her if she was ready for their weekly outing to dinner at Antonello's.

"Alice, you look stunning" Ron said. "I got you a little something." He reached into his pocket and slid a red box across the dinner table. Alice slowly opened the box Ron had given her. As she slowly but surely pried on it, she let out a giggle.

"You shouldn't have," she replied. "It's so gorgeous, this must have cost you a fortune!"

"Well, maybe, but you're worth it, Alice." Ron said with a big smile following by a quick wink. All of a sudden, I felt scared to death, sweating over what I had seen. A pearl necklace sat there, shiny as ever. I knew I had to compete but I didn't know how. I began to think to myself that there is no way Alice would replace me. Calming myself down, I felt a little bit better. Alice reached for the new necklace, pulling it out of the box. I couldn't be calm anymore. I closed my eyes only to feel her cold fingers on my clasp. This is it. My days on display were over. I was stuck into a box for the first time in forty years. Hearing the two of their murmured voices drove me insane. I forgot what it had been like to be trapped; hot and claustrophobic. I thought I would have been forever, but to my surprise, she took me out of that awful box. I laid on the cold countertop, wondering what would happen next. Would Alice ever put me back on? Was I replaced forever? Was she going to throw me away? Thoughts rushed through me. I didn't understand why this was happening, I have always been there for Alice, for everything from her wedding, to job interviews, to the birth of her children. What could this new necklace possibly have that I don't?

It seemed like weeks had passed, yet I still sat on the countertop in Alice's bedroom. Lost in thoughts about being thrown away, until she grabbed me. I thought I was getting a second chance, but in reality, I was just getting shoved back into the black velvet box that Bernard had bought me in. I hadn't been in there in forty years. Suddenly, I became uneasy. It had been extremely difficult to breathe. I started to panic at the thought of being suck in the stupid black box forever. I doubted that Alice would ever put me on display again. Seeing nothing but darkness in front of me made me feel as if these past forty years had meant nothing to her. Being able to hear voices mumbling was the worst part. Every time I heard a muffled laugh I grew extremely frustrated.

It was cold and depressing in there. At that point, I would have rather been thrown away than be sitting in Alice's drawer. She was a traitor and I could not even bare to think about Ron. To think I ever liked him was obscured. I thought he was a good guy because me made Alice happy, but now I wish she wasn't. I couldn't even tell how long I had been in the box anymore, but I knew the twins' birthday was coming up. I knew I was missing it, and selfishly, I hoped William would spend it with Bernard. Every night I heard roars of laughter from the living room, and every night jealousy bubbled inside me. Ron's single pearl necklace was nothing compared to me, a beautiful white diamond. But maybe it wasn't about how much I was worth. Maybe it was symbolic of Alice and Ron's relationship. I wish they had never met.

I felt a sudden movement, and a sense of comfort. It was almost like I was being picked up. The box cracked open, and a beam of light flashed at me. Before I could focus everything was blurry, then I saw Alice. I've never had that feeling of excitement before. I knew Alice would come around. Although she did betray me, I knew she would come back. All the hate I felt for Alice those few months disappeared. How could I ever hate Alice? She gave me this life. She just stared at me, and she was talking to someone too. Probably Ron I thought until I saw the jet black hair. Could it actually be Bernard, I questioned myself. Are Alice and Bernard back together? It was too good to be true.

"What do you think Bernard, don't you think she'll love it?" She asked him.

Who was she talking about, was Alice giving me away? That is even worse than sitting in her drawer. I was devastated once again.

"Yes, she would, but we can't spoil her and not William." He responded, squinting his eyes and staring at me.

"Bernard, I have not seen William in almost a year, I have no idea what he would like!" Alice yelled as she stormed out of her bedroom, with me in hand. And all of a sudden the air got tighter, like Alice had sealed the edges.

"Happy birthday dear William and Juliet, happy birthday to you!" Was all I could manage to hear; the sound was so muffled. How could I forget the twins' birthday?

"Present time!" I heard a voice yell. I recognized that voice, I think it was Juliet! There was a lot of crunching and ripping and laughing and 'thank you's.' I felt so left out. Until someone lifted me off the hard surface, and I could breathe again. A crack of light peaked through again, and I saw her. It was Juliet; I hadn't seen her since Christmas.

"Mom, you shouldn't have!" She broke down into tears.

"Well, I didn't really, your father gave that to me, when we started dating." Alice reassured Juliet. Juliet knew that, she always wanted me to be hers. She was so happy to have me. Finally, I felt joyful again, Like I had a purpose. My purpose was to make people happy. I finally realized that I had been with Alice too long, and was in need of a new owner, someone youthful. Just like Alice was, when I was given to her. Juliet wore me every day, and I got to move to school with her. I met all of her friends. They all were almost as in love with me as Juliet had been. She wasn't as boring as I once thought she was, Juliet goes to parties, and hangs out with friends almost every night. They were obsessed and insanely jealous of me. Alice may have betrayed me, but I could help but thank her, for repurposing me to someone who needed me.

※※※

It's Just a Phase

Christmas morning. Just an average holiday morning, cold and windy. Fluffy white flakes fell from the sky. As I glanced out the window, all I could make out was that everything was covered in white. The next thing I noticed was the big barn covered with icicles and lights. The gleam of the lights lit up the front of the barn, as the snow appeared brighter than ever.

I was always the first one up in the morning. Seven o'clock sharp, my eyes burst wide open, constricting to fill my eyes with light. A smile crept across my face once I realized that today was Christmas. I leaped up off of my bed, making a loud thud, slipped my fuzzy slippers on, and bolted down the hall to my parents room. As I sprinted through the hallway, all that I could think about was, *I wonder what Santa brought me this year?* As I approached my parents bedroom door, I shoved it open, belted out a large screech and jumped directly on top of both of them.

"Mommy, Daddy wake up, wake up! It's Christmas morning. Come on, wake up!" I demanded, jumping up and down.

"Kara, it's seven in the morning. You need to be patient. Give us ten minutes and then we can all go down and open presents," my mom spoke in a hoarse voice as she rolled over and opened her eyes in my direction.

***

As I sat on my bed, the same question had come across my mind, what did Santa bring me? I had been such a good girl this year, I did everything that was asked of me, I listened, I did it all. I cleaned my room and organized my stuffed animals. I even helped clean the house without having to be asked.

My mind filled up with all things that a little girl could think of on Christmas. I found myself looking out the window towards the barn, when I noticed something different about it. I watched as a shadow slid past the window that was positioned at the front. Nothing ever appeared behind the large, red doors. My dad would go out there to work on his car and to get tools, but besides that, the barn remained empty.

A year ago, we moved into this house, it was like a dream come true. I was a girl that wanted the big barn in my backyard, where I could look out my window and see my horses. After that, the dream of the backyard barn came true, the desire for a pony became stronger.

***

There was this time when me and my dad were driving around the town and we drove past this pasture with three horses in it.

"Daddy, daddy, look look look!" I screeched as I pointed towards the three horses that remained only a couple steps away from where our car was parked.

My dad had pulled over so that I could look at the horses. I sat there, and watched as the horses ate the tall, green grass. They are just so pretty. I've never seen a horse like that one before.

"They're so pretty, daddy, I've never seen one like that." I looked at my dad, feeling so amazed by the colors that they embraced.

One of the horses was like a light gray color. It appeared to have several different shades of gray. It was much bigger than the other two. But it looked like one of the horses that you see pulling that big wagon in all of those commercials on TV. The second horse was a combination of two colors- white and brown. It was really pretty because it had just about the same amount of each color. The last horse was my favorite. It looked to be the skinniest out of the three. It was this yellowish color but almost like a tan color too. It had white on all four legs and on its face.

"Daddy, I really, really want a pony like that one." I said as I pointed towards the yellowish, tanish horse that stood out in the middle of the pasture.

"Well sweetie, if you continue to be a good girl and do what is asked of you, maybe we'll talk about it." My dad said, turning the car back on to continue driving.

"But daddy, please. I really want that horsey. I've never seen one like that." I said sadly, as my eyes still remained, locked on the three horses.

"Kara, we are not going to have this discussion now. You have to prove that you can handle the responsibility. You will have to clean up after it, brush it, make sure that it gets exercise, and more importantly love it." My dad spoke in a harsher tone, not that it had scared me but I knew by the way he spoke that this was something that would bring a challenge.

The moment that I got home, I sought to help out my parents in any way I could think of. I wanted to show them that I could handle taking care of my own horse. The only way that I could do that was by helping out at home and making sure that I went to the store with them.

✳✳✳

"Kara, sweetie, it was time to move on. That house- it was too small for our family." My mom spoke in a soft voice as she placed her hand on my shoulder, attempting to comfort me.

"But, but, mommy, daddy, I don't want to leave our house." I said, sitting in the back seat crying desperately.

"I know that it's going to be hard for you to understand but this is what is best for our family. I am sure that you will love our new house once you see it. But, promise me you will try to like it." My mom questioned me in a comforting voice knowing that I was upset.

This house had brought so many memories into my life. I had a lot of firsts that I could remember. I remember my first play date, sleepover, pet, and more importantly the first day that I came home from the barn. This house may not have been the ideal house but, for its older characteristics, it had been perfect for everything that I had experienced.

The new house would have nothing better then what this house had offered me. All that I could hope for was a easy transfer and hopefully even better firsts.

Next thing I knew, my dad had locked the front door to what used to be our house. The engine rumbled and the car shook, it was time. The new house awaited our arrival.

Placing my hand on the cold, clear glass, I whispered, "Good bye."

Tears filled up my eyes, as I wiped a tear that had fallen down my cheek. I couldn't believe that was the last time I would see this house.

I stared out the window the entire time, watched every car, billboard, and tree pass by. The entire car ride, I remained silent, as I attempted to except what just happened. Why do we have to leave? What if I don't like it there? What if I don't fit in? What happens if I don't make any new friends, or get to experience the things I did at this house?

The moment I stepped out of the car, my eyes found their way straight to the house. It was humongous. A big, stained brown door appeared on the front as a tall, beat up looking fence ran along the entire property.

"So, Kara what do you think about our new house?" My mom asked as she stepped out of the car.

I shrugged my shoulders, as tears still formed in my eyes. I was still so upset; I couldn't believe that my parents were doing this to me. I couldn't even make eye contact with my parents so, I had kept my back turned towards them.

"Kara, there's something that I really want you to see." My dad grabbed onto my hand, as he pushed open the fence, we made our way around the house.

I couldn't take my eyes off of the house. It was so pretty. I couldn't believe that this it was my new home.

As we came around the back of the house, I caught a glimpse of something out of the corner of my eye.

"Ahhhhh, we have a barn now!?" I asked while I jumped up and down, feeling so much excitement.

I ran straight for the barn, slid the barn doors open and peered inside. I had taken in all that remained in front of me.

I couldn't believe that we had a barn-our own bard- in our backyard. Now we could get a horse to bring home. I could ride whenever my heart desired. I could look out the window whenever I wanted and see my horse. I was so excited!

***

Riding came into my life when I was just four years old and from the moment my eyes caught a glimpse of a horse, I knew that riding was a path I wanted to take. I was a little girl that took lessons at a local barn but wanted a pony of my own. Riding became a sport that I fell in love with. My parents were never too fond of the idea of me riding but, thanks to my aunt, they gave in. People used to tell my parents not to worry, that I was just going through a phase and I wouldn't be doing this for long.

***

The first time that I was introduced to a horse, was about three years ago.

The Ridgeway County fair. It was the biggest, and most popular fair around. It was filled with, games, food, and all kinds of rides. My aunt insisted that I go with her because she wanted to show me something.

I watched as building after building passed by. I stared out the window, and listened to my aunt sing a song, as the car projected the music throughout, even for me to here in the back. What does she want to show me? Is it something I've seen before?

"Step right up. Only five dollars to ride one of our ponies for five minutes! Yes, just five dollars!" A lady spoke loudly, as she stood facing out towards a crowd of people that stood around my aunt and me.

I couldn't take my eyes off of the large red and white tent. A tall metal pole stood tall in the middle with ropes that dangled from the tippity top. I stared at the ponies as they went round and round on the ropes while the pole spun. Next thing I knew, I felt a tap on my shoulder.

"Hey Kara, want to try something crazy?" My aunt said as she kneeled down to my height.

My aunt handed the five dollars to the lady that stood at the front of the tent.

"Walk this way, sweetie." The tent lady stuck one hand out to guide me down the path to the ponies, while she used her other hand to point where I should walk towards.

I was mounted on to this little brown pony and next thing I knew, the pony started stepping one foot after another. My jaw dropped and staring at my aunt I screamed out in excitement.

"This is so much fun! Go pony, Go!"

That was the moment that I knew that I wanted to keep riding. Round and round I went on that little brown pony, with a smile that stretched from ear to ear.

***

Every shooting star, 11:11, birthday wish, and Christmas list, "a pony" came first to my mind.

***

"Jacob, grab the lighter, please." My mom shouted from the kitchen to by brother, the sound of cabinets and drawers opening caught my attention.

I remained in the dining room, listening to the noises my mom made in the kitchen.

Hearing the doorbell, I stood up from my chair, I made my way towards the front door as I skipped.

"Grandma, Grandpa!" I said as I greeted them by wrapping my arms around them.

They were just the first to arrive, minute after minute, new people walked through the front door. Everyone greeted me with a hug and wished me a happy birthday. It lasted for what felt like years.

Next thing I knew, my mom was yelling from the kitchen asking if everyone was ready. The room went dark. Seconds later, my mom walked in with a cake. Placing it down in front of me, counted.

"On three, one, two, three."

I scanned the room, seeing the smiles that covered everyone's face. Tears fell down my mom's face.

"Mommy, what's wrong? Don't be sad mommy." I asked my mom as I turned towards her.

"Oh sweetie, don't worry. Mommy is just so proud of you and who you are growing up to be. You're just growing up so fast." My mom spoke in a softer voice, as she tried to hold back her tears.

"But mommy, I will always be your little girl." I said confidently as I tried to comfort my mom.

As everyone sang happy birthday, I thought about all of the things that I could wish for. I could wish for a new pair of uggs. I could wish for a ipad, cause everyone has one of those. No, I knew what I was going to wish for- a pony.

Loud clapping consumed the room as it echoed off the walls. I watched as smiles turned in to happy birthday, and as people started to shout and get louder.

"Okay, Kara, you can make a wish now." My dad spoke as he leaned close to my head, placing a kiss on my forehead.

"Make sure you don't spit on the cake." Jacob said giggling.

Closing my eyes tightly, I made my wish *I wish that I could have a pony of my own.* Ending it by opening my eyes and blowing out all 7 candles.

✳✳✳

Ten minutes must have passed because I turned around to the sound of my bedroom door creaking open and to the shaking of my bed as my two parents and older brother walked in. My brother disturbed my thoughts as he belly flopped onto my bed.

"Okay, lets go open some presents!" My father said in a joyful voice as he moved his hand, suggesting that I move towards the door.

My brother Jacob was ten years older than me. At this point in his life, he was looking into colleges and what he was planning to major in. He was always so supportive when it came to riding for me. Even though he wasn't as interested in riding like me, he always came to watch and even helped me with the horses sometimes.

Bolting out of my room and down the stairs in front of my family, all that I could think about was the tree and the one thing I hoped to see under the tree. My mind flooded with the items that I put on the list which I had made this year for my parents and Santa. I wanted nothing more than a pony to call mine, "a pony" appeared at least three times on that list.

***

I sat there. As I continued to stare at the blank piece of paper that rested in front of me. As I sat at my little pink table in my room, I focused on what to write down on my list for Santa. *Hmm, what should I ask for?*

Silence consumed the room as my little brain had gone to work about what I really wanted for Christmas this year. My hand laid flat on both the piece of paper and the table as I thought to myself quietly. *Well, lets see. I know, I'm going to write a pony a couple of times, cause I really want one. I'll also write an Ipad because everyone my age has one of those and I want to be cool.*

So immediately after that thought came rushing to my mind, I picked up the pen and slid my hand that grasped onto the pen across the paper. I started off by writing 'Dear Santa,' at the top. I went down a couple of spaces and continued to write, 'What I really want for Christmas this year is,' that was the moment that my mind became flooded with all of the things that I wanted.

I continued to furiously write down the list of things that I wanted as they came to the front of my brain. I had written at least twenty things down but the first three had been 'a pony'.

***

What turned out to be only about fifteen stairs, felt like an eternity as I longed to reach the living room where the presents would be. Once my eyes reached the tree with the presents, I screeched out,

"Mommy, Daddy, Santa was here! He brought presents!" I jumped up and down struggling to contain my excitement.

Running towards the tree, I examined all the presents that sat there, motionless. It was at that moment that I realized that nothing was moving. That automatically meant that there was no pony. *Was I not a good girl this year? I thought that I behaved and listened, what more could I have done?* Sadness had consumed me just when I quickly snapped back to reality.

"Kara, what's the matter?" My older brother questioned me as he realized how quickly my mood had changed.

"Hold that thought, I have to go get some firewood outside," my dad spoke as he dressed to bear the cold he was about to face.

My mom stood up and reached for a little box that appeared on top of all the rest. She placed it in front of me and told me to wait a second until she came back. All of a sudden, I heard footsteps as my mom ran back upstairs to retrieve something that she must have forgotten. When she first stepped back into the living room she spoke with a shortness of breath.

"Okay sweetie, you may open it now."

The box was little and wrapped with a bow and a sticker that said "no peeking". I slowly untied the bow and peeled the wrapping paper off the little box that sat in my hand. Not knowing what it was and still being upset about the fact that there wasn't a pony under the tree, I finally reached the box. Removing the lid to find tissue paper, I unfolded that and found a leather and snakeskin bracelet. I examined it, my eyes caught glimpse of what looked to be a name.

"Bella?" I read out loud, staring at the bracelet.

Really a bracelet? I was such a good girl this year. I don't even know whose name this. I looked up to see my mom with a grin from ear to ear, as she held her phone up, with the camera facing towards me.

I watched as my mom walked over to Jacob and whispered in his ears. She was too quiet for me to hear, but I guess that was the point of her whispering in his ear.

"Jacob, take this and cover Kara's eyes with it. I need you to guide your little sister outside." My mom spoke with an excited voice as she threw a bright white cloth at my brother. It was small and it looked exactly like one of our dish towels.

"Cool, I can make her walk into things." My brother stated as he began to laugh.

"Mom, now I'm scared. I don't want to walk into something."

"Don't worry, Kara, Jacob won't do that. Won't you Jacob?" My mom said, making me feel a little less nervous about the whole thing.

***

The next thing I knew, all that I could see was darkness. No sign of light to be found. The sound of the front door opening made my head spun in the direction that the sound came from. It was then that I felt someone's hands touch my shoulders.

"Ready squirt?" Jacob asked me as he rubbed his hands along the top of my shoulders.

"What are you guys doing and why can't I see it? I'm scared that I'm gonna walk into something." I said, concerned.

"Well, believe it or not, you're not missing anything yet and that's what I'm here for, to guide you." Jacob spoke in a very reassuring voice.

Step by step, I felt Jacob slightly pushing me left, right, straight, telling me to take a step up and down. He made it a lot less scary. All of a sudden, cold air hit my tiny body and that's when I noticed that we were outside. Jacob tapped me on the shoulder whispering in my ear,

"Okay, you can stop now. I'm going to take the blindfold off on three, okay? One, two, three."

The light was so blinding that the first couple of seconds I couldn't see because my eyes were trying to readjust. What I tried to make out was the blurry figure that stood right in front of me and as I looked out further into the distance, the big barn covered in white. Nothing was completely clear and everything had been so bright that I couldn't stare for more than a couple of seconds. I watched as the figure moved the slightest amount in front of me, side to side it seemed to sway. I listened to the crunch of the snow as I came to the conclusion that one of the crunches was much louder than usual.

Once they had adjusted, I looked forward and my jaw dropped.

"A Pony!" I screamed, and turned to my mom as she continued to hold the phone up. As my dad held onto the pony's lead rope. I felt a tap on my shoulder, and turned around to find Jacob who then handed me a note. Both my parents then encouraged that I read it out loud.

Dear Kara,

I would like you to meet Bella. She is a 15.2 hand American Quarter horse. Bella is 7 years old just like you and she was looking for a little girl to love. ou were such a good girl this year that I thought you would be perfect for eachother. This is because not only do little girls want to be loved, but so do ponies. Now with that being said, with a pony comes a lot of responsibility and I know you're up for the challenge. So, I want to wish you both happiness and good luck, have a Merry Christmas and enjoy each other. Not many little girls get ponies from me so, love her with all your heart and continue being a good girl. Now, you can see that not only being good, but having patience brings you big opportunities. Getting a pony is a once in a lifetime opportunity, so take it and run with it. njoy!

Love, Santa

"Now Kara, I would like you to meet Bella, your very own pony," my dad told me.

It finally clicked, it all made sense. Bella was my pony's name and that's why it was on the bracelet. I just couldn't believe my eyes, my dream had finally come true. Years of wishing and praying had finally paid off.

Redamancy

I came into Belle's life on a dreary Monday afternoon. The crisp, autumn wind violently ripped leaves from the trees, creating small tornadoes on the ground and leaving the branches bare. Clouds covered the sky, letting not a ray of sunshine through, making the day seem as if it were night. Hidden in a man's zippered-up jacket with just my head popping through, I was able to stay warm for the walk from the car to the front door. We climbed the steps to the front porch where the man knocked three times on the dark, wooden door. As we waited, he pulled me out from my safe shelter to peer into my eyes. Finally seeing his face for the first time in nearly 30 years, I examined his wrinkles and grey hairs. His hazel eyes drooped at the ends, with dark circles barely holding them up. He cleared his throat and shook as he struggled to speak.

"Please put a smile on my little Isabelle's face. She needs someone, she needs you, to help her through this hard time." Our conversation was cut short as a little girl with bouncy blonde curls threw open the door.

"Grandpa!" Her eyes grew wide when she looked up and saw me in her grandfather's arms. He quickly hid me behind his back and grinned from ear to ear for what seemed like the first time in a while.

"Now, now, Belle. Let me get inside and say hello to my daughter-in-law first, and then I will show you what I have for you." We stepped inside out of the brisk wind; a blast of heat from the fireplace warmed me up instantly. September 3rd, the magnets spelled out on the refrigerator.

Pictures of the little girl, Belle, and a middle-aged man who looked quite familiar covered the front and sides of it. After greeting Belle's mother, he sat down on the living room couch with me still behind his back and called Belle over to join us. He introduced me as "The Lost Teddy," once loved by her very own father, and then stored away when he suddenly became too old for stuffed animals and just old enough for cars and sports, never to find another person to love again; until now, that is. Theodore had called me Snuggles in the past, but Grandpa told Belle my name was Teddy, in honor of her father. Struggling to choke back tears, he held Belle's hand, "Whenever you miss your daddy, squeeze this bear tight, and Daddy will feel it up in heaven. While you won't be able to feel his hug, or hear him talk back, what's important is that he will always feel your love." That night, Belle fell asleep on the couch, squeezing me so tight I thought my eyes might pop off. I knew in that moment that we would be inseparable.

✳✳✳

Weeks passed by and soon the trees were completely bare of leaves, their arms covered in a thick blanket of white, along with the ground. I noticed Grandpa had been coming over a lot more often, at times staying so late that it just made more sense to sleep overnight in the guest bedroom and leave early for work the next day. Belle's mother came home one evening with "exciting news" of a new job opening at a hospital nearby. She'd been spending most of her time there, struggling to pay the bills with only one income now instead of two. This forced her to get Belle and I got a babysitter for the daytime until Grandpa came home in the afternoon. However, the careless 17-year-old did a lot more of sitting on the couch, watching television, and talking on the phone rather than paying attention to what Belle and I did. On days like those, we took off on one of our great adventures; building forts and playing make believe games was our specialty.

I could tell Belle was her father's daughter. I've had my fair share of adventures with him, Theodore, roaming the neighborhood, sometimes accompanied by friends and sometimes alone. His favorite place to bring me was often either the woods or his tree house. Deep in the forest we would build teepees and forts out of broken sticks and tree limbs, and have imaginary sword fights with "the bad guys." The tree house, on the other hand, had a more relaxed vibe. Sometimes, Theodore would bring his homework up, but it was much too difficult for me to understand, so sadly I was useless. Other times he would bring up stacks of paper and some crayons, and waste the day away drawing versions of me as a superhero. Eventually, we would act out these drawings in real life. Theodore and I had matching green capes, and we'd fly through the backyard without fear of anything that would challenge us. We would be off in our own little world until his mother would call him home for dinner.

Belle was quite obviously more girly than her father. Our outside adventures were more focused around the idea of princesses and dragons; me being the princess stuck inside the prison guarded by a dragon, and Belle with her pink cape and crown, the "princess superhero," as she called it, slaying the dragon and saving my life. While we often played outside, occasionally, we'd have a tea party in the warmth of the house and invite some of Belle's other stuffed animals, like Ellie the elephant, or George the monkey. They were always jealous of our relationship. Belle had Ellie and George since before she met me; they had grown up with her since she was a baby. However, her attention was more focused on my brown fur rather than Ellie's trunk or George's tail. I grew up with Belle's father before I grew old with Belle. In doing so, I was able to learn every secret that Theodore had, every aspect of his life. Belle and I clung to each other like we were joined at the hip; If she was there, anyone could find me along with her. I attended many family events with Grandpa, Mom, and Belle. We'd go to a cousin's birthday party, or a classic Sunday dinner with extended family members. I even made an appearance at Thanksgiving dinner. Mom was not too happy about that. Belle would act like she was feeding me some turkey or stuffing, accidentally getting it all over my face, and then shoved it into her mouth. She often avoided her family members when they attempted to talk to her, mumbling non-comprehensive words. Instead of engaging in some type of conversation with them, Belle would turn her back and continue to play with me.

The point is, I was Belle's best friend. Always her first choice, always the first she turned to when she missed her dad. My other best friend. My first best friend.

Eventually, the snow began to melt and flowers began to bloom. Days spent under a warm blanket in front of the TV shifted to running around outside, creating missions for ourselves in the woods surrounding Belle's backyard. With each coming day we woke up earlier and earlier, the morning sun illuminating our bedroom. Something must've happened with Grandpa's job, because he took the role of full-time babysitter. By the time we woke up in the morning, Mom was long gone, probably en-route to the hospital for one of her long shifts, and Grandpa was already cooking up a storm in the kitchen. The smell of crispy bacon and buttery pancakes wafted up the spiral staircase, luring us out of our comfy bed. Belle and I played with Grandpa throughout the day, taking small breaks for snacks and juice, waiting for Mom to come home in the evening.

***

The spring and summer quickly flew by, bringing us to the fresh scent of autumn. I had been with Belle for nearly a year, but it felt like it had been a lifetime. That day, Mom was the one to wake us, and she woke us up much earlier than Grandpa usually did. The sun had just barely risen above the tree line, and Belle was already up and getting ready for her day. However, that day was different. I could easily tell Belle's emotions, especially by the way she held on to me.

She pulled me close to her body and hugged me with both arms, and looked into my eyes, "It's a big day today, Teddy. Mommy says I have to go the whole day without her. Without her! And my only friend is you, you're the only one I know." Not being able to reassure her, I laid there limp, allowing her to softly pet my fur.

I've only felt Belle squeeze me in the same way she did today a handful of times. Mom had brought us to the doctor's office for Belle's yearly checkup. This was not too long after I learned of my late best friend, and I assumed it was her first doctor visit without Theodore alongside her. Belle squeezed me tighter than she did the first night she got me, ripping a small hole in my neck, though nothing Mom couldn't easily mend as she had in the past. Moms could always fix anything and everything. Even when I was with Theodore, his mom was able to patch me up in seconds after years of wear and tear. Her teardrops soaked my fur, darkening it and matting it down, as I attempted to comfort her.

The doctor laughed a little, "It's okay Belle, it's only a finger prick. It won't take more than a couple seconds." Allowing Belle to hug me with the strength of a hundred men, her breathing began to slow. I knew this is what I would have to do today. While most mornings Belle and I would go straight downstairs for breakfast and lounge in pajamas all day, today she hopped in the shower and got dressed, and pulled a backpack down the carpeted stairs, squeezing me close to her heart.

"Are you ready for your first day of Kindergarten?" Mom sounded enthusiastic, clearly attempting to get rid of the nervous look that encompassed Belle's face.

"I guess," my best friend sounded unsure. We arrived at the building a little after 8:00 AM, the clock in Mom's car read. The yellow buses filled the parking lot, but she managed to find a spot nonetheless. Still holding me as tight as before, Belle followed Mom into the brightly colored classroom filled with art supplies and books. Belle quickly looked around the classroom, her eyes darting from one corner of the room to the next, taking in all the new faces. She seemingly decided it was not for her, and ran into the bathroom while squeezing me even closer to her, "This is too scary. I can't do this, I miss Daddy," she muffled her words into my fur, matting it with her tears. It wasn't until Mom came into the bathroom that Belle softened her grip on my hand and wiped her tears.

"Now, Belle. I have to go to work and you need to stay here in school. I will be back at the end of the day to pick you up," Mom paused when she saw Belle's eyes start to well up again, "you'll be so distracted with activities, you won't even know that I left."

"What am I gonna do for lunch? Who am I gonna eat with? Can Grandpa come eat with me?" Belle rattled off questions while her grip on my arm tightened.

"Think about all the new friends you'll make! You can eat your lunch with them. They're going to love you as much as I do. Have fun, Belle, I love you!" Mom gave Belle a hug and a kiss before walking out of the room. She hugged me tight as her teardrops once again soaked my head. I laid there limp; my only way to help my best friend was to let her hug me close to her heart.

Day by day, Belle was finally able to find it easier to go to school without Mom. She soon began to stuff me in her backpack rather than holding me throughout the entire school day. This bothered me; how was I supposed to protect her when I couldn't even see what was happening? This was my responsibility now, since she was without the comfort of Mom or Grandpa. I'm the only one who knows everything about this precious little girl. I need to keep her safe.

I soon found out after a while that Belle didn't need me anymore. The first day of middle school was when this horrible news became clear. She woke up earlier than the previous school years to get ready, more excited than she had been in the past. Immediately after her shower, she turned blow dryer on, and the sound of Belle perfecting her golden hair for the school day filled the upstairs bathroom. She waltzed back into her room to get dressed and grab her backpack. This first day of school, though, she neglected to grab me. At first, I assumed it was a careless mistake; Belle had her father's memory, and was constantly forgetting everything. But then the second day of school came and went, and I stayed sitting on her bedside table, leaning against a picture of Belle and her father. This continued on for months. Staying seated on the table, watching the trees change colors, and watching my best friend forget about me. Years flew by, and there I sat, watching Belle grow into the amazing woman I knew she'd become, yet without me in the picture. She eventually started high school, leaving me earlier in the morning than she did in the past. I watched her come home everyday from school to do her homework, and then rush to field hockey practice. Many people came and went throughout these four years, paying me no attention. Her friend groups were constantly changing, but I noticed one friend that was always present. She must've been Belle's new best friend. My heart ached to see my replacement become closer and closer with my former companion. They spent nearly every day together, talking about boys and what they were going to wear to the next party. Belle's new friend was able to be there for her; she was able to give her helpful advice, while all I was good for was when she needed to squeeze me. I know I wasn't much help, but I thought I was a pretty good friend. I had been there for Belle since the beginning, being the only one who understood her feelings about Theodore's death. She was always able to talk to me about anything and everything, without me judging one word of it. Now, I was lucky if she even glanced my way. Maybe it's for the best. Or maybe not.

Not being able to protect Belle had to have been the hardest part of this detachment. Countless times during her high school career, Belle would be up until nearly three o'clock, whether it was doing homework or worrying about bullies. The worst day was when she and her boyfriend broke up. Never in my 12 years of knowing Belle had I seen her so upset, so torn apart over another person; except, of course, her father. Had this been when Belle was six, she would've curled up in bed with me, holding me all the way until morning. But times had changed, and Belle had moved on without me by her side, denying me the ability to comfort her like I had in the past with her father. The muffled sound of her cries echoed throughout her room; this broke my heart, hearing my best friend so distraught. A couple of times Belle had glanced over at me, giving me hope that maybe I would be lucky enough Unfortunately, there was still nothing for me to do. She didn't need me anymore. Her friends, along with Mom and Grandpa, were able to take my spot in her life, taking care of her whenever she needed taking care of. Time like this happened over many years, especially while Belle was in college. She would come home much too often; she became homesick nearly every week she was away, each day getting worse than the last. But not once did she reach for me. In her eyes I had no use anymore; I was simply a childhood toy.

In Belle's sophomore year of college, Mom and Grandpa decided it would be best to clean out Belle's old room. When I heard of this, I simply thought it would be the usual vacuuming and dusting Belle had done in the past, but boy was I wrong. Grandpa entered the room carrying a large brown box labeled "attic" and plopped it on Belle's bed. I felt quite uneasy; I knew what was going to happen next. A wave of deja vu washed over me as I recalled Theodore's mother doing this exact same thing when he left home. I felt sorry for Ellie and George; they were the first to go in. My heart sank when Grandpa picked me up off of the table; I thought maybe this time I would get the privilege of staying on the table. If you can even call that a privilege. I took one last look at Belle's room before I would be imprisoned. Her room had changed a lot throughout the years. She was always one to quickly grow out of everything; she painted her room nearly every other year, as if it reflected her aging. My table I rested on for years still had the picture of Belle and her father; I assumed that was the one item that could never be put away in a box in the attic. Dust had covered the table, as Belle had been away for quite some time, though one circle was clean, the area I had been. Maybe when she came back she would realize I had been there, but was gone now. I was brought back to reality as Grandpa placed me on top of Ellie and George, shutting the top of the box. I knew in that moment that I would remain here for a long time, much longer than I had preferred.

***

An old man finally pulled me out of the darkness today, lifting me out of the box and brushing off the dust bunnies. That's what I began to call it after a while. The Darkness. I could see nothing- hear nothing. Feeling that loneliness reminded me of my years on Belle's table, forgotten like a wilted rose. Just like the one Grandpa gave Belle on the night of her first Father-Daughter dance. After a quick glance-over observation, I realized it was Grandpa. His previously grey hair was hardly visible, thinner than the paper Theodore would draw on in his secluded tree house. Wrinkles covered his face, though this time he had no circles drooping his hazel eyes. In fact, a weak yet still charming smile spread across his face as he lifted me into the air.

"You've put a smile on Isabelle's face in the past, I trust you'll do this same this time," Grandpa pulled a small black bow tie out of his pocket and placed it around my neck. I was beyond confused, but it reminded me of when Belle and I used to play dress up, so I went along with it. We left the house in a limo that led us to a large building with flowers covering the grounds. Grandpa hurriedly half-ran into the building out of the autumn breeze with me tucked inside his jacket and closed the door behind us before the colorful leaves snuck in. We weaved our way through a swarm of people to a room tucked away in the back, ignoring all of the "hellos" along the way.

A woman in a long white dress stood in front of us, lace covering the skirt and extending along the ground to an elegant train. Her curly golden locks cascaded down her back, bouncing as she tilted her head while looking in the mirror, as if something was not right. Grandpa and I stepped to the side a bit, just enough for the girl to see us in the mirror behind her. Her eyes lit up like fireworks, and she whipped around, though careful not to disturb her hairdo. The same smile I remember from the first time I saw Belle crept across her face; a single teardrop fell from her bright green eyes and she gasped quickly.

Belle carefully wiped the tear and whispered, "Teddy, I've missed you."

Pronto

I n a matter of seconds, the smell of roasted nuts drew the attention of Jeffrey's grumbling stomach as he dodged oncoming strangers heading towards the bus stop. His pace was a bit faster than usual as he tried to make up the time bicycling. She was one of those new foldable jobies, the optimal method of transportation for people in the city who just happened to wake up a little too late.

It had all begun the night before when the party got a bit too wild. One thing led to another and before he knew it, Jeffrey was dancing on top of the china cabinet somewhere on the Lower East-Side. Granted, tomorrow was his birthday, so why not live a little? The question was answered that morning as he woke up sleeping next to the toilet bowl, only to remember that he'd been scheduled to work the morning shift at the cafe. As he got ready amidst aches and pains, he walked downstairs to find his neighbor sitting at the bottom step. Sheepishly smiling at her, he remembered the previous night's revelry. One never really knows who their neighbors are until its two in the morning and you're singing karaoke to Journey's Don't Stop Believing on the terrace. That'd been the end of the evening for Jeffrey- as the last note blasted from the speakers, as if on schedule, there came a rap at the door with the neighbor on the other side, asking, or rather, yelling, at them to turn it down. As the party ended, the last thing Jeffrey knew, he was seeing his food again as he stumbled into the bathroom and fell asleep. He winced as he thought back to the end of the evening, opening the front door pushing past his neighbor. Stepping outside, his eyes strained against the bright light of the sun. Fumbling with his phone, Jeff began sorting through the texts from the previous night as he began his trek to the cafe.

Making his way up the street, he was overcome by another feeling of nausea as he passed a taco stand. Bringing his hand to his nose in an attempt to waft the smell away, he groaned remembering the six tacos he'd eaten the night prior before he saw them again just hours after.

Mexican food itself had never proposed a challenge Jeff wasn't willing to taste. The mere thought of a cuisine that was built upon the fusion of indigenous, staple-ingredients always sparked his interest. The relationship between different combinations of flavors was simply unavoidable in a city of diverse cultures. Each component acting as a smaller part of a much larger jigsaw puzzle in an attempt to satisfy some stranger's senses was much less than a task for Jeffrey. Something about being able to create a physical and nutritionally attractive embodiment of art within food captivated his attention like no other. Plus, who wouldn't enjoy the ability to change the direction of someone's day with a good, hearty meal?

In an effort to stop the sudden urge to gag, Jeffrey clasped a hand over his mouth as heat began to rise up his esophagus. An overwhelming wave of discomfort settled over the concoction of filtered water and grain subsiding in Jeff's stomach as he felt droplets of sweat bead across the top of his brow.

Throwing up was never easy for Jeff as he had always hated the idea of being wasteful like that. The idea that some people went hungry, without the opportunity to eat, burdened him. With vendors and convenience stores around nearly every block, it might've seemed unnatural to go without grub in the city, but the maintenance of a livelihood in a roaring metropolis could never be performed independently, not to mention all other things unplanned. However, throughout most of his younger years, Jeffrey's mother attempted to do so.

For a single mother in the city, it wasn't the easiest raising Jeffrey. Day after day, trying to make ends meet was difficult as a maid. From the early morning until the sun set, Jeffrey's mother would try and clean for cash. The hours were exhausting, but a smile across her face always went a long way in helping others. Granted, sometimes people didn't appreciate their luxury, but on the off chance that someone felt generous, days became much easier. But while the job helped keep a roof over their heads, paying for a solid meal was hard sometimes. Jeffrey often fled to the marketplace with his mother's money stuffed in his pocket, wrapped in one of those stretchy yellow bands accompanied by a list of groceries that changed weekly depending on how well it went.

Each Sunday, the fresh fruits and vegetables would be imported and many gathered to get the best of the best before the new week started. Jeffrey always wanted to help his mother with groceries and began to become more accustomed with the food assortment as he enjoyed tasting the different foods at the marketplace. The variety of colors in each region's selection of produce prompted him to investigate the differences and try something new. With no one at home, the place became a home of its own for Jeffrey throughout the years as he began to meet new people in search of good food.

On one of those sunny Sundays while perusing the grounds of the marketplace, Jeffrey was startled by a stranger.

"Excuse me, sir." The man interrupted while Jeffrey tried juggling the tomatoes he had just picked up from the wicker basket.

"Hey! Watch it buddy!" Jeffrey yelped, extending his reach to grasp the plummeting oversized, red berry before slipping on what appeared to be some sort of screw. As the little metal piece rattled across the pavement, it slowed to a stop before the stranger's path.

Maintaining conversation and learning to hustle were important in a place where that was the only way to survive. Talking to strangers at first seemed out of the ordinary to Jeffrey, but as time carried on, communicating with people became less and less difficult as curiosity arose. In the meantime, with Jeffrey becoming older, he felt the need to diverge from his mother's support as he looked to find a job to support himself and contribute to the family's expenses. The idea that his mother kept on putting herself through hell frustrated him, and Jeffrey felt the need to find something he was good at. Normal schooling never seemed to be the right fit.

Jeff's heart rate continued to climb as the feeling continued to linger. "You can do this," he gibbered in a dazed-like state, hoping for the pressure in his abdomen to subside. Tomorrow will be a new day, he thought to himself. Jeffrey began to doze off into a slumber as his arms lay wrapped around the base of the can seeking comfort from the all-too familiar tiled floor.

As the sun began to peek through the blinds in the bedroom of the city flat, the sound of a hollow siren invaded the complex and heads began to turn on the streets below. The engine headed down the street as an eruption of horns arose from impatient drivers who rather get to their destinations on time than be bothered by a big red truck.

Jeffrey stayed laying face-down extended across the area of the bathroom until the sound of waves began to crash from the pocket of his jeans. A series of snorts and heavy breathing preceded the cue to get out of bed. With a triumphant grunt, Jeffrey sprawled out on the floor and screamed with the gratification of a good stretch. "How'd I get in here?" he questioned, in a state of half-consciousness.

It was one thing to just lay there all night, but getting up posed new challenges as Jeffrey's insides remained fatigued, twisting and turning with each and every movement.

After a few moments of struggling, Jeff attempted to regain balance, bringing all fours together. On his way up, Jeff managed to bump his head on the side of the porcelain throne before grabbing his scalp in pain. A circular bump began to come through. Rubbing the sensitive area, he winced. While raising his hand, Jeffrey caught a whiff of his armpit and began to feel his stomach turn again. He quickly plugged his nose and headed for the shower.

The bathroom had looked different since yesterday, but as the walls started to shapeshift, Jeff found himself nauseous again and this time he knew there was no way to avoid the impending doom that would lie ahead. With the courage of a thousand men, Jeffrey quickly slipped his fingers down his throat making sure to touch the punching bag in the back. In the matter of seconds, the deed was done. A feeling of relief instantly eased Jeffrey's aching body as the toxins, unofficially, left his system. Ehh, that wasn't so bad, he thought, as another burp began to surface, triggering the man to hunch over and let out a large belch of various scents.

Whilst cleaning up the mess he'd just made, Jeffrey reached into the pocket of his slacks and pulled out his cell phone. Jeff swiped on his device and within a few seconds, a symphony of different tones alerted the device and messages began to flock wishing Jeff the best on his own 25th anniversary of being alive. Wow, he thought, filing through collections of photos with friends and acquaintances, I really got it good.

Passing the mirror, Jeff caught a glimpse of himself and let out a laugh he unsuccessfully tried to suppress. A formation of black lines wrapped in plastic took the place of where his right sleeve should have been. On the left, a collection of mysterious stains ranging from pico de gallo to what was hopefully just queso covered the black short-sleeve. "Here we go again," he exasperated.

Jeffrey nonchalantly attempted to examine the damage done to his bicep from the evening prior, reaffirming its permanence and blanking whilst trying to understand the story behind it.

The plastic wrap unraveled with ease as Jeffrey gently tugged at the tattoo in a most curious fashion, being careful not to irritate the punctured skin. After a few moments of unraveling, the wound made contact with the cool air of the city flat and his muscle became tense.

For a moment, Jeff's breathing halted and his palms became sweaty as his attention wandered back to the mirror. With a solemn grin of satisfaction, Jeffrey exhaled and continued to get ready.

Jeffrey waddled into the shower in a zombie-like fashion and forced the handle three quarters to the left. Without warning, the head began to drip, followed by a rush of cold water onto Jeffrey's torso. "Ahhh!" He screamed in shock as his muscles tightened and his breathing began to dissipate. Something had been wrong with the building's water heaters and it was under maintenance since God knows when. For the time being, the only way to get hot water was to, "boil it like back in the day," according to one of the old timers in the residency. *"Happy Birthday to me!"* Jeffrey muttered under his chilly breath. In an attempt to combat the temperature, Jeffrey frantically washed his body in a routine-like fashion as if he had done it before. Morning shifts had always been Jeff's go-to.

Something about waking up and starting the day in the cafe, talking to people who came and went usually wasn't a burden. Employee discounts made life a lot easier, especially when Jeffrey needed the occasional morning pick-me-up. He quickly came to the realization that a nice cup of joe would accompany his breakfast while washing up and started to slobber a little. Hey, the paychecks weren't the greatest, but one thing was for sure, there was always food around to grub on.

The sound of glass and stone buzzed around the bathroom as Jeff's phone vibrated signaling it was nearly time to get ready.

Sooner than later, he hopped out of shower and began to dry off. A whirlwind of water drizzled around the room as Jeff violently shook his head into the towel that smelt a little less than fresh. In fact, the whole apartment wasn't the cleanest either. It was not like Jeff was a slob, but the place could definitely be spruced up a bit. Empty containers of what seemed to be Chinese food laid on top of the counter where food was to be made, but due to the circumstances, that was off the table.

Jeff began to make his way into the bedroom and out of the bathroom, scavenging for a clean pair of grey slacks and a top to coalesce the contemporary atmosphere of the place.

Pronto wasn't the fanciest of diners, but Eric, the son of the boss, always made it top priority to look the part. Something about the importance of neutrality got to him and the restaurant reflected the family's ideals.

Sitting on the edge of the East River allowed for masses of customers to come in which usually allowed for better tips, especially when the weather was nice. And, tips always helped the ever-increasing rent required to survive in the city.

***

Immature Independence

"**A**nna, remember what I said—"

"Do not go past the sidewalk," I finished for her. I beamed at my mom to let her know I was listening despite the fact that I was strongly refraining from rolling my eyes. Again and again and again she told me the same thing. 'Don't go past the sidewalk, don't play near the street.' I was not a baby like Joey, he was four and wouldn't listen to Mommy like I do. I am seven years old.

I will.

Her eyes narrowed slightly, lingering a moment longer before she unlocked the glass storm door. My hand itched to reach out and do it myself, to feel the cool touch of the metal and have the latch come undone in my fingers, but hearing the satisfying click was enough for now. I was free.

I hopped down the wooden steps two at a time and raced to the middle of the front yard with my four barbies and their Barbie Dream truck. We settled where the grass was a little more worn than the rest of the yard right next to the round garden with the pink and yellow flowers. My favorite were the pink lilies. It was the perfect spot to play summer vacation and send Barbie, Ken, Dolly, and Stephen to Costa Rica.

"Oh, Ken! This is such a nice vacation!" I voiced for Barbie. The other two nodded in agreement.

"You're welcome Barbie! Only the best for the best girl in the world!"

The deep voice I used for Ken made me laugh. I took the doll's tiny hand and made it reach for Barbie's even tinier one. It made me think about my boyfriend in school and my brows furrowed. Ex, actually. I found him talking to Lily Porter and I don't believe in integrity or whatever it's called when you're not faithful to your boyfriend or girlfriend.

The four barbies sat comfortably on the grass against the stone edging of the round garden.

"Boo!" someone shouted in my ear. I shrieked and jumped up. Behind me was Grace Thomas, laughing. I didn't like Grace Thomas very much. She always smelled funny and played weird.

"Grace!" I shouted angrily. Just then, my mom appeared at the door with her hands on her hips. She was smiling big. Like really big. The same big that she uses when Joey and I are being too loud during her and Daddy's garden parties in the backyard. I wonder what brought this on.

"Grace!" she called happily. Grace turned around.

"Hi, Mrs. Abasolo." Mom just kept staring at her with that smile. I wonder if she didn't like Grace. After a moment of silence, my mom spoke.

"What brings you here?"

"I was just walking around the neighborhood." And if it was possible, her smile grew bigger.

"You know it's not safe to walk around alone Grace. It's very dangerous near the streets. Especially when you want to cross!"

"It's okay, Mrs. Abasolo, I was careful. My mom and dad don't care if I walk by myself because I'm seven and I'm big enough." My mouth fell open. Mommy would never let us talk like that. How come I wasn't big enough to be by myself! There was snapping in my face.

"Anna?" Grace asked again. I looked at her confused.

"Your mom asked if we wanted to play inside?" I looked at my mom over Grace's shoulder. Her eyebrows reached the middle of her forehead and I knew. No stomping my feet this time. We didn't have a choice.

I smiled weakly and looked at Grace. "Sure."

Before Grace could touch my toys I picked them all up and carried them inside. I didn't want her to break anything before we reached the playroom. As we passed my mom, I moved my shoulders away so she couldn't touch them as a way of saying thanks. I heard her sigh and it made me feel sad. But I was angry too. After setting the truck and dolls down in the playroom, I turned to Grace.

"We have to wash our hands first. My mom always says after we come inside, that's what we have to do." Grace gave a halfhearted nod as she looked around the room. I don't know why she always did this. It's not like she hasn't been over before. The two of us went to the main floor bathroom to wash our hands.

"I like your soap," Grace commented. I looked at it. It was just the regular pump soap that smelled like vanilla. There wasn't much to like.

"Uh, thanks," I mumbled. After we finished, the two us tried to walk back to the playroom but my mom stopped us again.

"Anna, Grace, why don't the two of you come have a snack before you play. Joey is already sitting at the table." My little brother waved to us from his seat. Grace waved back and looked at me.

"How 'bout it, Anna? Then we'll have lots of energy to play." I clenched my fists.

"I don't want to have a snack! I don't want to have a lot of energy and I don't want to play with you!" Grace took a step back, hurt. Sheepishly, I glanced at my mom. She was not happy.

"Anna Jamie Abasolo," she started. "Go to your room."

I opened my mouth to speak. "But Mommy—"

"Listen to what I'm saying and go!" Without looking at anyone I raced up the stairs to my room. I couldn't let them see me cry.

***

Ages later, I heard a light knocking at my door. I rolled over to the other side so I wouldn't be able to see whoever opened it. They sat on the edge of my bed and placed a hand on my shoulder.

"Anna," Mom's soothing voice called. I refused to look at her. "Anna?" After no response from me, she sighed again.

"Anna remember when I told you we have to be nicer to Grace?" Oh yeah. I had forgotten.

"Tell me what I said about that." I rolled over on my other arm and flattened the fur on my pillow to be met with eyebrows only going up slightly.

"You said that we had to be nicer to Grace because she doesn't have as much stuff as me and Joey do." My mom nodded and put a hair back in its place.

"You know Daddy and I love you right?" It was my turn to nod. "Well, Grace doesn't know that for sure with her parents. Sometimes moms and dads aren't very nice to their children." I thought for a moment.

"You mean like when Joey and I don't listen and you and Daddy yell at us?" My mom opened her mouth but laughed instead.

"No, Anna. I mean there are times when good children like Grace do listen and they still get yelled at." My mouth fell open. There was no way that was true. My mom didn't know what she was talking about. "Do you understand?"

I nodded anyway.

"Good," Mommy smiled. She kissed my forehead. "You remember that we're having a garden party tonight, yes? I want you to go downstairs and pick a dress out and get showered. Grace is watching TV with Joey." I frowned slightly and she gave me the look. I shook the expression from my face.

"I'm going to get ready. Be nice to Grace, she's staying for the party." With that, she stood up and walked down the hall to her own room. I stood up and made my way down the stairs.

As I walked in the family room, Grace stood up and smiled nervously. "Hi Anna. I'm sorry we didn't get to play earlier but I—"

"Is that my dress?" Grace raised her eyebrows and looked down.

"Yeah, your mom let me shower and pick out a dress—"

"That's my *favorite* dress," I seethed. I couldn't be nice to Grace after that one. She went too far. Grace started wringing her hands together and blinking rapidly.

"I uh, I mean I can, I mean, I mean I can get another—"

"Why are you here!" I exploded. I knew why she was here but I didn't care. That was *my* favorite dress. "You can't come here just because your parents are mean to you!" Grace stopped. The blinking, the wringing.

Stopped.

I don't know what happened but Grace didn't seem nervous

anymore. She didn't seem mad at me either but she definitely wasn't happy. Even Joey stared at the two of us, not saying anything.

"Grace, I—" She pushed past me out of the playroom and into the foyer. I followed her as she walked towards the laundry room.

"Hey what are you doing?" I didn't know what to do as Grace looked around all the piles of clothing. She even opened the dryer which turned out to be empty. Suddenly I heard my mom.

"Anna do you know where I left my silver earrings?" Grace looked at me. She was going to tell. Before I could do anything Grace pushed past me again and marched straight towards my mom.

"Mrs. Abasolo I have to go home," she declared. Mom blinked in confusion.

"You're not staying for the party?" Grace shook her head and glanced at me.

"I just remembered that my mom wanted me to help cook tonight. My grandma is coming over. But my clothes are still in the wash." My mom nodded, disappointed.

"Well, okay. You can take some of Anna's old clothes." Grace started wringing her hands and glancing at me again.

"Are you sure? I don't want to take anything that's not mine." Mom waved a hand at her.

"Nonsense, Anna doesn't wear any of this. Isn't that right, Anna?" I nodded. "Then that settles it. Take anything you like, sweetie. And let me know when you're ready to leave so I can walk you back." Grace nodded obediently and started sifting through the clothes I didn't wear anymore. After my mom left, Grace's face changed again to that not mad-not happy expression. Without looking at me she whispered.

"Is it really ok for me to take anything I want, Anna?" I nodded vigorously before remembering she wasn't looking.

"Yes."

Silence.

"Can I get you a bag for the stuff you're taking?" I was eager to get out of there. When Grace agreed I turned swiftly on my heel and walked back into the kitchen. I searched under the sink for our paper bags and pulled out the biggest one I could find. I felt bad about the dress and wanted to make up for it.

"Here you go." Grace pushed a stack of clothes inside the bag and kept a shirt and a pair of shorts in her hand. Once again she spoke without looking at me.

"Where can I change?" I pointed towards the bathroom we were in earlier and she went. I decided to be helpful and take the bag she left and bring it to the door. It was heavy. Before going back to the kitchen to wait for Grace I decided to check on Joey. He was still sitting on the couch but now he was staring at something out the window.

"Joey?" I called. He didn't look at me. "Joey? What are you looking at?"

"Those look like my cars," he commented.

"What cars?" I walked towards the window to see what he was pointing at. Sure enough, life sized cars raced by on the street at all different speeds. This wasn't a normally busy street yet I rolled my hands together like Grace at the thought of being hit. Joey always crashed his toy cars on purpose but imagining that for real life made my palms sweaty.

"Hey Joey why don't we play with your toy cars!" I grabbed my little brother's hand and pulled him away from the window. The two of us crawled in search of his possessions and bumped into a pair of legs. Grace's.

"I'm ready to leave now," she mumbled. I stood up and shook my head.

"They're, they're out there. They're out there Grace you can't go outside." She looked over my shoulder through the front door window.

"I don't see anything." I turned around. Sure enough, the streets were empty.

"But they were just there... I saw them! There were many dangerous cars!" Grace didn't look convinced. I backed off. "I'm going to tell my mom you're ready to go."

I took Joey by the hand and led him up to my mom's room. She wasn't in there which meant she was in her bathroom. I knocked on the door.

"Mommy, Grace is ready to leave." After a minute she opened the door and a wave of her expensive perfume wafted through the air. The Parkers must be coming. Joey started crying.

"What's the matter, Joey?" Mom asked as she picked him up. She raised her eyebrows and looked me.

"Anna?"

"I don't know Mom, we were just looking for his cars because we saw many on the street and then Grace wanted to go home and the cars were gone." Mom frowned. I didn't like it when she did that.

"Maybe Grace should wait a bit before leaving." The three of us exited the room and went back downstairs. There was no sight of Grace.

"Grace?" I called. Nothing. As Mom went to check around the kitchen I felt the need to open the front door. So I did. Nothing looked out of the ordinary...

Except Grace was about to cross the street with the heavy bag. I opened my mouth to shout but nothing came out. Just as Grace took a step onto the street my mom appeared behind me and screamed her name as a car whizzed around the corner.

Gravity

eter Dolor was hunched over the toilet in the basement of the venue. The stone on the walls that appeared once white, had a garbage juice brown color to them. His taste buds were once again exposed to the flavors of rum and pizza followed by a sour aftertaste. There was a banging on the door that startled him.

"Come on, Pete. I know you're having a tough time in there, but we got to go," said John who played rhythm on guitar.

Peter grabbed the half empty bottle of rum and swung open the bathroom door. John looked at Peter's drained face.

"How do you feel?" asked John.

"Like crap," Peter mumbled, "What a waste."

"You drank too much before the show?" John shouted.

"No, of course not, you moron. I'm just a little nervous for the show."

Peter moved past John to the backroom and there he saw it. Its solid black aside from the dark oak fretboard. Instead of using a standard strap, Peter preferred the bolted on chain that's as silver as the four dense strings. Peter's bass had always had a rattle to it ever since he bought it. Bass guitar wasn't his first choice, but it became his instrument out of necessity of the band.

They all gathered on the stage to practice before the show and the room was empty. Peter dropped his pick repetitively.

"You alright there, butterfingers?" asked Rad, the lead guitarist.

Peter responded by doing an aggressive flick of his hand under his chin.

Each strike of his bass was followed by a thunderous and bellowing sound, as the floor would shake. They played as if they were one unit rather than four people, each person perfectly jumped to each note and chord. And then, there was Peter. He kept missing notes as he seemed to stumble a little over his bass.

"Peter, for Christ's sake. How are we gonna play tonight?" Rad asked.

"How we play every night pretty good, but kind of crappy," responded Peter.

"You can't keep doing this, you have no reason to be this nervous." Rad said, shaking his head. "You're a great bass player, and I know you are because you can play pretty good even when your buzzed for crying out loud."

"Alright, alright, alright, just shut up and lets get this show over with."

Rad said under his breath, "Yeah sure...idiot."

"Excuse me?" Peter said, his eyebrows furrowed.

"Nothing Peter, I'm just messing around with you. But don't forget you can let off a little steam at the party after the show."

Peter just let out a small chuckle.

They practiced until it was almost time for the show because they wanted a short break. Everyone made sure their instruments were tuned. Peter went to the back room to put some extra picks in his pocket and he saw the bottle of rum right where he had left it, staring back at him. Peter snatched a handful of picks and took one last slug from the bottle before he went back to the stage.

"Hello everyone, we are The Sons of Surtur," announced Peter. "Enjoy the show or don't, I do not care."

The small venue responded with a loud cheer.

"1!...2!...3!" the drummer shouted, tapping his drumsticks together.

"Ahhhhhhh!" Peter screamed while the band started to pick up speed.

They played vigorously into their first song. Peter didn't have nearly as many slips as he had during practice and the bass continued to rattle as the packed venue roared. The thunderous, rattling bass caused the mass of people to shake the ground beneath them. Everyone bobbed their heads in unison as the second song started, and everyone was going wild.

Peter looked out to the mass of people shouting for him as beads of sweat started forming on his head. Standing on the stage, he felt his knees start to wobble as they grew weak underneath the weight of gravity and lights that shone down onto the stage. The walls of his chest seemed to be closer and closer, restraining his breathing. Sweat was soaking into his shirt as the fans chanted his name. As his head spun, he resisted being pulled to the ground. Peter's heart was pounding, and he darted his eyes around with each mistake to see if anyone noticed.

After the show, the band had to pack up the van and head to the party at John's house. When they arrived, the party had already started. Walking up the sidewalk, they noticed that the door ajar. It looked as though they'd left it open for anyone to come join in the fun.

"Alright boys, just leave your stuff in here. I don't want any halfwits busting any of our stuff." John said, stretching his back, placing his instrument to the ground.

"I was terrible tonight," Peter sighed.

"You really weren't, Pete, don't beat yourself up," John responded.

John reached out his hand to give him a pat on the back, but Peter hit away his hand as if it were an obnoxious gnat.

"Shut up! I know how bad I was. I messed up like 20 times- save me your pity."

"Definitely not 20, but even if you did, none of those boneheads out there can hear your small mess ups," John assured.

"Of course they did," Peter shook his head

"I really don't think they did," Rad interjected, "They aren't exactly scholars out there."

Peter grabbed his bass and jumped out of the back of the van and said, "Whatever. You guys go ahead in I'm gonna go through the back."

"Okay, Pete, just don't be a stranger. I'm sure there are some girls in there that would love to meet you," teased Kenny.

Peter just headed towards the back of the house while the rest of the band entered through the front. They burst into the house and stood tall. Everyone praised their arrival with loud yells. "You guys played awesome!" one said holding up his arm with the rock on symbol, "Great show tonight!" another said.

Peter snuck in through the back door and slowly made his way past the kitchen. He was cautious of his black leather boots from stomping too loud, and made his way down the basement, shutting the door slowly behind him. The basement was silent and dark except for the muffled clamor from the party. He sunk into the couch and started to play his bass to himself. He didn't bring his amp to not attract any unwanted attention. The bass was so low and quiet, that the rattle could be heard more clearly. He created a riff and started bobbing his head, and played it repeatedly. Trying his best to ignore the obnoxious rattle, he closed his eyes and put his feet up on the table and consisted his practice. His peace was disturbed once he heard the basement door creak open.

"Anymore booze down here?" asked the stranger.

Peter darted his head towards the stairs, "Get out of here!" and continued to play.

The stranger laughed as he entered the basement, "Not before you let me help you fix that."

"What, the rattle? You know how to fix it? I could never figure it out," said Peter.

"Of course I do, and I'll do it for free, so your next show doesn't suck," said the stranger in a snarky tone.

Peter smirked as he stood up handing the bass to the stranger, "Alright, let see it then."

Peter paused for a moment, "Hey, I don't remember seeing you at the show, and I don't think I've seen you around town. What's your name?"

"You can just call me Tony. And you're Peter right?" he replied.

"Yeah I'm Peter."

The two shook hands but Peter looked at him with one eyebrow slightly raised, unsure what to think of this man.

"Alright Tony, so how do you fix this thing?" Peter said crossing his arms.

"Are there tools down here?"

"Yeah, actually, right in here." Peter reached into a drawer and pulled out a tool box, handing them to Tony

"So why aren't you upstairs with everyone else?" asked Tony

"Why would I be up there with all those fakes? Not a single person knows who any of the bands members are personally. I bet they don't even know our names," Peter said.

Tony started tightening one of the screws, "Not me, I know all you guys, and I've actually been to quite a bit of your shows too, but I don't usually come to the party's because I'm more of a lone wolf. I figured I'd come here to meet some of you guys for once."

"Well I'm glad you did; you seem pretty cool actually. And if it weren't for you I would just be here alone with this rattling bass." Peter responded.

"Yeah, me too. I can't stand those people up there, following the herd, like just another cow. Every one of them. I understand why you chill out down here." Tony said screwing in another bolt.

"The girls are usually drinking too much; they ain't so hot throwing up everywhere."

Tony laughed loudly and asked, "Do you drink?"

Peter replied, "Who doesn't"

Tony said, "I'm pretty much finished here. You want me to grab some beers and bring them down here."

"I can always go for some beers." Peter chuckled.

He grabbed the beers from the fridge in the kitchen and brought them back to Peter.

"What do we drink to?" Tony asked.

The two clinked their cans together.

"Nothing. We just drink."

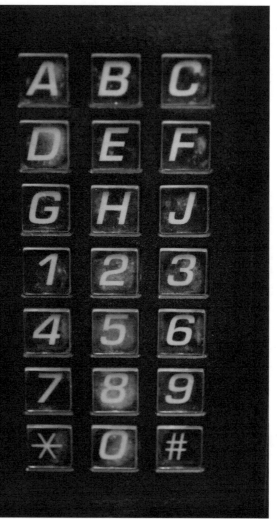

Fish and Chips

Justine lived a life of lists, everything down to the numbers and exactly as it should be. She worked at the local Burger Joint called 'Fry A Lot Burgers' just outside of the mall.

Justine's daily routine consisted of waking up at 6:30 sharp; she'd wake up and brush her teeth in bed, all the while trying desperately to shut off the incessant noise of the alarm clock blaring from her dresser. After a few smacks of the hand, the sound would subside and Justine would get dressed and head to work for her daily 7:15 shift.

On her walk to work, Justine would pop in at the local Subway. The vending machine there was Justine's first stop of the day, a bag of Lays chips had been Justine's breakfast for the past six years; it wasn't healthy, but it worked. Due to her job and the bad hours she had, Justine didn't really have a social life, let alone a romantic one. She lived through her work almost vicariously. The thing that Justine liked the most about the chips was that they had a little fortune on the back of the bag. They normally made either no sense or were badly misspelled purposely. This particular day was a little different, Justine got up and put her clothes on first and brushed her teeth in the bathroom, none of this was on purpose, Justine just couldn't believe what she had done. On her walk to work, she stopped like she normally did to get her chips, as she watched the chips slowly feed out of the slot and into the bottom of the machine everything felt normal. When she grabbed the chips out of the machine she looked at the fortune on the back. The fortune read, "change will save your life." Shoving the chips into her purse, Justine continued on her way to work. Walking into work was pretty standard. Beginning her shift, she took an order at the register as her boss called her into the back office. He was notorious for having a short temper and not being the kindest man, so she thought it could be nothing but trouble. As she walked into the door, she saw nothing but a smile across his face. That was something that Justine just assumed didn't exist. Her boss, Mr. Sergey, was a grumpy old man who typically lived to frown. As she sat down he opened with "Congratulations, Justine! I put you up as one of the two picks for manager. I'm retiring and have been asked to choose who is going to take the position. You will each have a week to run the place as if you were the manager and you're allowed to make any changes you want, good luck!"

Justine stood there, shocked. She never thought she would hear those words come out of Sergey's mouth.

"If you don't mind me asking you, who is the other person up for the position?" asked Justine.

"Neil," Sergey replied bluntly.

Rolling her eyes, Justine let out a sigh as she tried to force a smile. Neil was the one person who she couldn't stand more than Sergey himself. He was constantly cracking jokes, being inappropriate, and most of the female employees just found him to be creepy. Yet, despite all of this, whenever Sergey was around, he was the nicest person ever-the epitome of a yes man, agreeing with Sergey, no matter what he said. Justine knew going against him was going to be a challenge.

Despite the daunting difficulty that earning this position came with, Justine knew she needed to give it her all-she really wanted this. Thinking back, she remembered how often she'd felt stuck in a rut while working at the register. She consistently questioned what her future would look like within the company. The lack of mobility and promotion had taken a toll on her-just three years ago, she had been diagnosed with depression and while she'd been going to therapy to cope with the issues that it presented, it always seemed one step forward, two steps back. She'd progress with her doctor, Dr. Grayson, but the very next day, all the progress would be washed away with french fry grease as she'd throw on her apron and walk into her dead end job. This promotion would be the thing to break the cycle.

Justine walked into work the next morning ready for her first day as interim manager. No longer was she wearing a Fry A Lot apron; now she donned a nice button-down shirt and khaki pants. Justine looked far better than she could remember, and her face showed it. Gleaming and smiling ear to ear, she had a new found sense of self-worth. She started by calling in the staff and giving them a pep talk for the week.

"Alright guys, first thing on the docket for today is simple, just remember always be wearing an apron while on the clock," said Justine as she furrowed her eyebrows and darted her eyes across every employee.

"Moving on, I feel like customer service could still be taken up a few notches, Eric I'm looking at you," chuckled Justine. Going through the day, Justine was much more hands-on than normal, even greeting customers at the door with a smile and a friendly greeting. Engaging with every member of the team was something Justine felt was very important. Throughout the day, she would make rounds and pop in to check on the cashier's and try to make every team member feel equally valued, something Justine never felt. The next few days made Justine look better than ever. She was waking up in the morning with a feeling of self-esteem and self-worth and that showed in her high energy when she'd begin each shift.

The last day of her week managing was just rolling over into sunrise, and on cue, Justine's alarm was wailing. Smacking the stop button on the alarm clock felt like hell. The feelings that she had all throughout the week were falling apart, the thoughts of Justine's life before that week came flooding back to her, the reality setting in that the last seven days would determine her future with the company. Panic had started to set in and Justine could feel her heart start to beat faster and faster, her breathing became short and rapid. The pale-faced and wide-eyed Justine slowly pushed the scratchy old comforter off of her. Trying to control her breathing, Justine walked into her bathroom and flicked the light. Looking in the mirror, she did not see the same person that was greeting customers at the door yesterday or the person she'd grown accustomed to see the prior six days. Turning on the faucet, she put her hands out under the water. The splash of the ice cold water hit Justine's face and doused her back. A lot was riding on that day and Justine being acutely aware of that, wanted to end her trial week on a good note.

Turning onto the street that Fry' A Lot was on was something that Justine was very familiar with, that'd been the final turn on her route to work for the past six years. Looking up at the Fry' A Lot, her heart dropped. There wasn't a single car in the parking lot, the restaurant was completely black except for the closed sign flickering in the front window. Justine was sure that they were supposed to be open right now. Frantically, Justine ripped her phone out of her pocket and shakily typed in her password. She opened up her email praying she would see an emergency closure email from Sergey. While the first email that popped up was an email from Sergey, the quick moment of relief came to an abrupt halt as Justine opened it and read, *Justine don't forget to schedule shifts for Friday, it's getting late.* Justine received this email at 10 the night before. She had gone to bed early at 9:30 PM in hopes of getting a good night's rest for the big day, and had completely missed the email from Sergey and forgot to schedule any employees for the day.

Pushing the brass key into the worn out lock and turning it revealed a completely desolate Fry' A Lot. The registers were locked, all the lights and machines were dark and unplugged. Running to the employee kitchen, Justine hoped to find even a single employee waiting for her. To Justine's dismay, the kitchen was just as dark as everywhere else in the restaurant. Frantically, Justine picked up her phone and began punching in the numbers of her employees and coworkers praying for a response. Not a single one. The blank dial tone that played after every missed call rang through her head like an old dial up phone.

Justine sat down on the front steps and put her head in her hands and started crying, she just let it all out, knowing for sure there was no way that Sergey would pick her to be the permanent manager after that large oversight.

Walking back to her apartment, Justine felt utterly defeated. She could feel the tears start to form in the corner of her eyes. It started slowly with a single tear rolling down her cheek. As the realization of what had actually happened continued to dawn the emotions that had been bottled up and forgotten began to resurface, and with that, so did the tears. Walking down the busy street, people passed by without so much as a glance at the visibly upset Justine. Looking up to see the vending machine, she walked over to the worn down appliance and slid a crumpled dollar bill slowly into the slot. Feeling the belts slowly pull the dollar out of her loose grip and out of her control into the gadget, she punched in the three numbers corresponding to her chips. The metal slowly twirled, releasing the bag as it fell to the tray, ready to be eaten. Grabbing the bag from the machine, Justin turned them over and glanced at the fortune on the back. It read, *Do not underestimate yourself. Human beings have unlimited potential.*

Above the Knife

The night before a big surgery was always difficult. Preparing to operate on the brain and to make sure everything would run smoothly was something no surgeon took lightly. Continuously picturing exactly what steps he would have to take next, he planned what he would have to do if anything were to go wrong. That was how every surgery was for Mark, and after a while, it was no longer nerve-racking. However this one was different.

When he would awake in the morning, it wouldn't just be any other patient he would operate on, it would be Allie. Ever since seeing her walk past him in their middle school library, he declared her, hands down, the most beautiful girl he had ever seen. And with a simple smile, shining brighter than that flashy yellow purse she always carried with her, she caught his eye for the first time. The yellow was just the right pop of color that made her glow a bit more radiantly than usual, even on her worst days.

This same crush redeveloped just over a year ago, when she moved onto the same street as Mark. The light blue house that belonged to Allie was just two doors away from his; she'd been living there alone for quite some time. Allie seemed lonely, aside from her newest addition, a little white maltese, Minnie, who never broke the routine of being the high pitched, alarm clock on Mark's days off. Mark always thought about bringing up how irritating the little rat was, just for an excuse to talk to her, but Allie loves her dog, and he didn't want to risk screwing anything up with her. Thinking about how perfect Allie's long brown hair was, with it's soft loose curls, Mark always had something planned to say before he spoke to her, in order to decrease the chances of making a fool out of himself, by spitting out compliments about her or her luscious hair. Because he'd known her since middle school, Mark didn't realize the feelings he pushed away throughout college, and everything he had felt for her, everything he thought he had forgotten, could all come rushing back when she caught his eye again for the first time, for what felt like forever, stepping down out of the moving truck last year.

Running through his head, whenever he had down time, memories of the small conversations they shared were all Mark thought about. To him, the little things were most important with her. A week before the surgery, hearing the chime of his doorbell ring, Mark jumped out of bed to make his way to the door.

"Oh, hey Allie, what are you doing here?" He managed to spit out, running his fingers through his hair fixing himself, hoping she wouldn't notice the bed head.

"Hey, Mark," She said flashing that perfect smile, ear to ear, "I know it's early, but I was wondering if you had an extra seat on your way to work this morning? My car's battery just died, and I know it's a lot to ask because you're supposed to go in for a couple more-"

"Of course I can bring you!" Mark interrupted.

He couldn't get over how beautiful she was. She always went on and on, which made his heart feel all warm inside, and he loved that about her. The best was the way she sang in the car. Absolutely the most delicate, soft tune of sound ever heard, filled with so much passion and soul. Her voice in the car that morning- that gentle hum- was a simple thing he wanted to look forward to everyday.

Working at the same hospital as her, Mark was blessed with every second he got to see Allie, cherishing even their smallest interactions. The bun she wore appeared elegant, even though it looked purely effortless, with the couple of loose strands that fell down, framing her face. Walking by her in the lounge after his lunch break was the perfect time to see her. She worked as a pediatric nurse, and with Mark being a neurosurgeon, they didn't really cross paths too much so when they did, it was a real treat for him.

Allie and Mark were still close, even if they didn't see eachother everyday. And the fact that they both lived alone made grabbing food together the best way to get out and have other social interactions outside of work. It didn't hurt that due to their professions, their work schedules lined up as well.

If he wasn't head of neurosurgery, he didn't know if she would have even wanted him to operate on her anyways. It wasn't that he was nervous. He'd done that surgery over a 100 times. He just needed to forget the fact that it was Allie, and treat it as any other patient. Thoughts flooding his head, Mark couldn't stop thinking about operating on Allie. She had hydrocephalus, so it was nothing Mark couldn't handle and there wasn't much that could go wrong. He just had to drain the fluid and do what he had to do and get out. Yet thoughts continued to run rapidly through his mind. But this wasn't new, overthinking was just something he did for about any situation. That's what Mark kept telling himself anyways. It was simply being prepared. There was never anything wrong with being overly prepared.

Rolling over onto his side, the bright blue numbers jumped out at him. Mark's eyes slowly begin to reopen adjusting to the blinding light, as his vision became clear again, reading 12:45 on his alarm clock. Annoyed with himself, Mark let out a sigh, frustrated by the fact that the constant stream of thoughts running around his mind continued to keep him up. Quietly relaxing his breathing, he shut his eyes as he drowned out the questions racing through his brain and fell asleep.

As he managed to pull himself out bed, he knew it was surgery day. Mornings had always felt different. Not necessarily in a bad way though. Mark's motivation felt high, yet there was that feeling in his stomach. That tightness of churning indicating how he used to feel before each band concert from the 4th grade all the way up through college. For Mark, the butterflies weren't there because of fear of the audience; he was never shy in that way. Instead, it was about how his performance would turn out, and how well he ended up doing. That continued to happen up until the point where he was so impatient for the concert to start, just because he would want to know the ending.

To him, it was important no matter how confident before a surgery, to never make any promises, which made it hard for Mark when thinking about what could happen to Allie.

Horrific images soon became the only thing Mark saw. Going from blank white, and flashing to the red splatter, the images repeated through his mind. It was then that a knife appeared, the scalpel Mark had used to cut into Allie, which was all he could see. He was standing above her, standing above the knife, and it was as if as soon as he made the first, very small incision, the blood would not stop pouring out. The simple hole he had to cut into her head, went nearly a little too deep, and Mark couldn't do anything about it. His heart started racing and his breathing quickly became choppy. Listening to the beeping of the EKG slowly faded away as everything suddenly became nothing. White noise. Standing there frozen, Mark looked around to search for help. Nurses and assistants ran over, trying to stop the bleeding, but all efforts were useless. Glancing downward to see the blood on his quivering hands, Mark had covered what used to be blue gloves, which were now red. Feeling hopeless, he realized there was nothing left he could do, and Mark accepted the fact he just killed her. He didn't want to believe it, but standing there, holding her blood in his hands, there was no other option. Sweat dripped down Mark's forehead and back, which gave him a feeling as if it was soaking through his clothes. After attempting several times to wipe it off, woke up to the relief it was just a dream. Letting out a huge sigh, Mark tried to catch his breath and calm down. Glancing over to his bedside table, a weight began to lift off of Mark's shoulders reading the time, that satisfied him to know the surgery hadn't begun yet. It was not even possible such a small incision could make anyone bleed out that way, Mark reassured himself. Continuing to check the time and date on his phone telling himself it was all just a dream, Mark snatched his car keys off the coffee table, and walked out the front door.

Entering the hospital, his eyes began to feel dragged. He decided to stop and get his usual coffee at one of the little shops they had for the patient's family members- actual coffee. Black coffee. Nothing like what had become a popular trend of more sugar or sweetener than the coffee itself. Passing several of his coworkers, Mark got many "good mornings" thrown at him. Was this morning good? Mark's conscious had mixed thoughts. Yes, it was, you'll be fine. He heard his 8th grade self reassure himself.

After scrubbing in, Mark entered the white operating room just like any other time, but was still pushing the underlying truth of Allie being his patient, to the back of his mind. It was just a dream; there was nothing to worry about, Mark tried telling himself. The anesthesiologist had already prepared Allie, she went under, and her head had just been shaved in the appropriate spot for the incision, so he was ready for the operation. Knowing exactly what to do, Mark wouldn't have anything standing in the way, especially now that it was time to begin. As he slipped on the blue rubber gloves, a flash of the red image appeared and then vanished as he shook his head and blinked, trying to find it. It wasn't real. There was nothing there. I'm just imagining it, Mark said to himself as he stepped forward and slowly picked up the scalpel, shaking softly. Breathe. Mark reminded himself. He began to imagine her laughing, which helped him relax and calm down. Coming back to reality, Mark realized the hole had been properly cut, and he had nothing to worry about. I knew it. It's all just in my head, I've got to stop thinking so much about it, Mark confidently thought with hope. Preparing to move forward with the craniotomy, he knew his next step. All he had to do was go forward with the implant, to prevent the cerebral spinal fluid from going to her brain.

Looking down at the scalpel, Mark started breathing heavily. His heart began to race, faster and faster, and when he finally did what he was trying to avoid, focusing his vision directly on the tool, it became a weapon. The image of the bloody scalpel was there, but wouldn't go away this time. Unsure what to do, a loud metal ching sounds, as he flung it out of his hand and heard it hit the ground. All the other eyes in the room look at him to see what was going on. Each sound in the room started to become mute, and the shaking of Mark's head from side to side turned into shaking of his whole body. Backing away from the table, his hands covered his pale face, and Mark bent down with embarrassment to pick up the scalpel.

As his hearing started to come back, he heard the voice of one of the nurses begin to ask about the strange thing he couldn't come up with an explanation for. How was he going to tell them he was in love with his patient?

"Don't worry, I'll get a new one." The other nurse said, as Mark thanked her with a soft smile.

"Are you okay Mark?" His assistant nurse called out, wearing a look of concern on her face.

"Yeah, I'm sorry, I don't know what happened." Mark responded, still trying to believe he just freaked out like that.

Knowing how bad the stunt could have become, Mark shook his head, trying to pull himself from the thoughts his mind kept having, trying to regain some sort of focus. Grabbing the new scalpel from the nurse, he looked on and began again.

Thinking about her helped. The whole time Mark felt more relaxed the more he pictured Allie. Thinking about the life he wanted to have with her someday and how good of a husband he would be to her brought a smile to his face. But then reality started to kick in. Allie would never fall for him, he thought. That wasn't fair. It's not fair and he needed to do something about that, by letting her know how he felt about her. He decided that when she woke up he was going to tell her. Mark planned confidently. Trying hard, Mark pushed the emotions deep down, at least for a little while longer, as he completed the surgery. With each minute that passed, he quietly became more and more confident in his decision, constructing the exact words in his head that he'd say to her when she woke up.

Finishing the surgery, he scrubbed out, and made sure to ask the nurse to page him when she woke up. He was really going to do it.

***

Grabbing the door handle to her room, Mark was never so sure of something in his life. He was going to march in there and tell Allie exactly what he'd been rehearsing over and over again, waiting for her to get out of the recovery room. Opening the door, Mark's eyes locked onto Allie's. She was glowing for someone who just had a major surgery, but that wasn't a surprise to Mark. The surprise however, was when his eyes drifted off of her and onto the man next to her in the chair. Mark's smile began to fade, as Allie looked up at me and flashed hers.

"Mark! This is Anthony, my boyfriend." She introduced him to the tall man, as Mark felt everything inside of him shatter.

A fake smile and awkward small talk would be the only thing Mark managed to get through. After just feeling as if his heart had literally broke, he wished he was the one that needed an operation.

Delicately Damaged

Like the past few mornings, I awoke in the living room, laying on the couch, quivering from the cold. My eyes danced across the room until I found my blanket on the floor. It must have slipped off sometime during the night. The clock on my phone said I still had a couple of hours before dawn. Damn. I slept even less than I did last night. Exhaling, I glanced at the TV, centered on the wall and surrounded by family photos, and realized it was still on. I couldn't even remember what I was watching and honestly, it didn't even matter. The TV was just there to play in the background, to distract me just enough from reality to allow me to doze off. My father had recommended sleeping pills- the ones he used- but using meds never was my forte, my body was deteriorating fast enough as it was. I mean, all of our bodies are slowly deteriorating, some faster than others, but we are all going to end up the same. Spoiler alert.

I turned off the TV, and sluggishly walked up to the window. My garden always looked eerie after midnight. The lack of light, combined with the overgrown bushes and tree branches, really generated a creepy image. I tried keeping the garden neat, for as long as I could, but after a while, I just did not have time for it anymore, mostly because of school and my constant therapy sessions.

It was October, the month when nature slowly died, as if having Halloween wasn't sinister enough. Waving to the left and right, the wind was very strong today. Poor Max, he must have been freezing in his little house. I still remembered the time Grace, my sister, and I had painted his house red. He was just a little baby when we had gotten him for our sixth birthday. That was such an exciting time, begging our dad to buy us a dog for weeks, even though he always said we were too young to take care of a living being. While he had a valid point, his opinion seemed to change. One unexpected day, we finally got a puppy. After all the excitement, came the arguing. I wanted to name him Wolf, Grace wanted to name him Moonlight, and like the spoiled little children that we were, we both started crying. The name Max came weeks later, when our mom started calling him that, naturally we all just went along with it. And now, twelve years later, that same pile of bones sleeps in our garden, in the same red house that we made him. I never thought that he would live this long. I also never thought that he would outlive my beloved sister, Grace.

A couple of hours later, I awake again, this time by the sound of footsteps coming down the stairs. Poking my head above the couch cushion I saw my dad, fully dressed up, as he stepped into the living room. His eyes looked tired as his arms hang at his sides, carrying a black suitcase; it must have been time for one of his work trips again.

"Hi dad, where ya going this early in the morning?" I mumbled, lifting my head from the cushion. His eyes met mine as sadness poured from his tired face.

"I need to go. Work. I have a meeting" he said, tying his right shoelace with his shaky hands.. He seemed kind of out of it.

Silence. He stepped closer to the front door, putting his hand in his pockets. Once he realized he had grabbed everything, his hand pulled the door opened.

"Have a good day honey" he faked a smile, looking at me with a blank stare.

"You too. Love you, dad," I sighed.

"Love you too," he looked at me one last time and shut the door behind him. A whiff of fresh air entered the room. It must have been below 30 degrees outside. My dad had been weird, since Grace's passing. Unlike the rest of us, he was trying to speak and make the days brighter, but he hasn't been the best at it. Making jokes was his usual way of spreading positivity and doing that now would be very inappropriate. I felt sorry for him. He did not even have time to fully express his feelings of grief. Work had been killing him, he couldn't even take a day off. At least that's what he said. But this wasn't anything new to him, working all the time was his habit. We barely got to see him. That's probably what was killing him the most, the fact he did not spend enough time with us, with Grace, before she died. He wasn't even in the country when it all happened. His priorities were never put in the right order, and as it seemed, that has not changed, even now, when his daughter is 6 feet under us all.

Looking up at the staircase I noticed my mother, glaring at the front door, barely blinking at all. She seemed completely emotionless. After a few seconds, she walked back into the dark hallway and a slamming door echoed throughout the house.

Laurelie, my mother, has been behaving differently as well. In the morning she would stroll down to the store nearby. She would bring a bag of goodies and a pack of cigarettes. The rest of the day, she would lock herself in her chamber, watching the TV and smoking. Sometimes, the room would stay silent, and she would read a book for a few hours, with the only sound being the flipping of the pages. By midnight, the pack of cigarettes would be empty. Our phone kept ringing on the first day, so she unplugged it from the wall. Not even the outside world spoke to her. The only person she would speak to was her sister, my dreaded aunt Agatha. She rarely ever came to our house before, but lately, all I ever heard was her pitchy voice, yapping about all the fancy places she had been and the amazing vacations she and her daughters had taken. I stayed away from her as much as I could, but listening to her seemed inevitable. I would roll my eyes, as she spoke about Paris and I would stare at Grace and giggle when she would do the same. But listening to her luxury life wasn't even the worst thing about her, it was her condescending attitude. She tended to bring over her daughters old, worn out clothes and gave them to us as gifts. As if we could not afford clothes for ourselves. And even though she has been this was for years, for some reason she was allowed to enter my mother's room and I wasn't. I tried approaching my mother, on that very first day, I grabbed her by the hand and asked her how she felt, but she just pulled her hand away and walked out of the room. I knocked on her door a few times as well, but, no answer. I guess she couldn't bare to look at my face.

The house felt empty. My dad was gone and my mother might as well be. The silence started getting to my head so I decided to leave. I quietly grabbed my purple coat from the hanger, placed my feet within my boots and walked out of the house. It was cold. The ground was muddy and the sound of my footsteps echoed throughout my garden.

"Good morning Faith, how are you?" looking up I see my aunt Agatha, stepping through the big black gate and entering our front yard.

"Good morning, to you too," I fake a smile, just out of courtesy. As always, I hid my emotions away. No one needed to know what really went in my head, as if anyone actually cared.

"How are you holding up?" she spoke, stepping closer to me, piercing through my comfort zone with every step.

"I'm doing better than my mother. You came to see her?" as mean as that sounded, I meant it in the best way possible.

"Yes, she needs someone close to her in times of need. Someone that she cares about." she gazed at the front door. I buried my nails into my hand as hard as I could. My eye began to twitch. Breathe, just breathe, I repeated in my head.

"Oh, okay, whatever. Just ring the doorbell, she should be out in a few minutes," I said, slowly stepping away, from the devil in makeup.

"Sure, see you later," I heard her say, as her voice got closer to the door and further away from me.

I watched her for a few seconds, judging her every move and then continued following my adventure. Closing the gate behind me, I walked onto the sidewalk. The town of Liltree, a loud, but small place in which everyone knew one another and everyone knew all the gossip. Nothing could be hidden in a town like this, absolutely nothing. The news of my sister's death spread like wildfire. Everyone was eager to find out how and why it happened. Some people probably knew the truth, but most of them probably heard a overly dramatic story told by a person who hadn't even been there. That seemed to be the case for many happenings around the town of Liltree, but, it really did not matter. Gossip cannot bring my sister back, whether it was good or bad.

I strolled past the post office located across from the ancient library, and walked into the Liltree intersection. My feet froze. I couldn't breathe. The sound of cars and people got louder and louder. The wind blew my hair over my eyes as I stared at the school bus across the street. The bus driver was smiling as the little children walked in and said their barely audible "good mornings." I felt my eye slowly start to twitch again as my entire body started to shake. For a slight moment I felt like I was going to pass out, but I came back to my senses as the bus drove off. It was less red than I remember it being.

I turned around and walked the other way. The park was awaiting me. Crossing the street, I walked onto a trail made of dead leaves. The storm must have been very strong around this part. The trees were bent, and the flowers completely demolished. What a tragedy.

Stepping through a maze of pinecones, I finally found myself in Liltree park. What a gorgeous place. I sat on one of many benches centered around the crowded parkway. The flowers were now dead, so instead of being the usual color parade that Liltree park usually was, it was now a mash off depressing brown, red and orange. The park felt empty, but I saw some people strolling down the many trails, taking different paths to different destinies. All of the footsteps and chirping of birds gave me a sense of peace. I loved coming here. So many memories from a single spec on this planet. So many games played on this very same ground. Oh how me and Grace loved coming here. Countless hours spent running through the leaves and rain. Hours and hours of playing princesses with our many dolls and teddy bears. Many secrets being told and shared with our friends, on the blanket that our mother made us. That's what I will always remember this place by. It was our place. In our heads, it was just ours. My eyes began to flicker and I yawned myself to sleep.

I felt something touching my hand, something wet. I slowly opened my eyes and to my disbelief I saw a furry little sheep licking my fingers. Startled, by my sudden movement, the sheep jumped a few feet back, looking at me ever so curiously.

"Hey little buddy, how did you get here?" I said, slowly moving my hand towards the sheep in a welcoming matter. I did not want to scare it away.

A sheep? In Liltree? I looked around left and right, but not another sheep in sight. Odd. Was I still dreaming? I rubbed my eyes a few times, but, it was still there, staring at me.

"Is this your sheep?" I asked a blonde woman walking by. She remained quiet as she swooshed past me. Rude.

"What are you even doing here?" I asked the sheep, gently. To no surprise I got no response.

"I know what I am doing. I am running away from that bitter house that I live in. It's only there now to haunt me and remind me of all the great memories I had with my sister."

The sheep chewed the grass beside me as I spoke. The thunder echoed throughout the gloomy park. A storm seemed to be on the horizon. I felt raindrops starting to descend onto my face.

"I know that they say that twins have a deep connection, but is it possible that a part of me died that day too," I sat there, staring at the sheep, overrun by too many emotions. I wasn't crying nor was I mad. I felt my empty soul consume me.

The sheep curled up to me as the mud beneath our feet was covered in our footsteps. I snapped out of my trans and pet it's head as I continued rambling on.

"I remember when it was our first day of high school, and how both of us were scared. But everyone get scared of new beginning, that bring strangers and unfamiliar surroundings. All of it just causes so much stress. Once our first three periods were over I remember walking into the cafeteria, petrified because of the fact that everyone in that room was going to judge me and sitting alone seemed like the worst way to start off the year. And then I saw Grace, sitting on the other side of the room, surrounded by people clinging to talk to her. Making friends came so naturally to her, she did not even need to try, she just radiated with positive energy. Once her eyes met mine she waved at me and called me over and introduced me to all of her friends. Just like that she made me feel safe. It's true that everyone loved her, but I loved her the most. She was my light in the dark, and the only person that would be there for me in times of need. I might have been the older one by a few minutes, but she was definitely stronger than me.

And there I was sitting on a bench talking to a sheep in the middle of a rainstorm. Yup, I've completely gone mad. At least the clothes on me made me feel cozy and warm. Hidden beneath my purple coat was my favorite T-shirt that I got from from Grace for our last birthday. It was handmade by her. It was just a simple black shirt with the writing saying "Faith*". Most people misspelled my name so she decided to turn it into a shirt. Funny and clever - she was perfect.

"I know it's gonna take me a long time to recover, and that life will never be the same without her, but I know that it will all get better soon. It has to," looking up at the grey colored sky, raindrops shower my face, washing all of my tiny tears away.

"Sometimes I still feel like I can hear her. The internet says that it's normal to imagine dead relatives, so maybe I haven't gone completely insane," I smirk at my own joke, as I notice an old man staring at me concerningly as he walked by.

I've never had someone die before, well not this significant at least. Can you believe that I still havent walked into our room? Seeing all her stuff, her bed, her pictures... I am afraid it will all be way too much to handle," taking a deep breath I finally decide to get up and take things into my own hands.

"I guess there is only one more thing left to do. See you later sheep. Thank you again."

I got to the gate of my front yard faster than I have ever before. Pushing the door wide open, my eyes see my mother talking to my aunt in the kitchen.

"How are you feeling today?" Agatha asked in a fake high pitched tone.

"The same, I'm just really nervous about the funeral. I don't want to leave this house."

"When is the funeral by the way?" she placed her left leg over the right, whilst smirking at me as she saw me enter the house. I rolled my eyes and darted towards the stairs.

"It's tomorrow. We had to wait a few days, so the entire family could be here," I heard my mom say as I walked up the wooden stairs. Stepping onto the landing, I entered the dark hallway. I walked by my parent's room, the bathroom, and the guest bedroom and finally found myself at the end of the hallway, standing in front of my room. I twirled the handle and stepped inside. The curtains on the windows covered most of the sunlight that beamed into the room. And there it all was, just like I remembered it being on that horrible day. All of our posters were still on the wall. The pictures of Grace and I were still standing on their designated shelves. Our closets opened ever so slightly, clothes dripping out of them. Grace's phone and clothes placed on the work desk next to the computer. The phone must have died over time. And there they were, our beds, mine still not made, and Graces bed tidied neatly, with her many pillows placed in order of height, and sitting right by them, Grace's favorite childhood toy - Charlie the sheep.

✳✳✳

Nekros

Dearil shuffled across the room to close the window. Winter was coming for his town of Syracuse and the old man was eager to keep the cold out. As his feet dragged and his arms swayed, he couldn't help but smile at the ancient picture of himself and his wife hanging on the wall he passed. Their two young faces smiled at him, frozen like that forever, but it only left him feeling warm.

Upon reaching his destination, Dearil started to push, yet no matter how hard he tried, it wouldn't budge. The window held its ground in protest but the old man's 88 years of determination made him stronger. The window screeched, its hinges crying in pain and finally closed with a sudden bang, echoing slightly throughout his old house.

Just as he released a breath, a crack filled his ears.

Dearil turned around to view what he had done. The picture. It lay there, motionless on the floor, a hard seam running right through. Immediately he raked his hand through whatever little hair he had left. His brows furrowed deeply and his teeth pressed against each other but his shoulders dropped after he realized it was only over him. Dearil's fingers traced lightly over the crack.

His wife came out unscathed.

"Lorelai?" Dearil called. There was no response. He waited to hear her answer but soon, shook his head. He couldn't figure out why he had done that. And because there was nothing he could do for the picture right then, the man hung it back up on its hook. His wrinkled hands lingered on the sides as he watched his own face, and his wife's, stare back at him, and a yearning for a different time flooded into his mind.

"Looks like I'm going to need to fix the window," he mumbled. "It seems a little stuck." Silence. Day in and day out brought an unsettling quiet for Dearil. His eyes wandered around the empty room and that familiar sensation of loneliness filled him once again. Not only was he lonely but he constantly felt *alone*. Perhaps it was his own fault. He knew Lorelai wasn't the company she used to be and his children did live close by, but he preferred to stay inside. Luckily for him, he was due for a visit from his youngest daughter. She always brought him what he needed for the week on Sundays at exactly 5 p.m.

Dearil dragged his feet over to the stove to see what time it read. 1:18.

He shrugged and ran a hand through his hair as he held the counter for support. That wasn't as late as he usually slept. Perhaps it was because this was the first night in three weeks where he didn't wake up in the middle of the night. For once, falling asleep was surprisingly easy.

He stood behind the counter of the little kitchenette that oversaw the living room. His eyes grazed over the room past the tiny, brown grandfather clock that sat happily on the counter, its golden arms ticking away, the picture on the wall, the large bookshelf next to it, and finally the window. A little black bird sat on the sill and pecked at the last remains of feed from when the window wasn't stuck. He thought about searching for the bag that was hidden somewhere but decided not to.

The cold would get in.

The crow, he determined it to be, pecked at the window pane causing the old man to cock his head. It stopped and slowly turned its bird head to stare at him. Almost as if it knew it was being watched, the bird caught sight of something else and flew away. He shrugged.

"Ah, well," Dearil mumbled. "I guess I'll eat something."

"Dearil?" a voice called. He stopped dead. "Dearil?"

"Lorie?" The old man looked around the room in all directions.

"Come to me, Dearil…"

"I'm coming, Lorelai!" He hurried over to his bedroom and threw open the door. But when he got there, he didn't hear anything else; everything had gone silent. Another tear slipped.

"I thought you were calling me, my Lorie sweet."

No response.

Dearil gripped the door handle as questions raced through his head. Why had he done that? Why did he react this way? He knew how things were, didn't he?

Dearil stood in the doorway of his room without a sound. His stomach tightened slightly, chasing his appetite away. Just like a drain plug being pulled and the water rushing to escape, his energy suddenly slipped and he struggled to hold his own body. Slowly but surely, he inched towards his bed and collapsed next to where Lorelai was to lay.

***

Looking up at the clock, it read 4:43.

Where had the time gone, he thought to himself. His stomach growled in response causing him to rise out of bed and shuffle into the living room and then the kitchenette. He let his hand glide over the counter in search of something to eat. A peach.

"You know, in Chinese culture, eating a peach during their new year represents immortality," he said to no one. His old hands steadied the small fruit on the counter and his knife sliced down the center. It slipped right through, like a knife on butter, causing him to stop.

Spoiled.

"Oh well," he started. "It's not Chinese New Year anyway. And I'm not even Chinese!" He heard laughter and it made the corners of his mouth tug in both directions. You'd expect a laugh coming from someone as tiny as Lorie to be just as so, tinkly and light and tiny. But it wasn't. Her laugh was bigger than she was and that had quickly become his favorite thing. He could listen to it forever.

"Thank you, thank you, I'll be here all day!" he joked some more. Lorie laughed again.

To continue with lunch, the old man settled on bread and butter, fruit, and a cup of coffee. Slowly he reached for the bread in the basket and sliced a chunk off only to break it in two. He then grabbed a pomegranate and cut it in half. He was ready to bring both to the little table they had nestled up against the counter but he stopped. Instead, Dearil only took his.

"Bon appetit." He sat down and rested his chin on his hand.

"Oh I'm not very hungry right now." Dearil said. He moved the food around his plate just as a child did when they were being picky. "I suppose I'll start with the fruit." He went for the seeds first. He always liked the seeds.

Putting the fork down, Dearil got up from the table, bringing his plate to the sink. The plate slid from his hand quickly, as it reached the tub filled with warm water and drifted to the bottom, with a muffled clank. Derail shook his head, mumbled something to himself as he reached his arm, elbow deep, pulling the plate from the sink to expose the chip that had broken off at the bottom of the basin. As he placed it down on the dish towel, he heard a knock at the door. Looking up at the small grandfather clock, slowly ticking time away, he read the hands to be 5 o'clock. Dearil wondered who could be at the door.

"I'm coming, I'm coming," he sounded, walking to the door. Twisting the knob, the door remained steadfast in its closed position. Letting out a heavy sigh, Derail let go of the knob and reached up to the padlock just above. He always seemed to forget they'd put that on there. His kids were always trying to protect him. As he unlocked the pad, and twisted the knob, his daughter's face stood at the other side, ready to greet him.

"Hi Dad," Morana greeted as she banged the snow off her boots. When had it started snowing? She kissed him on the cheek. "I brought you your groceries."

"Thank you, my dear. You are such a great help to me and your mother." He stared at her face and realized just how much she looked like Lorelai.

Morana smiled sadly.

"Of course, Dad." They stood there silently. "Did you eat today?"

He nodded. "Actually I just finished." The two of them looked into the house at the abandoned table. He looked back to his daughter. "Your mother didn't want to join me," Dearil explained, hurt. Morana frowned deeply.

"Of course..." she trailed off.

He glanced at the groceries still in her hands. "Let me get that for you."

"Thanks, Dad." She gave him a couple of bags and picked up the rest. The two of them brought them to the counter. "Oh, Dad," she started. He turned to her.

"I just remembered I brought you something. I'll be right back!" Dearil watched his daughter move excitedly out of the house. He waited a minute, alone, until she came back holding a box. The front door was still open, letting all the cold in. "Look!"

He leaned over and peered into the box. Inside was a beautiful black cat, probably about a year old. He looked up.

"What's this?"

"Why, it's a cat, Dad. I thought you could use a companion." His brows knitted together.

"I already have your mother." Her smile faltered.

"Well, I mean *another* companion. Cats are great house pets. Very low maintenance." Dearil looked down into the box again. The cat stared right into him with its big yellow eyes.

"I suppose it is kind of cute." He looked up. "Thank you, my dear." Morana smiled.

"Go on and pick him up, Dad. They said his name was Houdini but I guess you can change it." The old man reached into the box making the cat squirm in his arms. It jumped and before either of them could react it ran out the door, taking a right towards the cyprus trees down the street. His daughter glanced back at him and then took off. Dearil blinked a couple of times, trying to process what was happening. The cat just ran out the door and someone was running after it but he couldn't remember who.

"Oh Dad, I'm so sorry. I had no idea that was going to happen." He looked up, startled.

"Lorelai what are you doing here? I mean Morana," he corrected quickly. She took a step forward.

"Dad, I've been here for maybe 10 minutes now. I just tried to get the cat I was going to give you but I'm not as fast as I used to be... don't you remember?" Morana frowned deeply as she watched her dad think.

"Why don't you go home now," he replied. "I'm sure your children are wondering where their mother is."

Morana swallowed and quickly closed the front door. She took off her coat and forced a smile.

"Dad, why don't we sit down." He nodded slowly and followed her to the couch. "Before I talk about the bigger issue, let me just ask you something. You know that Azrail is 21 and he's my youngest, right?" Dearil shook his head. He knew Azrail was only 8.

"I don't want you to feel like I'm abandoning you, or that I don't care about you, but have you ever thought about moving into a retirement home? You're getting much older now and you're here alone wi—"

"Morana I do not want to continue this discussion any further. I am just fine taking care of myself and your mother and I wish you wouldn't even bring this up without her being here."

"But Dad—"

"I insist. Go on."

"No, Dad, we really have to talk about this—"

"I said enough! Respect your father and your mother!" His daughter stared back at him, hurt and concerned. She stood up and walked towards the door with the empty box in her arms. Dearil sighed heavily.

"Morana I... Say hi to our grandbabies for us." His daughter smiled weakly and nodded.

✳✳✳

Pins dropped and could be heard in Dearil's house at that time. He longed to talk to his wife but she was particularly quiet and distant since his fight with their daughter. He was alone and not even the cat would've filled what he was lacking. As the old man brushed his teeth, he suddenly felt his heart ache. Weights were placed on his arms and he turned to sit on the toilet before falling on the ground.

"Dearil," Lorelai whispered. "I wish you would come to me. Why don't you?" He shivered.

"I don't know if I could do that, Lorie..." Suddenly, a feeling of dread washed over him.

"But Dearil... don't you love me?" He nodded rapidly and wiped a tear from his eye.

"Of course I do!" His breathing picked up and Dearil clutched his chest. His heart ached and ached and he felt tears sliding down his face. "Yes, Lorie, I love you more than anyone in the world!"

"Then come to me!" He shook his head.

"I can't, Lorie! My house! The children!"

"Dearil!" It screamed. He covered his ears. *"Dearil!"* The voice was raspy and loud. It shrieked and shrieked and shrieked. "Come to me!"

"Oh, Lorie!" He cried. Dearil rushed into his room and fumbled around for his shoes and coat in the dark. He hurried out of his house, not caring if he were to fall at his age.

He ran past the raven and he ran past the cat and he ran past the cyprus trees. And finally, he ran to her.

Dearil fell down in front of the gravestone marked with his wife's name.

Lorelai Singer
1930-2018
A singer in skill and a Singer in name
With the most beautiful voice around

"I'm here Lorie, dear. I'm here." And as the snow fell, Dearil laid in peace, ready to join his wife in death.

Passing Memories

Morning was soon to fade away and the thought of getting out of bed was still a challenge. The alarm clock read 11:28, however no light seemed to be entering the bedroom. The heavy, red curtains stopped any light from bleeding into the house. The darkness of the room forced my head down into the pillow. My eyes became heavy, and my breathing lightened.

Blinking my eyes awake once more, I turned to face the alarm clock. I felt frustrated once the numbers focused into my vision.

"12:47? How could time have passed so fast?" I questioned myself. Perhaps it was time for me to get out of my bed. Forcing myself upwards, I slipped into my memory foam slippers and proceeded to the window. Throwing open the curtains became a clear mistake to me as the light blinded me. Raising my arm to shield my eyes, I took a step back and tripped over my own feet. A loud crunch sound shot through me, my head hitting nearly everything on the way down. My ears began to ring as I laid there in utter shock. The muscles in my body started to clench, moving them becoming a sudden challenge. While laying on the floor, I realized that the ground was actually quite comfortable.

Seconds after, the tensing stopped. Then confusion started to fill my mind. How could my body be so relaxed, yet above my shoulders, ache to the point where I couldn't feel? All emotions that filled my mind before were gone. I was forced to make a decision; to get back up on my feet, or stay lying on the floor. My head began to feel foggy as I stumbled to the bathroom, hoping that maybe if I found some medicine, it would help stop the throbbing pain. A faint, high-pitched ring started to roam around between my ears. Gently guiding myself to the wall, I flipped the light switch. The light in the room seemed to be worse than the light from the outdoors, the fluorescent bulb giving off an artificial look that didn't help my headache in the slightest. However, this time, my feet did not fall from beneath me. Pulling the mirror towards me, a clear white container appeared on the second shelf of the cabinet. I grabbed two orange pills and brought them toward my mouth. Suddenly, the sounds of clinking in the sink erupted. My eyes darting to the area of the sound, I saw the last two pills in the bottle fall down the drain.

"Maybe there's an extra bottle in the kitchen." I thought, my eyes starting to go dark from all the pain. My forehead burning from ear to ear, I wobbled on over to the kitchen.

"Come on, where is it? Where is it? Where is it?" I was pacing around the kitchen in a desperate search for some kind of pain relief. "I'm pretty sure I got an extra bottle. Where did it go?"

It was no use. I couldn't find it anywhere. Waving a white flag, I slumped down on my couch in defeat. I turned towards the coffee table where a silver picture frame sat. My hands curled around the cool frame as my thumb rubbed over an inscription that read 'Gloria and Semaj, May 15, 1949.' I could have cared less about myself in the photo, rather, my eyes were glued to Gloria. She looked perfect, no one could have looked better than her. Her long brown hair was in an elaborate updo. The dress seemed to match with intricate lace going from her shoulders down to her wrists. I liked her dress, but it was her face that was the most beautiful. Her smile lit up the entire church that day, and how when we looked into each other's eyes, I was still as blown away as I was the first time we met. I began to hug the frame, relaxing more into the sofa. My eyes fluttered shut as I continued to relive that day, not realizing that I began to nod off.

I opened my eyes to look at the dusty, wooden clock on the wall. It read 2:32. Assuming it was afternoon, I began to walk towards the kitchen after placing the picture frame back in it's spot. The humming of the fridge caught my attention, and the door seemed to pull my hand to it like a magnet. The cold air poured out of the fridge onto my bare shins. A spine tingling shiver shot up my back. Immediately closing the door, I noticed a packet of oatmeal peeking out of the cabinet, most likely left open from my prior search for medicine. Opening the packet of oatmeal, the aroma of cinnamon poured into my nose. Turning on the nozzle to the faucet, a wind-like sound came from the boiling pot. When the pot was finally filled, it found its way to the stove. Waiting for water to boil felt equivalent to watching paint dry.

I sat on the dining room table, my legs feeling weak from standing for so long. I sat at the head of the table in my usual spot and picked up another photo of Gloria. She was so beautiful. She was 78 when the photo was taken, but had the same strikingly blue eyes she had when she was in her twenties. Her hair cut short, barely passing her shoulder when straightened. This picture was on display during the memorial, I thought to myself, I miss her so much.

A high pitch whistle rang through the house signaling his water was hot enough. My head started burning again, as the familiar stinging in the eyes returned.

Standing up, my legs began to wobble beneath me. Feeling in my legs began to fade with every step I took forward. An immense pain started to fill the area between my ears. Almost three steps from the stove, I collapsed.

***

There were a pair of icy blue eyes nearly inches from mine as I woke. A groan escaped my lips as I sat up to rub my face. The woman backed away and watched as I gained some consciousness. Trying to be careful as I stood up, I realized the pounding in my head had stopped. There was no pain, my fingers began flexing, I shook out my legs, I even jumped a little bit, but felt nothing. A giggle echoed through the air, causing me to look back up at the woman standing before me. Suddenly, all of the blood seemed to drain from my face. Her hair was too familiar, her wrinkles were too familiar, and her eyes were much too familiar. Shutters shot through my body as I tried to take a step back.

"This isn't real, this isn't real," the woman reached out, the ring still on her left hand, "this can't be real!" I nearly yelled as I ran towards the bedroom, not realizing how easy and pain free it was to sprint across the house. My hands in my head, I rocked back in forth at the edge of my bed.

"This can't be happening. This can't be happening. Oh my god, this can't be happening."

Gloria put her arms around my shoulders. Her intentions were to help calm me down, but it was to no avail. I was hyperventilating.

"Shh it's okay. Everything is going to be alright." Her hand rubbed up and down my back. I've missed that feeling for too many years. We sat for what felt like hours. My mind racing, I had so many questions I wanted to ask, but didn't have the will power to interrupt this moment. I decided to only ask the most important one.

"If I'm dead, how are we still here?"

Our eyes locked. She was unaware of how to answer.

"Do you want to see something? It's difficult to imagine without seeing first."

I nodded and we both stood up. The feeling in my feet was surreal. No more pain. No more locking. No more falls.

We walked down the hall and into the kitchen.

"No... No, no," My fingers grabbing onto my hair, "no, no no!" My vision blurred from the tears forming on my eyes. I jerked my head away before I could fully make out everything. The sight was too much to take in.

"That's you." The obvious remark from Gloria didn't help.

I slumped next to my body. We looked identical, except one of us was curled over the kitchen floor, and the other was hovering above my own corpse.

"But I'm alive. I can feel myself breathe. I can walk. I'm alive." I didn't know what to think.

"No, honey. Your brain filled with blood when you hit it earlier this morning. You are dead. You just need to accept it. Do you know how hard it was to watch over you mourning my loss for a decade? You may have died alone, but now you have me. You have me forever." She held out to me, gesturing to help me up.

"What do we do now?"

"We can do whatever we want. Go wherever we want. We can do anything together."

We held hands, walked through the closed door, and down the street. No one knows I'm dead, I thought. Curiously, I asked,

"Who's going to find my body?"

Gloria nudged him before speaking sarcastically,

"Really? You are reunited with the love of your life after years of being lonely, and you are worried about who is going to find your body?" I gave a sheepish smile in return, I hadn't realized how much I had missed her sarcasm.

We walked on down the street, our legs not feeling any bit tired. We just kept walking. The sun started to set, and in the glorious red sky, I leaned into my wife, as if I was going in for a kiss, but instead went to her ear and said,

"Uh honey, I left the stove on."

Should I Stay or Should I Go?

As the dawn of the new millennium is creeps upon us, and the end of my high school is lurking. It was time to make a lifetime decision and answer this question. Should I Stay or Should I Go? Do I go to college and live up to my parents expectations or do I find my own path and find what makes me happy. What's so great about living in the United States is that you can do anything you want with your life. The sky is honesty the limit on what you can be: A Rockstar, a Superhero, or just simply living the dream. My parents expectations for me were always high. They have always wanted me attend college, specifically Florida State University with my brothers Chuck and Lonnie, but I've always been so hesitant about to college. Every semester my mother would always pull the report card from the mail and see a big line of C's and D's. School was a struggle, not just academically but also socially. Even I was involved on the football and wrestling team, nobody ever acknowledged me. Maybe it was because nobody liked me or maybe it was because people saw me as freak. Whatever the reason, all that neglect made withdraw into my own world.

Most of my free time as a child was spent reading and doing a lot of daydreaming. The fourth grade, became one of the highlight points in my life. During one of my reads in the library, my teacher at the time, introduced me things called comic books. They were stories about superheroes saving people from the dangers of the world, in which my addiction grew quickly for them. No one would have ever suwanting to be something great when I grow up. it's all what I wanted to be at that point. And joining the military was probably the closest thing to being a superhero.

Even though I was little hesitant at first, an application ended up being submitted to join the United States Marine Corps sometime after Thanksgiving. I'm expecting a response for them any day now. Hopefully I'll get in, but the only issue is I haven't even told my family about joining the joining the military, nor do they know that I applied. Who knows they'd do if they found out? Probably yell the heck out of me, if I'm being honest. My parents aren't obnoxious and abusive people, they could be loving people at times, but it's fair to say that they're strict and demanding folks who only listen to what they want, and don't really care about their kids want. It's probably what drove my family apart, was all of that weight, and all of that tension being on pressed up against each other everyday.

After my parents divorce, Chuck and Lonnie had already for college. My mom, my sister Jane, and I had moved into an condo right outside the city, while my dad moved into an apartment across town. And although things weren't perfect, my hope was to be gone by the time school year ends. Hopefully, my family will be okay with me living the dream,being stationed in the military, rather than stuck in school for another four years.

As many of these thoughts were pondering in my head, my mother yells, "Jack sweetie, breakfast!" After noticing that it was 8 o clock, I immediately got out of bed, dragged a comb across my head, and found my way downstairs, seeing Jane enjoying some pancakes while my mother was whipping up another batch or me. Before even going to eat breakfast, I went outside to check the mail. My gut was telling me that this is going be a big day full day full of surprises and wonders. Seeing that a large envelope from the marine was sent, I came back into the house, and walked into the kitchen, and threw the mail on the table.

"Good Morning Mom," I said while giving her a hug. "Good Morning Jack. Why were you just outside?"

After grabbing myself a small stack of flapjacks and a big bottle of syrup, Jane said, "He was just getting the mail mom." By the look of my mother's face, she was probably expecting for me hear back from one of these colleges.

172

"Oh, I bet today is the day we hear back from Florida State." I said laughing my head.

But to tell you the truth I didn't apply to FSU, there was no desire to go there or any college to be honest. Other than few applying to a few local community colleges for backup, my mind was pretty made up in joining the military.

"You know what mom, you're right this might be the day," I sarcastically said. "Why don't we take a look at what came in the mail."

My mother began perusing through the mail slowly. You could easily see the boredom on her face as she was seeing the same old bills and newspapers until she spotted the envelope, and laughed.

"Ha Ha Ha, Jack are the marines still trying to recruit you, because I'm pretty sure I made it clear to you and the school that you don't belong in the marines."

"Could you give a quick reminder on why I shouldn't be marine again," I said.

"Well, you know your father and I really want to go to college Jack, preferably somewhere in Florida, it's important. You won't be stuck like me, cleaning houses for a living and living in a cramped apartment."

"We live in a condo mom, and all of us are still lucky that dad chips in for the rent, even though he doesn't have to." There was a brief awkward pause. I took quick glance at Jane, she knew she wanted to get the hell out of there, and began eating her pancakes a lot quicker.

"By the way, that's not a recruitment letter, it's a feedback letter on whether I made it into the military or not." While in disbelief, my mother vigorously opened up the letter and read,

"Dear Mr. Ryan, on behalf of the United States, we would like to thank you in taking an interest into serving our country. We are pleased to inform that pending on your physical, you have qualified on becoming a member of the United States Marine Corp."

It took my mother a moment to let the news sink in, she looked up back at me with disappointment, she had no words to say to me. My mind began to boggle a little, it was a bit surprising to my mother not get angry and yell at me for once. Jane took a peek at the letter, then grabbed my hand.

"Jack I think it's great. You're gonna do great in the marines."

"Over my dead body," mom said

"What do you mean ma?"

"Jack you're not gonna do it...I'm not gonna let my baby go out there into the military and wind up dead somewhere in the middle east six months later."

Jane interrupted, "Mom do you see you those pictures on the refrigerator."

"Yes Jane, I see those pictures of spiderman and superman," my mother exclaimed.

"Yeah, and there's a reason why those pictures are up there instead of A+ report cards." I began to smile a bit. My sister actually understood me.

"Mom you need to get that through your head that college isn't for everyone, and Jack can do whatever he wants with his life."

As my mom and sister continued to bicker and things escalated, I quickly grabbed the letter and my car keys and slipped out the back door without being noticed. The thought of being able in the room any longer would have made sick. That whole fiasco itself was like airing of grievances on festivus, and not in a funny way. Sometimes the chaos was a bit too much for me to handle. It was easy to say my mind became a bit stumped on making a decision on joining the marines or not. The decision itself became an extremely difficult for me because there are three things I honor in this world: God, family, and my country. So the thought of losing my family was absolutely dreadful to me. Getting my entire family to be on board with this before the decision was essential and became a mission it self. I drove to the nearest payphone and called up my twin brothers Chuck and Lonnie. Despite the fact, that they two of them are goofballs who whose only hobbies really included getting drunk, getting high, and getting laid and probably don't even care what I do with my life anyway. It was crucial for me to at least let them know about joining the military. After walking into the payphone and putting a quarter into the machine following the rubbing off of the gum and gonorrhea off the phone, I dialed 720-654-7460 to call my brothers. The phone rang for a few seconds until my brother Chuck answered, "Hello"

"Yo Chuck, it's brother Jack," I said.

"Hey Bro, what's sup," replied Chuck

"Are you and Lonnie free right now, I really need to talk to you," I asked skeptically

"In person?" Chuck questioned . "Yeah, I really kind of busy Jack. The boys and I are throwing a huge party tonight to celebrate the end of midterms."

"It'll just take 20 minutes I promise," I stated.

"Fine, meet us at Jimmy's Diner down on Dixwell Ave," Chuck said. "I'll see in you in 45 minutes."

"Okay, see you then," I answered.

Jimmy's Diner is located right down street from FSU, about a thirty-five minute drive away from my house. My family and I used to go there every sunday after church to get breakfast. Even though the diner was a bit far away from our house, they have the best damn eggs in the damn state. So driving up there was always worth the trip. Not to mention, the place holds up so many good memories. Sundays at Jimmy's was probably the one day of the week where the family never fought. Everyone always got along on that day. I'm not really sure why. It might've been the fact that it was the day of the lord, or that fact it was the one day everyone could forget about all of their troubles through a couple of laughs and one large plate of food. I pulled up to Jimmy's diner around 3:30 pm. Chuck and Lonnie spotted me coming in the restaurant, and both simultaneously gave me immediately gave me one big hug.

"What's sup bro...It's been so long," Lonnie graciously yelled.

"Hey Lonnie, it's good to see you guys too." We both sat down at booth and quickly took our ours.

"Listen, I don't wanna waste any of your guys time because it seems like you have a big night ahead of you so here it is... How would you guys feel if I joined the military?" Lonnie and Chuckie both looked each other and began dying in laughter. That became a nunsense.

"What the hell is so funny?" I said. "Nothing, nothing...It seems like a good idea in way."

"How so."

"Well, I know I shouldn't be talking because Lonnie and I aren't smartest ducks in the pond, but you're really cut out for school little Jack."

"I know I was never great in school, but I passed."

"Yeah barely, but then again the army may not it for you either"

"Why not?"

"Cause it's suicide Jack. You're not cut out for it"

"Shut up Lonnie, let him join the army if he wants to, we're gonna be dead by Y2K anway."

Lonnie laughs and says, "Yeah, you're right"

The waitress brings out both of our meals out. The lady serves Lonnie Chuckie a plate of eggs, pancakes, sausage, bacon, and home fries. While I ordered a batch of egg whites and turkey bacon, symbolizing my new future commitment. It was a little ironic that my brothers were calling me dumb, yet they couldn't pick up a little sign when they see one. Not to mention, that they barely passed school as well. We spent a period of about five minutes of scarfing down our food. Once the three of us were well into our meals,

Lonnie asks, "So make you wanna join the army anyhow? I never saw you playing playing war or wrestling around with the other kids.

Chuckie interrupts, "Yeah, you were always in your room drawing comics or superheros, or whatever?" said Lonnie.

"Because that's all I ever wanted to be."

"Be what?"

"A hero."

They looked at me, and smiled they both knew that what I just said, was probably one of the most corniest things that they ever heard of.

Chuck says, "You know that little Jack, if you wanna go ahead and join the army, do it."

"Are you serious?" I replied

"Yeah, you have one life, do whatever it is that makes you happy." He sarcastically said

"Thanks guys, I'm glad to heard this. Now all I have to do is get dad on my side."

"Ooof, Good Luck with that one, anway we gotta go."

"Good seeing you little bro, we'll see you on the other side when you're dead."

My brothers immediately darted out of the restaurant leaving me by myself. I wonder if it ever occurred to them that they left me with the check, despite the fact that they ordered the most food. They probably pulled that crap on purpose just to piss me off. Should've seen that coming, knowing my brothers by now. Whenever the family would go out for breakfast, Chuck and Lonnie had the tendency to order the most expensive things while the rest of us would just order a normal meal.

After paying the check, I left the diner, and began to move on to my next objective- telling my dad about joining the army. The idea itself became a bit frightening to me. I had no idea what to expect from my father. His opinion had always meant the world to me, and was usually right about everything. Even going back to my early years in high school, where he coached me when I was on the football and wrestling team, my father could always see my disinterest for sports, but always forced me into doing it. He believed that being part of a team would be a good thing for me and sure enough, he had been right.

I pulled up to my father's apartment following a half hour drive. After walking up the steps, it occurred to me that last time I was at father's apartment was right after my parents split. So coming back was a bit odd for me. When reaching the top floor, I walked up and down the halls trying to find room 104. It took me a moment to find as I spotted it behind a small corner. I glanced up and down the floor, took a deep breath, and knocked. No one answered. I knocked again, and still no answer. Right before my fist hit the door for a third knock, my father answered. He looked as if he had just woken up as he was wearing a robe with many stains on it.

My father looked up at me confused and said, "Jack? Is that you?"

"Yeah dad, it's me," I replied.

He puts down the bottle and says, "What brings you here?"

"Oh, I was just in the neighborhood, and I'd thought I would stop by." I awkwardly said.

We stared at each other and said nothing. It was as if we both forgotten had to talk or that the fact that he kind of felt like a stranger now.

"You wanna come in," He said.

With a slight hesitation I said, "Uh, Sure."

We both walked into his living room, and sat down on his couch. I tried my absolute best to ignore the fact that the apartment was an absolute mess. Clothes everywhere, beer bottles all over the floor, with a few sticky counters as well.

"So why are you actually here, Jack? Did your mother tell you to come and ask for more money?" My father said. Although the question itself offended me a bit, I again ignored it.

"Dad, other than these last two years, you've always been there for me. You've told me right from wrong and taught me so many lessons that will carry with me for the rest of life."

"Okay and..." my father said starting to become slightly annoyed. His lack of care angered me bit as I said, "Okay you know what, I'm just gonna cut to the chase. I got accepted into the United States Marine Corp. I'm actually thinking about doing it, and I'm hoping that I will get your blessing." My father walked up from the other side of couch and walked into the kitchen. He opened the fridge, and grabbed a beer.

"Dad, what the hell happened to you?" I said. "Whatever happened to guy who told me to never give up and would push me to boundaries I never knew I had?" My father looked directly at me and took another sip of his beer.

"That guy is long gone, and that old war hero is all that is left... And if you want the truth, here it is. You're mother took everything away from me: my home, my money, my kids- it got me fired from my job. She ruined me!"

A tear began to roll down my cheek. It was hard to try and make up some words to say.

My father continued, "So going back to whole army thing, you can go for it... And again Jack, I love you son, but to tell you the truth, I don't care what you do. Both the good lord and your mom took everything away from me, and you were never there for me these last two years. You never called me. You haven't even checked in on me once. So go be a doctor, a cop, or some sort of war hero for all I care because you clearly don't care about me."

At that moment, my heart collapsed. I'd let down the one person who had made a huge difference in my life. There were no words for me to say him. Nothing could fix the pain that my father had already been put through. I left his apartment without saying another word.

That day had become a huge disappointment. What was supposed to be a good day, turned into a whole line of disappointment. I drove back to Jimmy's diner and ordered some pancakes. As that became the only pace to go to, since I didn't wanna go home to my disappointed mother, it was probably the only place that could make me feel a bit of joy. The diner again would always bring me back to the early 90s, which was a much better time in my life. Hopefully, the new millennium would bring me nothing but happiness. But it's tough to say where I was gonna be in the following year. I was excited to join the marines at first to try and make a difference, and yet the only one on my side at the moment was Jane. If only wish God would give a sign to tell me what to do, because I was stumped.

All of the sudden, the sweet smell of melted syrup and butter struck my nose. The steaming hot aroma of the cinnamon on the pancakes made my stomach start to rumble. And just like that, all of my troubles seemed to disappear as the waitress brought my pancakes. I began to devour my long stack of flapjacks one by one. The poor golden-brown fully treats didn't stand of chance against me as it felt like I hadn't eaten in a week. While in the middle of one of the greatest meals in my life, a group of people beginning to gasp and shout caught my attention.

A women had just fallen from her chair and began choking on some food. One the relatives, "Help, somebody, help."

Sitting in my seat in a state of shock, I had no idea what to do in that moment.

The husband shouted again, "Help, she's choking!"

In an act of desperation, I pounded on her chest multiple times as I wrapped my hands around her stomach. Eventually, the ham that was stuck in the lady's throat, came hurtling out. The lady graciously thanked me, and her family came up me and gave me a big hug.

As my body relaxed a bit, the man turned to me and said, "You're a hero."

Plane & Simple

"Don't forget your luggage," said the man driving the big black suburban- he even stepped out of the car to open the doors for us.

"Oh yes, son grab your bag." my father said scratching his head anxiously. Father handed our driver a check, "whoops, almost forgot this," he added, forcing a smile.

Stepping into the airport, I felt nostalgia from the last time we went on a plane. The last time I went on a plane I was three years old. I don't remember much from it but I know it was the last time we were with my mother, all together, as a family. Trailing behind my father, my bag dragging on the floor due to its heavy weight, I followed my father to the kiosk in order to print our boarding tickets. I could tell he was stressed. Whenever he's stressed he rambles, and I mean rambles.

Patiently standing next to my father as he fumbled through his pockets looking for something, "What are you looking for, I can help," I said.

"My wallet, where is it? Did I leave it in the car? Check my luggage!" standing...staring at my father I could see the pain piercing through his eyes.

"It-it's in your hand, father." I stated with as much patience as I could let out.

Father opened the wallet and began punching buttons on the screen, "it's going to be a long day," he mumbled under his breath.

When the tickets finally printed, we headed to the restroom. The line was pretty big; it seemed like everyone in New York was headed somewhere. I wonder where? Minutes of waiting felt like hours passed. My father finally got to the front of the line, I sat with our luggage as he ran into the bathroom. Walking out I noticed droplets of water on his shirt, and his forehead glistened. Hmm, who's he trying to impress, I thought to myself.

"Okay, let's go," he picked up his luggage and started towards the security line.

That line was huge; there was children sitting on suitcases waiting to move, and people sitting on the ground crawling inch by inch when the line moved. One lady had fallen asleep standing up, her head held up by the handle of her suitcase. You can imagine how uncomfortable that was. Standing against his suitcase, my father tinkered with his phone. I bet he was texting my Uncle Jimmy; that's really his only friend. Crazy part is, he's not even my uncle, he's just good friends with my father. I guess they've known each other since high school and yada yada.

"Dad," I said trying to spark a conversation. "When we get up to security do I have to take my belt off or no? It is fake metal, I think?" Right after I said that it hit me- my father had given me that belt for my last birthday. He's going to be so disappointed.

"It is real metal, I paid good money for that belt, son. Take it off for security."

After an hour in the security line, we made it through, and yes I did take off the belt.

"Shall we grab a bite to eat?" I asked my father, he needed something to distract him.

"Uh yeah, yes we could go to this little pub right by our gate, we have a bit of time to kill." For a moment there, I thought my father was finally feeling less stressed, but that was not the case.

As I sipped on a Coke, my father gulped down his third beer.

"You are going to have to use that tiny restroom on the plane if you keep drinking," I said as my father poured the last sip down his throat rolling his eyes at me.

"Ma'am, can I get another one," father grabbed the waitress' arm as she walked by.

"Uh, yes, I'll grab that for you right now." I knew what she was thinking, my father was a drunk and I was just tagging along. It's not like that; he just gets nervous- it happens to everyone right?

"Dad le-lets go sit at the gate I wanna charge my phone," I insisted trying to get my dad as far away from the bar as possible.

Guess it doesn't help that we chose a pub right across from our gate. Sitting there waiting for my father to finish his final beer, I couldn't help but notice the happy families sitting at the gates. One little girl was snuggled up on her dad's lap reading a book, to pass time I guessed. I bet they were going on a family vacation with palm trees, family photos, and laughter. I was stuck at a pub with my drunk father.

Over at the gate, I was able to plug in my phone. It was already fully charged but I had to plug it in for my father's sake. Beginning to read a book I had brought along for the trip, I looked up to my father walking away, where was he going? Wondering if I should yell to him, ask him where he is going, instead I just sat there and watched him leave. I figured he was headed to the bathroom, who knows with him anymore. He came back a few minutes later with a brown paper bag.

"What's that?"

"Just a few refreshments for the plane"

"Oh cool, did you grab me a water?" I said grabbing the bag to peak in. Of course, it was filled with alcohol. Father was right; it was going to be a long day.

***

Walking onto the plane it was more than obvious my father was drunk. He continuously dropped his luggage on the floor. At one point he decided not to pick his bag back up so I ended up with two heavy bags on my shoulder. I should've taken gym class more seriously. It took us five minutes to actually get seated because father made it his job to talk to every single flight attendant.

"Anybody ever tell you you look like Cameron Diaz?" father said to one of the flight attendants.

"Dad, lets go sit down."

"Hold on I'm talking to my frie-"

"Now." I stated sternly.

Luckily for my father, our seats were only six rows away from the bathroom, which I knew he'd need sooner than later.

"Come on dad, sit down," I said gently after coming to my senses.

"Okay, son. Have I ever told you you're the best?" father replied slurring almost every word.

"Yep." I said even though the real answer was no. My father never complimented me nor did he even talk to me on a regular basis. Sitting down after shoving both our luggage bags in the tiny overhead compartment I noticed my father had begun to snore. But he hadn't put his seat belt on and that was a safety issue. Reaching over to buckle his seatbelt, he began to open his eyes.

"Get off me!" he raised his voice.

Closing his eyes immediately after.

"Dad, it's me, you need your seatbelt on, come on wake up."

"I don't need a seatbelt," he mumbled.

"Yes, you do wake up!"

We went back and forth for a few minutes until I gave up, he wasn't going to budge so I figured I'd let the flight attendants handle it. Before take-off I ran to use the bathroom. Returning after less than five minutes, father was yelling at the attendants.

"Sir," the flight attendant approached my father, "Sir, put your seatbelt on please, we are going to take off shortly."

"Take off? No." my father replied to the flight attendant.

"Yes sir, we are going to take off soon. Please put your seatbelt on."

This was going to get ugly quickly.

"No, get me off. I'm not taking off." my father began to raise his voice.

"Sir, i'm going to ask you to calm do-"

"No! Get me off this plane right now!" he yelled.

"Dad? What're you doing," I budded in as I returned from the bathroom.

"Mason, good you're back. Listen buddy, we have to get off this plane right now." my father spoke with such wide eyes, implying that something was wrong.

"Dad, you are fine. We are going to take off- everything's going to be okay. Buckle the seatbelt." I said gently, trying not to draw any attention

184

to us, although the whole plane was listening including the pilot who was supposed to be preparing for take off.

"No," father screamed, shoving me into the flight attendant. Instantly he began for the door screaming, "let me out, let me out."

He approached the plane door, which was now closed and separated from the gate. He started banging on it. Everyone on the plane was watching some were laughing, while others were trying to help. Two taller, strong looking men tried to restrain him from banging on the door.

"Sir you are going to have to calm down or I will have no choice but to kick you off," the flight attendant yelled as my father continued banging on the door.

"Dad."

"Dad, mom wouldn't want you to be like this." I said hoping my father was listening, "drinking your problems away. You're stressed dad; you need help".

Suddenly everything went quiet. The banging stopped, the men restraining my father let go, it was almost peaceful. My father stood there staring at me. I couldn't tell if he was about to scream at me or continue to bang on the door.

"Dad," I said quietly approaching him.

Out of nowhere my father began to cry, dropping to his knees covering his face with his hands.

"I-Im sorry, I'm so sorry, Mason."

Dropping to the floor I began to hug my father, "It's okay dad, I love you,"

"I love you too," father said.

The people around us, once snickering at my father looked on with softer smiles. A relief seemed to flood the whole plane as we got ready to take off. After a long, emotional embrace, father and I climbed back into our seats and buckled are seatbelts. Seconds later, one of the flight attendants offered us waters,

"I'm glad to see you two are doing good, would you like waters?"

"Yes please, thank you!" I said grabbing the waters.

Father was still recovering from his previous outburst. I figured it'd be best for me to do the talking. Gulping down the ice cold water my father began to snap back to normal. The pilot came over the loudspeaker.

"Ladies and gentlemen this is your pilot speaking, we are just about to take off. I'd like to take a moment to thank you for joining us on this trip, now sit back, relax, and enjoy!"

I looked at my father who began to fall asleep on my shoulder and sighed, "It's going to be a good day." I smiled.

❋❋❋

Completing the Journey

Laying on the foot of the bed, her sweet scent filled my nose as food entered my thoughts. Everytime she points in a direction, her kid Tom will follow her finger. If Tom does not follow, Rachel's voice will echo throughout the house and Tom will go to his room where a big wood door separates him from everybody else. Sam started talking, interrupting my thought with his deep, crackling voice. His voice can get much deeper, like if I don't "gentle" or even when Tom doesn't follow Rachels finger. Sam stopped, allowing Rachel to talk again, it was all just as confusing as before.

"When should we make Yoda's last vet appointment?" I heard my name and perked up. Then they talked more.

"I am not sure, but Tom has to know before we take Yoda. We couldn't possibly tell him after, could we?" Sam adjusted the position he was laying in.

"No, Sam! We have to let Tom know, and lower your voice. Do you really want him to find out this way?"

I didn't know what they were talking about, but everytime they say the vet, I have to go to this place with other dogs; which is nice, but there are also cats. That's not as nice. Then there are some other animals there that are weird. Once I go into a separate room, some other person is all over me, so I don't want to go again.

Jumping off the bed, my paws brush on the ground, as my back leg jolts with pain as I let out a small yelp in surprise. I twist my head to my tail leg looking for a small cut or something else that might have caused the pain, ready to lick it away. But there's nothing there. How weird. This sudden pain sparked nerves throughout my body, just like when I was a puppy.

I was at this very small place with a bunch of my siblings. More and more came, making the area even smaller. One day the man had put me in a box. He walked around with me, causing my balance to fail, especially when the box rattled and shook around. I then nervously waited in anticipation, there was a slam, then a loud noise sparked a vibration all around me causing me to rush to the other corner. I had felt a motion, yet it was different this time, less choppy. The movement came to a halt, and my nerves were trying to burst out of me. A dim light penetrated the box and rested on my face. The choppy motion started again, only to stop shortly after. It was almost as if everything had paused for a second. The noise I'd heard before sounded again but this time it didn't sound as close; almost as if it were further away. The noise then faded away and more of those noises filled my ears. The darkness filled the box, but so did emptiness. I was the only thing in there, which seemed unusual since I was always in a crowd. Eventually, the darkness disappeared. Allowing light to fill the box. Revealing two people who I now know as Rachel and Sam but at the time, fear froze my paws. All I could do was look away hoping they wouldn't hurt me.

***

Fortunately, right as I approach the door, Tom comes in, so I use my snout to push the door, allowing me to run right by him. I stopped at my food bowl first, sniffing for my meal. Nothing. I only go two times during the day where there is actually food. Walking around my "toy" as they call it was too still. My paws would leave the ground and shortly return as I went to grab it. Upon reaching it my teeth felt the smooth, yet also rough texture of the toy. I had to get it in the air. Then once in the air, it would come back down and go right up again. It memorized me watching it go up then down while I ran rampant to try and get it back. It is like a squirrel running away but I can catch it and then keep on chasing it. Sometimes it's even better than a squirrel for that reason, and that I can use it inside as well. I felt content with chasing the toy for now, so I continued on my way downstairs. I got one paw on the step to go downstairs to the door when I heard Tom.

"What?! No. No. No. He can't... but why?" His voice portrayed grief and it seemed like tears were ready to fall. You could hear the gasps in between almost each word and it made me remember the time he also sounded that way when he was with those other smaller people.

***

He was playing with those other people in the backyard on a cool day, so I joined them outside to enjoy the weather before the ground gets higher with white, tasteless fluff. He and the others started playing a game where they ran around just to touch each others shoulders, then run in the opposite direction. Tom was being chased and he was running fast, when he tripped over himself. Putting out one arm, Tom landed and a loud scream rung into the air with the same tone. His friends froze as I ran over.

"Owwwwww, Mommy! Mommy, my arm!" Tom continued to wail "Yoda, my arm!"

I licked his face, hoping to help him stop crying. I laid right next to him, all curled up until Rachel and Sam came. Sam picked him up, and directed everyone else to follow. I was all alone in the backyard, curious as to where they went and what happened. I knew he was sad, but I was not sure why. He came back later with a rough and bulky object around his arm.

***

I stopped and turned back to the bedroom. Walking in I saw Tom curled up in Rachel's arms, while Sam was rubbing his back. They all heard me enter, Tom swerving his head last, then started to cry more, running over to me. His arms swooped around my neck and stayed there repeating,

"Yoda, I love you. But why? It's not fair."

I had no idea what he was talking about, but I loved it when he hugged me like that. My tail was going all over the place. That made

Tom look up and start to laugh, but this was a tear filled laugh. Shuffling out of her bed Rachel created the same lock with her arms, but around Tom and me.

"I'm sorry Tom, you are right. Yoda doesn't deserve this, but life does this to people. This doesn't mean Yoda will be unhappy. He will go to a wonderful place with treats and bones, fire hydrants, and many other good dogs."

"You promise Mommy? I want Yoda to be the happiest dog ever!" Tom perked up, the thought of me in this wonderland Rachel was talking about put a huge smile on Tom's face. "What about when I got mad from school. Remember mommy, english class. I ran right up to my room. I started crying more and Yoda followed me in. He put his head right on my back, near my head, warming me up, staying there until I stopped crying. He helped me be happy. I want him to be happy and feel cozy. He deserves it. I love him so much!"

✳✳✳

Tom was in his room where I get yelled at if I enter. It took me a while to learn that's why they yelled at me, so I don't go in there. Rachel and Sam sat in the room with the loud and colorful box. The box was dark and silent now, so the two talked.

"I just got off the phone with the specialist. They believe that Yoda has cancer." Rachel talked in short bursts, holding back tears.

"Cancer? Really, cancer. Why didn't they suspect that sooner?" Sam's voice got deeper and louder than normal.

"We could have done more if they didn't screw us like this. So what, it's too late now? They solved the puzzle, but there is no glue to keep it together. Why are they specialists if they are so slow to find out?"

"Listen, Sam, we didn't go straight to the specialist." Sam interrupted her,

"You're right. It is that overpriced, lets not jump to any conclusions yet. I am going to call him and give him a piece of my mind."

Tom walked out with a worried look weighing his face down, making Sam calm down.

"Daddy, why are you yelling at Yoda?"

"Tom, I'm not yelling at him. We got some more news and I am just angry at the vets. I am so sorry I shouted like that."

"What did the doctors say, Daddy?" Tom looked up at Sam, then down at me.

"Yoda has something very bad Tom, and the doctors found the bad thing too late," Sam sighs and directs his head down, "so you might have to say bye to Yoda sooner than we thought. I'm so sorry Tom, I know this is hard for you, but just remember the good times you and Yoda have had and where he will go. Everything will work out." Sam rested his hand on Tom's shoulder while he finished talking.

I heard my name a lot, so I cocked my head to the side looking at Tom, trying to understand every word that I know. I really only know my name.

At that moment Tom perked up and ran into the kitchen. I remained by the black box, but my attention was directed at Tom. A squeak followed by the crinkle of the bag my food was in meant I was going to have to do some odd task, but after the task I get my food in the bag. Thinking of this, I hurdled myself up, but my back leg had a shooting pain worse than anything I have ever felt. I let out a high pitched scream and Rachel hurried to come to me.

"It's okay Yoda, lay back down. Everything will be okay."

I knew she was speaking to me, I just didn't understand it. While she talked her hand beat against the floor. Knowing that she wanted me to lay down, I followed her gesture.

"Oh I know Yoda, you must be in a tremendous amount of pain It mus-"

Tom leaped out of the kitchen.

"Yoda, do not get up, but I have a treat for you." Tom's face gleamed with excitement.

I wanted that treat so I started to get up, but Rachel put her hand on my back with just enough resistance that I knew not to continue to get up. Tom continued walking to me, treat exposed in his hand as I thumped my tail against the floor and try to shimmy forward.

"Here you go Yoda. Gentle... gentle... gentle Yoda."

Each gentle grew slightly louder and more firm. I knew that when Tom says "gentle" I have to watch out for his hand. I practically licked the treat away from his hand and then ate it as fast as possible so no one would steal it from me.

***

I learned about gentle when Tom was younger. He was with Sam and Rachel playing, when Sam brought in food, which they call a treat. Sam handed the treat to Tom as his face lit up with excited curiosity. Tom grabbed the treat, hesitated with it, then put it right in his mouth.

"No Tom, no!" Rachel jumped into action, pulling the treat right out of his mouth, but it was too late. Tom's facial expression turned sour and his cheeks became bright red while tears flowed down his face. Rachel picked Tom up, cradled him until he calmed down, and gave him the treat. She made sure to help hold the treat this time. Rachel, holding the treat and Tom's arm, put them right in my face. I smelled the food and heard Rachel say gentle, but not knowing what that meant, I went in and snatched the food, and some of Toms finger. Tom started to cry again and Sam stepped in looking right at me firmly saying "gentle". He smacked my snout and repeated gentle. At that point I got what he was saying. From then on I would gentle so I don't make Tom cry and I don't get hit.

***

It was the next day and Sam was getting dressed later then he would normally in the morning. The room usually isn't bright from the sun when he gets dressed.

"Hopefully this doc will be able to help Yoda feel better for the time he has left." Sam stated as he buttoned his shirt.

"Or maybe he will say that they were wrong and we don't have to put him down." Rachel gained a hopeful shine in her eyes as she said this.

"Rachel, we have to accept the fact that Yoda has cancer, we can't change that in the stage he is in." Sam rotated to look right at Rachel, putting out that hopeful shine.

Sam walked downstairs, out of boredom and curiosity, I followed. As I walked to the door that opens to let me outside, Sam didn't follow.

He went into the other room, confused, I followed him. As I was walking the jingle noise started. That is the thing that goes around my neck when we go to the other outside, where Sam is with me. They call the other outside a walk, so I enjoy walks. They use a leash, which is what jingles to control how far and fast I can go. Sometimes the leash makes it so I can't sniff people to know if they are safe for Sam and Rachel. I try to chase squirrels because I need to catch them, yet I never do, and the leash keeps me from trying in the other outside. Especially since I don't run as fast as when I was young. I went inside the room where Sam was standing and I started to jump around him.

"Easy Yoda, calm down." Sam struggled to put the leash around my neck, but once he did I went right for the door.

***

"Alright Yoda, after examining you today I know how to help. So Sam, since we have tried to make the cancer go into remission, I am here to focus more on making Yoda comfortable. I have a pain killer pill that will help him. With this pill we have to stop the remission process and just focus on making Yoda happy with his time left."

"Alright doc, I mean I would rather Yoda be comfortable then live painfully."

"That is normally what my patient's parents choose. He will be happy, his pain should decrease ten fold and he will be pain free and normal right up until the end. I know this is a hard time, but we should schedule Yoda's last appointment."

I got so bored, so I stood up, shook, and tried to walk out of the room but my leash tugged my head back. Sam pulled me closer "It's alright Yoda, we're almost done here today."

I wagged my tail and calmed down. I like when Sam talks to me in a calm voice like he is now. I don't know what he is saying, but he isn't mad, which is nice. I know when he is mad because he will stand straight up, while raising his voice and pointing at something. He can be even more mad then that.

One time there were a case of markers in the room with me. Nobody was home and the door was shut. I smelled many good things that captured my attention. I sniffed around, my nose to the floor, until I came face to cover with the markers. They smelled like food, so I went to eat them. After biting into almost every marker I stopped, wondering why I smelt food but was not able to eat anything. When everyone got home they saw me, the punctured and torn markers, and my fur. Sam got so mad that time that he hit my nose. After that I knew it wasn't food and that I shouldn't have tried to eat it. Sam's calm voice is much nicer.

As Sam held my leash back to open the door, a scent flowed into my nose, mmmmmh. Saliva was forming in my mouth forcing me to lick my snout. I couldn't wait for Sam to let go so I ran in. A quick resistance didn't stop me as Sam let go of my leash, my nose ten steps ahead of my feet leading me right to Rachel.

"Yoda" Rachel paused, "Sit"

I bent my back legs so they rested on the floor.

"Good boy Yoda, Who's a good boy? Who's a good boy?"

Rachel's voice was in a high pitch and she was leaning forward, which meant she was happy. After waiting, she showed her arm, which had a bone. Impatiently I inched forward without lifting my back legs. Rachel finally handed me the bone, which I grabbed and ran right to the door to go outside. Rachel and Tom followed shortly behind me and let me out. Running out all I did was lay down. After laying down and chewing on my bone I realized that Rachel and Tom were still there. Tom, nearly in tears again, was talking to Rachel.

"I am so happy that Yoda likes his bone. I wish we could do more, what else could we do by tomorrow?" Tom jumped in his own skin while asking.

"I think the best thing to do would be to just love him as much as possible. Think of it as a good thing okay? He won't be in pain and he will be with all of his other doggy friends."

I didn't listen very much because I was focused on my bone, but then Tom walked over with his arms spread wide. I did not want him to take my bone so I grabbed it, got up, and ran to the other side of the yard to lay back down. As I ran away I watched Tom stop and giggle.

The next day I woke up to Tom's arms wrapped tight around me. He was warm and his breathing was light. He was whispering, but so softly I couldn't make out what he was saying. Rachel walked out of the room with the bowl of water in it and called my name.

"Alright Yoda, it is time for your appointment."

Right as Rachel said that Sam got up and wrapped his arms around her and Tom squeezed me tighter. Rachel walked out of the room right to my leash. Hearing a rattle, I realized it was my leash so I hopped up to run over but pain resonated through my leg.

"Sit Yoda, please don't make this harder than it has to be. I am sad enough already." Sam stood right next to Rachel with his arm around her while she talked.

"I know, but it will be alright, let's just go now." Sam spoke with a sad tone as he motioned towards the door.

Tom stood at the end of the room looking at me with an upset look haunting his face. I attempted to walk toward Tom, but my head jerked back due to the leash around my neck. Tom screaming "No! No! Don't take him yet. Just one more minute." as he ran over, he dropped, sliding right into me. While hugging me, I felt the leash tug, so I turned to Rachel. It must be time to go in the car now, so I followed the leash. Tom dropped his arms but followed directly behind me out the door. Sam opened the door to the car, so I went to hop in. I was able to get halfway in and then I felt Sam's arms push me the rest of the way up. Before Sam shut the door, Tom put his arm out, I licked his hand and then he rubbed the top of my head. Tom stepped back so Sam slammed the door shut.

Looking out the clear part of the door in the car is weird because I see everything moving, but my legs are not doing anything. I looked back at Tom as he stood by the door until I couldn't see him anymore. My head drifted off watching things fly by, and then I saw a squirrel! I pressed my snout against the clear part of the door. I just thought about chasing the squirrel, just running and running like I used to be able to do. That would be nice.

Misunderstood

The morning sun peeked through a crack in the blinds, nearly illuminating his entire bedroom. Checking the clock and groaning at the location of the hands, Anthony dropped his head back onto the pillow; it was only 6:42. Eighteen more minutes until it was time to start the day. He shut his eyes to fall back asleep, only to awaken to the blaring sound of his alarm clock going off in what seemed like only three minutes later. The big hand touched the seven while the little was on the 12. Anthony hit the clock once, twice, three times as his feet swung off the bed, slowly but surely, and hit the cold hardwood floor. Twenty long minutes later of repeating his shower routine three times led him to the kitchen to eat the most important meal of the day, but only after throwing back a glass of orange juice along with a couple of pills. Anthony slipped on a pair of rubber gloves, the kind that would be found at a hospital, before reading that morning's newspaper; the pages were without a doubt horribly dirty and contaminated. Going gloveless and having to wash his hands three times would have disrupted his morning routine substantially. Grabbing his house keys left on the empty mantel, he twisted the door handle three times, before grabbing his beaten-up cane, and headed out for his morning walk.

Though it was still early in the year, spring had come quickly; Anthony sported a light jacket to protect himself from the slapping wind, popping the collar and smiling to himself as he recalled a lifestyle, humming the tune of "Mr. Lonely" and taking his usual route to the neighborhood park, careful not to step on the sidewalk cracks. Even years of therapy and medication could not get rid of the feeling he got when his foot came down on a sidewalk crack, or walked into an unorganized room. The cool breeze carried the voices of children, followed by conversation between parents regarding information that everyone acted to care about, yet it was clear that no one truly did. Anthony scanned the area before carefully selecting the park bench he would sit on that day. Tearing open a wipe package, he thoroughly cleaned the seat before slowly lowering himself onto the wooden bench. The atmosphere changed almost instantly; parent's fake conversations lowered to whispers while their eyes flickered between Anthony and their children. The once welcoming ambience quickly shifted, and it seemed as if the sky had begun to grow darker with every minute the elderly man was present. While they thought they were being discreet, Anthony's hearing aid allowed him to hear every hurtful word.

"He's back again," one parent shuddered and gathered her two kids, "Layla! Nick! Come on, let's go home. Maybe we can come back after lunch."

Another parent rolled her eyes, and turned to her husband, "I've had enough of this. How are we supposed to let our kids have fun if we have to worry about this creep everyday? I think you should say something to him."

"What do you expect me to say? He's just an old man sitting on the bench, until he actually does anything, we can't exactly complain," the husband seemed unbothered by Anthony, but nonetheless felt he should speak to the daily park-watcher to please his wife. Anthony never quite understood why he was so feared and hated. Yes, he would be at the park nearly all hours of the day, after breakfast, lunch, and right before sunset, but he had never meant any harm. Sitting there and watching the children play and grow up throughout the years helped him through the lonely days. His memories of seeing children age and soon leave the playground were interrupted, "Hello Sir, I'm sorry to confront you like this but my wife is concerned about you being at the park all the time. Her and some other parents are convinced that you're some type of threat to the kids. You seem like a normal guy, maybe if you just speak to them and tell them they have nothing to worry about we can all feel more comfortable." Anthony's eyes grew wide as he began to perspire and he felt his heart beat faster and faster. Nervously tapping his fingers on his knee and gripping his cane with his wrinkly hand, Anthony rose from the bench as quickly as his old joints allowed, gave the man a short nod, and went on his way. The husband looked utterly confused and turned to his wife, "You're right, he's a weirdo. It's probably best if we just keep our distance."

Anthony returned home for lunch after struggling to make one more lap around the block to clear his head with his nearly split in half cane. Turning his house key three times, he opened his door to emptiness. The same emptiness he felt every morning when he woke up; the same emptiness he felt every night before he went to sleep. It seemed as though he could never escape it. No matter where he went, the emptiness swallowed him. While others came home to family members and pets, Anthony opened the door to his tidy house, complete with bare walls and pristine surfaces. He quickly washed his hands, counting his ABC's, once, twice, three times. Anthony grabbed a towel to dry his freshly cleaned hands and made a sandwich, cutting each side of the bread nearly straight. Before he was able to sit, his doorbell rang, echoing throughout the entire house. Hobbling over to the front door, Anthony quickly turned the handle three times and swung it open to find one of the many judgmental parents standing on his porch holding a stack of mail.

"Hi, I'm Kate, I live across the street. I think this is your mail; well, I'm assuming it is since the address matches this house's," the two stood in awkward silence for a while before Kate spoke up again, "are you busy? Do you mind if I come in?" The parent stepped in before Anthony could have a say. He grunted and rolled his eyes, sarcastically gesturing her to enter his home. The nosy girl couldn't have just left the mail on the steps and gone home? She handed him the mail and quickly observed the room, seeing no pictures covering the bare walls. "Do you live alone?" She questioned, though had a feeling she already knew the answer. She noticed the walls were bare, with no holes in the wall left from nails hanging up family photos.

"Yes," his answer was originally short and aggressive, but then he continued, "It's just me. No one else."

"Do you have any kids?" Again, Kate knew the answer before she asked the question.

"No. No kids. No wife. As I said, it's just me," the subject was touchy for Anthony; he never talked about it to anyone. The majority of the time he hardly even talked to anyone. Everyone Anthony had met seemed to have the same preconceived idea that he was a creep. However, the old man noticed Kate was not as bothered by him as other parents. Could it be possible that he would be able to have an actual conversation with someone in the neighborhood that did not see him as some old creep? Anthony gestured toward the kitchen table, though this time in a much less sarcastic manner, "Kate, take a seat. Would you like some coffee? There should be some candies left in that jar over there," he nodded towards the center of the table, eagerly waiting for Kate's response; if she decided to take a seat and talk for a while, Anthony would finally make a friend in this judgmental neighborhood. However, if she declined the offer, she would walk out the front door as the same person everyone else on the block was.

"Yes, please, I'd love some!" Kate sat down and started the conversation off. Though from two separate generations, both Kate and Anthony had plenty in common to keep the conversation going. The two talked for hours about anything and everything; it felt as if they had been old friends, catching up after being apart for many years.

Anthony checked the time when his stomach growled and saw that it read 6:00pm. "Look at the time! Are you hungry? I have lots of food in the fridge that I can whip up for us," he knew it was a long shot, but Anthony needed to make sure he would not lose the new friend he had just made.

"I would love to but I have to go home, my family is waiting for me to make dinner and I have to pick up my daughter from lacrosse," Kate gathered her purse and phone, dialing one of the other parents in the neighborhood as she said goodbye to Anthony, "Lori! Hi! Are you busy right now? Can we talk? It's important."

***

Days and weeks passed by, and Anthony's trips to the park, hobbling with his half-broken cane, seemed to become more enjoyable, thanks to

Kate. While not all of the parents favored his presence, it seemed like Kate was able to convince a select few of Anthony's innocence through his loneliness. Now, instead of remaining on the bench during his visits, he was walking around, talking to Kate and other parents, and even playing with some of the children. Eventually, the parents were all able to see that Anthony was not a creep, but just a lonely old man who had no love and no children.

June 12th came much quicker than he thought it would; another year passed, another year older. Anthony was typically used to having a quiet birthday, sitting at the park and enjoying the blooming summer breeze. That day, however, was quite different. As Anthony arrived at the park, he noticed balloons and streamers covering the playground and benches. He found Kate amongst the crowd of parents and indulged in conversation.

"Hi Kate, how are you today? Is it one of the youngster's birthdays?" Anthony questioned.

"No, it's yours! Did you really think I would forget?" Kate shook her head while smiling and grabbed a present from behind her, "This is for you, from us," she stepped to the side to reveal the remaining parents from the neighborhood. Anthony's heart started beating faster and faster and a smile formed across his face, showing his wrinkles on the sides of his mouth and the corner of his eyes. It's been years since he's received a present, and especially one on his birthday. Even when he was little, he can remember barely getting as much as a cake. Some years, if he was lucky, his parents would give him a small gift, but typically nothing too expensive. He was often the forgotten child. Being the youngest in a big family was hard; everything that belonged to Anthony had also once belonged to his older brothers and sisters. Even the cane he used now was from his older brother that passed years ago. Anthony tore back the wrapping paper to reveal a smooth, hickory cane.

His eyes welled up as he looked over at the group of parents, "For me?"

"Yes, finally a cane of your own, and one that's not broken," Kate laughed and gave Anthony a hug, "Happy 80th Birthday."

Bruto

The mist of the mornings in Antioch were quite an eerie sight; not my first time here, but surely my last. Through the mist, however, the sun poked its head out from above. As the ship turned, some of that light slipped through the iron grates, revealing those who didn't survive the trip. I was one of the stronger ones, those who had been accustomed to abhorrent conditions. The stench in the room made many of the others gag, which would sometimes manifest into low sobs and howls. As I looked away, the suns rays faded and the room returned to darkness. Looking away, I saw a metal helmet pop around the corner of the brig; it seemed to be carrying a large wad of keys. The man came closer, and upon inspection of our cages, he stood by as if he was anticipating something. From the darkness emerged a large group of armed soldiers, armour far more ornate than that of any of the Syriac conscripts. If I had to guess, they must've been from the Roman consort; they were here for me.

Surprisingly, the chains were light and much more pleasant than expected; not a single mark left on my wrists this time around. In addition to this newfound hospitality was a much better cart for transport, which meant less time hunched over in an open cage to avoid the burning sun. This cart stood tall and had dainty wooden seats with an upper canopy to keep us in the shade. Who ever bought us must've taken great care in our transport, to which many of the others said that it was a sign that we had a good master. Something to ponder on the way I guess. But my attention was drawn away once more, this time by a great steed. In front of the caravan stood a tall white horse with a figure I couldn't see. He stood just under the sun and it made it very hard to see with the light in my face. As he drew closer I could just barely make out the details. He himself was much shorter than the Syriac or Coeliac men, rather he was much less dark and more olive-like in his complexion. The man had oddly curly hair and had mounds of armor on, lined with golden tress'. He looked like the soldiers I saw as a kid, of which we called them the *Opal'khoai*.

✳✳✳

Artorius Ovidius Erastus he was, man in figure but a caring brother at heart. He was like a father, of which I never truly had. His fatherly nature with all of his funny and immature moments always made me feel like alien to where I came from. No longer did I have to worry about eating or the clothes on my back, and even sickness was far less frequent. What a luxurious life we live today, with the works of Ovid and lifestyles one can pursue, just divine all over. But with luxury comes the sin of gluttony, though many of us in Ostia cannot run from it. Master Artor loved when I painted him, each stroke bringing his smile tighter and more pompous, and subsequently his posture. I loved painting as well as it calmed me down from the constant commotion of life.

Master Artor was standing on his plinth, when he suddenly aborted his pose, drawing around the desk and sat down slowly on the couch.

"Brutus, do you remember when you first arrived here, from Antioch?" He leaned over my shoulder and inspected my work.

"Ah yes, was a liberating day, however it was quite different from what people had described the process. " I stopped my work and sat staring at the color palette.

"I'm glad you still have it so clear in memory. But there is something I have neglected to discuss with you..." He seemed rather standoffish, retreating a step in dismay.

"What is it?" Feeling a bit insecure I looked to master him, but quickly returned to my canvas to avoid eye contact.

"I just wanted to explain to you something I should have much earlier than now. I miss when you were young and only now do I finally accept my ignorance, that is my ignorance that all along you have been a slave. It clouds my thoughts, the problem with that is that it is now clouding my judgement." His eyes began to pain, the stare he gave me said it all.

"And, like me, there are others who are nice and caring to their slaves, but few. And look at your arms; can you spot a signum?" Seeing me look at my arms, he muttered. "That's right, there are none, and that was a choice I made very early on. I did not want you to feel as a slave, and because you were so young, I didn't want to scare you. You were like a son, Brutus. And all those precautions, all to hide my guilt." He retreated into his chair and began to hang his head in his hands. I sat down next to him and held him close. Never before had I seen him so weak; my role model.

"Just rest now, I cannot bear this image. Would my acceptance suffice?" Leaning over, I put a hand on his shoulder and sat with him for a while.

"Oh Brutus, my guilt lives within me, let me bear it alone. You need not accept anyone but you, you are your own master." His tone was weak and and trembling, and I could sense the lie. But the last words sat in my head for quite some time.

✳✳✳

My dreams became reality in what felt like a year long transition. One moment I heard banging of my hammer building my dream home along the water, to a rather piercing ringing of pots and pans being smashed together out in the hall. As I woke, I nearly jumped out of bed and sprinted to the atrium. Passing the frescos I came into the compluvium and saw Marius on the verge of crying with mistress Ophelia crouching over him. She looked to be treating a burn of some sort, nasty sight it was. Coming closer I began to see the extent of damage he had, and a wonder how he had the strength and resilience to clap those pots together.

"How did this happen Marius? Speak up will you!" Mistress Ophelia began to sob.

"I was on an errand when a band of brigands came through the forum. They held torches and spears. Armed to the toe they were, and without opposition. They destroyed everything and stole the goods. I tried to save a few others, but I was run out of the city. They slaughtered many, but our courier was drawn in the forum. I believe someone snuck away and sent word to Rome. Please let me be silent now?" He groaned and settled back down and began to close his eyes.

"Do not sleep now, we must tend to your burns and get them wrapped. Brutus, fetch the gate keys and seal the entrances. Gather Artorius. " She spoke with great volume and determination, for anger ran deep in her eyes. Running out of the hall, I called for master and headed for the study.

"Speak child, what is it you need?" He sat wide-eyed with a smile.

"Come now master, and maintain haste. We haven't time to chat! We must seal the gates and gather the children. The town has been overrun with brigands! Where are the keys to the gates?"

"I have them here," handing them to me, "go set up the cart once your finished the gates. We will ride out to Rome in a few hours. It will be noon when we arrive. " He split from me and ran to the bedrooms.

As the sun hit me, I began to feel just how anxious I was. The sweat was profuse and my blood rushed like crazy. Each gate was heavy and hard to push, each one was around 12 feet tall and made of solid oak casted in iron. And with four total gates, we were sure to withstand an attack, at least for a while. Nearing the stable, I tacked the horses and put the canvas cover on the cart. The wagon was already being armoured up by the blacksmith Syphax and the stablehand Maxim. Once that was all complete, we led the wagon to the back of the villa where the family had all of their belongings packed. As we drew closer I could see the angst and despair in their eyes. Their faces were grim and it was very telling of the true danger we were in. From around the barn came two of the younger slaves with a stretcher for Marius. They quickly vanished inside, and after a short pause came loud yelling of agony and pain. The yelling reminded me of my home city, Memphis, when the southern Berber tribes burned my hometown.

For about an hour we remained packing the wagon with our things; master walked out of the house towards the cart signalling me. I stopped and stuck my head around to seem him better. "What is it you need, sir?"

"Nothing, I just wanted you to follow me for a few. I have something to show you. " He seemed considerably less anxious than earlier, and had a sort of *'you're going to like this'* face on. As we past by the barn, I caught a glimpse of something shiny through the cracks of woods slats on the forge-house. As I squinted I could make out the image of some pretty ornate armour. Immediately I was consumed with a feeling of strength and masculinity. Master Artor looked back at me and noticed my faint excitement and said, "Ah damn, you've already caught my little secret. This is something I've been waiting to give you... I guess just not for this reason. " His words faded somewhat into a saddened tone. Coming into the forge-house felt awesome; I had never been in here before. In the center of the room was a full set of armour, much like that of the Roman soldier, however this was different. It wasn't made to mimic real soldiers, rather it was made to show strength in our family. I knew this because I had read some of the old family books in master Artor's study.

Master carefully put each piece on the long oak table, tentatively arranging each in a specific order. "This is my gift to you... *son*. For many a time I have wanted to bestow this set upon you, but it was never the right time, and now isn't either but we have good reason. " He looked at me with pain in his eyes, and it felt like they were reaching deep within me. "With the threat of brigands encroaching on our property, we must suit you up as the next defender of our family for I must stay here and defend my livelihood. " He pointed to his study and continued, "Those books amass the total knowledge and understanding our family has, for it has been handed down for generations. Today I want to commence manumissio in front of our scholar, Alius. " I immediately was taken aback; truly dumbfounded. He moved to the shelving and began to shuffle around through the stacks. Suddenly, he brought out an old and dusty wax tablet.

Walking over to me he said, "Alius will document it and seal it for me. Then it will be given to you as a sign of your freedom. Don't lose it though, for those who haven't gotten word of your freedom will seek to end it. " The words rang through my head, nearly burying me with the pressure.

"Make it to the emperor's secretarius and have her send word to all cities in the empire. Then you will have your newfound freedom codified. " He began to hustle. With quick movements, he carried in a chest and opened it at my feet.

"Put these leather undergarments on, they will keep your armour steady and will help defend against arrows that penetrate the iron. For the most part, it is light so it won't weigh you down much. " He pointed to the chest and instructed me on how to assemble the armor. With my new set on, I felt invincible. Yanking me by the arm, he led me to a shiny piece of reflective metal. In it I could see myself, looking like the caesar himself, the epaulettes had handmade gold and bronze markings of our family. At this moment I knew I was not a slave at heart.

As I came to the front of the house, the family gasped in awe. Many of them smiled while the mistress seemed deeply saddened by the sight. From behind I could hear some rustling, and so I turned. To my surprise, Alius and Master Artor held a large sword case. With a nod from master I knew it was mine, and I didn't hesitate. Opening up the box was like being in the sweet shops of Rome and Alexandria. The sword was a short sword much like the ones found in Memphis, and when I realized this, I nearly collapsed. He had went through great lengths to make this sword, and that is what truly made me feel special.

✳✳✳

It was nearing noon when I found myself in the observatory deck. I was sitting with a pitcher of wine and a book, and beside me sat my helmet and sword. Out over the horizon towards the town, I could just barely make out some riders. For a moment I thought they were just passing, but within a minute, they began to head in our direction. I quickly jumped up, put my helmet on, and strapped my sword around my waist. Downing the rest of my wine, I hurried down the stairs.

"Master Artor! Send the wagon and grab me my horse! The brigands have found the villas! They are just above the horizon on the town. " I shouted and bolted for the side entrance. Upon exiting into the muster grounds, Master sat proudly upon a white stallion, dressed to the toe with armor like mine.

"Ahh you still have yours on! I was afraid you'd have taken it off by

now. Come now, we must get the cart our and set off for the brigands!"
He said as he put his helmet on.

We quickly set the wagon on the road and prepared the family.
Leaning in on the cart, I said, "Okay now, listen here. I'm going to meet
you in the forum in Rome in two days. For now I must stay and help
Master and the others. You all must alert Rome, and I trust Alius will
take care of you guys. Now be gone and don't look back. We will be
safe... I give you my word."

Watching them leave was hard and very distracting. For once I was
very depressed, but I was in no position to brood. Sensing my despair,
master Artor came 'round and patted me on the back. He slowly turned
to me and said, "I have one wish son, just one, that you must follow.
Consider this as my final command before I truly set you free."

"Yes, Master?"

"When we charge into that stampede, I want you to keep riding
forward and don't look back. I want you to ride all the way to Rome and
I want you to forget the villa. We are too outnumbered and it's almost
guaranteed death. Let me gain my glory and let you live another day."
He looked more serious than ever before, for this was a dream of any true
Roman. His eyes were all I could pay attention to as they peered into my
soul. "You have served your family well, but now it's time for us to give
back. " I could see the tears in his eyes, but our emotional moment was
cut short with the sound of horse hooves. It was time.

We braced hard, nearly shaking in our armor for the army before us
was massive. The moment before the signal was eerily quiet on our end;
we held steady for what felt like an hour. As they approached, him and I
gathered close, careful to inspect their lines. Scanning the field, I began
to make out the faces and insignia held by the riders. But, with a quick
turn of my head, I saw him nod and give me the go ahead … and we
were off. As we sprinted, I could feel my heart beating in my chest, hard
and powerful. My horse began to kick it into overdrive, his heart too
beating rapidly. As we got closer I felt a deep fire and rage build in me,
and it began to take over. Using the spurs, I had the horse nearly ready
to buck me. Drawing closer, they were now nearly 100 feet ahead and
closing in fast. Their lines began to collapse and encircle us; I quickly
drew my sword and held it ready for impact. Closer and closer we got,

our horses at full speed. Then finally, I lost control. When I drew aim, I swung hard and fast. My anger became rage and rage became fury. I began slicing all who came close. But that was my mistake- leaving my guard down left me vulnerable and nearly lost me my arm. Instead, one of the men sliced through my side plate cutting a deep slice into my ribs. Quickly my rage became fear, an immense rush of anxiety. Looking back, I could see master being surrounded, and yet he looked to me and shook his head. "Leave, leave now!" He shouted as I kept riding. Clutching my stomach, I leaned forward and let the horse take me east.

This was very painful to hear, but within a few minutes, I could hear his final screams of pain as he succumbed to the hoard. I paced for ages away from the villa, and when the sun showed signs of the evening I had to pick up the pace. But riding became monotonous and it felt like I was never actually going to reach my destination. And eventually my morale wore thin, and I stopped riding. Upon dismounting, my horse walked to the side and began to eat the grass. Before it got darker, I pitched a small tent and started a fire. I had some food, but not much of anything. Just some salted pork from the town butcher, and a few apples for the horse. Quickly night overcame our camp and we had nothing much more to do than sleep.

In the morning I woke up much earlier than I had anticipated, pretty much as dark as it had been when I fell asleep. The air was cool and misty which made the armor feel stiff. After some stretching it loosened up enough to remount. With haste, I ate and tended to the horse, and then left for Rome. Within an hour or so, the riding felt much more leisurely and quiet, which led to some cynical introspection. I felt guilty for feeling so peaceful but how could one feel so at home in such a time of grief? But my attention was broken once more, however this was much more nice for a attention breaker. On the horizon was another town, much larger than ours. If I had a guess, I'd say it was Veii, the old Etruscan town. It seemed quite different from other Roman designs but pleasant it was. But as I got closer things began to seem odd.

Nearing the north side of the town, I saw a large group of men in front of the gates on foot. The men were armed with various weapons, and many were of different groups. There were triarii, retiarii, and even Roman soldiers in the group. They were standing as if ready for a battle, but as I looked to the hills, I could see why. Coming down on foot was a large mass of brigands this time with real armor. The men at the gates stood still, and I wanted to go with, but I had no time for that and plus all of my strength was depleted in the other battle. I had to get inside soon and get my wounds treated. So instead I turned and headed for the southern entrance.

Meeting me at the southern gate was a large mob of disorganized Roman soldiers who gave me a hard time. They began questioning my presence here and why I had returned. They were surprised to hear that my town had been sacked as well, and they began to fear. But they relented and let me inside to get help. When I went inside the gate was shut and locked, no one was allowed in or out of the towns walls. For now I was safe, but who knows what they'll do to Veii if they can destroy Ostia so easily.

As I came closer to the doctor's hut, I felt my head begin to spin and could feel my body become weak. I held on to my horse for dear life until I made it to the hitching post. When I let go of the horse, my legs buckled and I collapsed, unconscious.

***

I woke up in such a stupor, one like I'd never had before. My head pounded, I had the shakes, and my whole body was sore to the touch. As I looked around, my eyes became less foggy and my vision returned. With the extra clarity came the realization that I was alone. The blackness of the hut was actually just the remains of the burnt wood and fabric. In the back of the remains of the hut layed two skeletons of feet poking around the marble surgical table. This alone made me lean over and puke. Quickly I got up and looked around my surroundings. The hut was nearly gone, burnt to the ground with small smoldering poles still holding firm. My mind was beginning to worry, but I had no time for that, so I made my way to the old doorway. Walking out of the ruins was quite a sight; the whole town was smoldering, and so I looked down at my body and hands. And with tears in my eyes, I saw all the burns on my arms and legs, god only knows what's under my armor. But one thing I noticed was the old wound was now cautourized by the flames.

The whole situation was dire, and I needed to scavenge for something that would allow me to get away and treat my wounds.

Looking around the town was exhausting but very easy as everything was almost above eye level now that everything was burnt. By the time I made it back to the hut, I had only gathered some wraps, herbal oil, and some basic food. As I sat down, I remembered my horse and when I realized he wasn't here, I began to cry and weep wildly. My horse, my body, my emotions, and my head were all messed up. This whole situation was awful and there was nothing I could do to fix it. Eventually the fatigue of the emotional stress knocked me out cold.

***

Morning was much better, the soreness was still there, but it had subsided. For a moment, I stood trying to remember the day or even the hour, but in vain. Before I did anything else, I cleaned my wounds and scars and covered my burns with herbal oil. It was taught to me that many of the herbal medicines would stave the pain and allow for gladiators to continue fighting even with semi-extreme wounds. Then I wrapped my whole exposed body with linen wraps. After an hour of drinking ashy well water and eating burnt bread, I began to scavenge again. However, this time I made it to the northern side. Upon arrival, I found most of the homes were still in tact and almost untouched by raiders. I assume now that the brigands sieged and burnt the southern half when the gates were closed. But then if they didn't take anything, what was their purpose? A question that would take hold of my mind for the next few days. My emotions took over again, and I began cautiously entering the buildings and searching. In a few I found coins and food, as well as clothes and tools. On my first round, I got myself a travel sack and filled it with only essentials, which meant medical supplies, food, and any extra clothing for when I got to town. After about an hour of searching, I finally reached the very edge of the town near the gate. The gate was still sealed, however the door to a house was open wide. As I approached, I drew my sword and tiptoed to the doorway as I peered in. The small atrium and hallway were void of any life. I slowly made my way towards the bedrooms where each step became an increasing whisper of sound. With every foot gained, clarity ensued and so I was only able to make out what I was hearing once I was only but five feet away. Snoring began filling my ears which quickened my pulse for a moment. I pressed my back against the wall slowly careful not to creak, and ever so slowly peeked an eye in. With a quick glance, I could make out two men on cots, another three on the floor, and one more against a wall. With a quick transfer to the opposing wall, I peered into the room adjacent and had a similar sight. They must've taken refuge in here to assure there were no survivors. With my pulse quickening, I had to leave and fast. I turned to the door and hugged the walls all through the atrium. As I came to the door, I heard some faint rustling from the bedroom, to which I leapt outside.

With my heart beating out of my chest, I ran all the way down the main street until I found a break in the city wall. The break led out to a small hillside horse ranch, quaint in nature but new in age. Outside was a pile of burnt corpses from the raid, but inside the stables were many fine steeds, but at the end was a beautiful black horse. Making my way into the stable-side, I began layering the tack, carefully taming the horse. He responded hesitantly but with some coaxing he relented.

Mounting the horse, I took a moment to sit and calm myself; I realized that I had not taken even a single moment to assess what had just happened. I had been attacked and followed, my family included and on top of all of that, I was burned in a fire that I managed to sleep through. If that's not enough then I don't know, but I can't believe I was still there.

***

It was a late sun, the air was humid and less pungent than the countryside. My back faced the sky and my face was buried in the horses mane. Groggily groaning, I mustered the strength to shift my head sideways to see the road. My head bounced up and down to match the cadence of the horses gallop. With my vision clearing, I noticed the outlines of large walls spanning the horizon. As I pulled myself up a bit, I saw the 'SPQR' text upon the streamers upon the walls. "*I am safe finally, free from brigands,*" I said to myself nearing the gate.

"Hold foreigner!" the projected voice boomed from above. As the horse slowed, a small group of soldiers came and checked the horse.

"He is badly injured sir, seems like he is a survivor of the coastal raids," the guard shouted to those above.

"Very well, send him to the medicus and get a translator if needed. Bring the scribe, the iudex will need to hear this, " the voice slowly faded and so did my consciousness.

***

Days must've gone by, the walls went through cycles of light and dark. Above my cot I stared, watching the dust float through the air. My body was sore and badly burnt, and where the armor was melted on, they had cut and removed to allow my skin to reheal. It was painful and agonizing but with each day that passed, I felt better and better. After losing count, time became untrackable.

Upon my final day in rest, the medicus came in and sat beside me, "How are you fairing? You've been here for nearly two weeks, and it is time you get out before you get stuck. " This medicus was alpha and stern, keeping eye-contact for the duration of the pause.

"Of course, I must take today to start leaving my bead, and on dawn I'll be gone. " I looked up at the ceiling again, trying to think about where to find my family.

As I sat up, a knock echoed through the halls, followed by the fast footsteps of the nurses. In the distance, a low grumble of a man could be heard, but muffled with these walls. The nurses seemed eager and were talking quite fast. Just mumbles from my end, frustrating when you can move closer to hear. From the end of the hall, one of the nurses ran and burst into my room.

"Brutus, yes?" she whispered to me.

"Yes, but why the suspect behaviour? Has someone broken in?" I looked seriously at her, trying to decode her eyes.

"You have a visitor, a very wealthy man by the name of Erastus. Marcus Aedifexus Erastus of Macedonia." She looked quite worried but wouldn't budge.

From the sounds echoing through the halls, I could hear that this visitor party was quite large. Before I could gather myself, the family emerged looking gaunt, all but one of course. In front of my family stood a tall lanky man, much larger than Master Artorius, smiling with a very shy grin. He was very proper, but seemed to be a bit alien to the family.

"How are you faring Brutus? You seem to be in quite the shape," one of the older slaves chuckled.

"Fine Alaerius, just charred on the edges." I smiled back at him. "More importantly tho, how are you all? And whom am I in the presence of?" I looked at Mistress Ophelia.

Locking eyes she said, "We are just fine, Artorius' cousin Sabinus Sabinus has taken the role of man of the house for the time being. The family is set to vote on the estate later on this week."

Sensing the fear in her eyes, I left the subject for later. From around the back of the crowd came a large and pudgy *boy*, seemingly important. With his beefy chest puffed out, he boomed over to me, "You, slave! Venī me! When will you be fit enough to work again?"

"I'm sorry to disappoint sir, but I am no longer a slave; rather, I am a free man." I looked back at him, waiting for a response. At first he seemed very shocked that I had spoken to him so clearly, but his expression soon became very twisted.

"And what proof do you bring? Do you have a sign or seal? Your weak father is gone now." He leaned in, a sign of a challenge.

"No sir, my tablet was burned in the siege of Veii. But the scribe was witness. " I remained calm, as to not cause more tension.

"Is this true?" He pointed to our scribe.

"Aye."

"I'll give you this week to find that tablet, or else you're mine." He quickly turned and stomped off, to which the many eyes in the room now shone on me.

***

The next day was spent in the forum with Syphax, finding new equipment for the forge room. Passing each stall was intriguing, many faces and many backgrounds from which they came. I had heard so much about this western city, from the depths of the far east, many would talk about their aspirations of someday reaching this heavenly land. But here I am, nearly a decade later, standing here and yet still I have to struggle for my own life.

Syphax and I spent a while taking inventory of the traders in town this week, hopefully we could set him up a new forge to work in very soon; I didn't want him to leave the family if Sabinus was to sell him. But all of this thinking and walking was making me hungry.

Drawing near the butcher and cook tents, I could smell the beef in the air, drawing me nearer. Sitting down at the stone table, I conferred with Syphax on what to get.

"I reckon that stew is good, or even the stuffed chicken." He was practically watering at the mouth.

"Here," I said extending my hand. "Take a few denarii and grab us a bowl or two, I'll find a place to sit." Leaving Syphax behind, I stepped toward the street, looking around at the grey stone tables. From down the road came a cacophony of sounds, mostly grief-stricken shrieks and sobs. Leaning around the column, I could just make out a wagon with bodies shoulder to shoulder, coming closer to me, I was just barely able to catch sight of the crest on the shoulder. Following the golden tress across the chestplate and up to the epaulettes, around the swirl plate covering the underarm, and right up to the golden eagle upon the neck brace. That was oddly familiar. From behind me a hand rooted itself on my shoulder; Syphax whispered.

"I know this must be very sentimental, but look at that armor! It looks like the set that was given to you from master Artorius." His eyes widened and looked to me. I could sense his insecurity.

"I must get closer, give me one moment." As the words left my mouth, I quickly parted to safety of the wall, down to the side of the cart. Peering in from the back, I could see they were not in fact dead. Rather they were very badly wounded, and swaddled like babies.

"Master Artorius! Is that you?" I whispered to him, leaning in as to hide my face.

Rolling to his side, the man took a moment, groggily opening his eyes and looking me up and down. Once he gained some sense of his surroundings and muttered,

"Brutus! How delighted I am to see you... have you seen the magistrate yet?" He smiled wide.

"Sir, you have a gaping hole in your side and you're here asking me if I talked to magistrate, how selfless!" He chuckled and groaned as he sat himself up.

"Well, did you?" He looked around at the crowds near the forum.

"Well, no actually, the fire at Veii incinerated the tablet and my armor is a bit damaged." I looked down and began to feel my eyes get heavy.

"Non-sense, when I make it to the house I will sort this out. You hear?" I nodded and walked closer, all before a guard put his hand in front of me.

"Stay back." The guard pushed me away before the horses began to march the caravan up the street. Waving to master Artorius, I turned and headed for the table with Syphax.

***

Life in the city was certainly weird, filled with varieties of people from all over the empire, all here for the same reasons. At least that's what I thought. Chores became quite hard and unpleasant with the new son in the family. He was demanding and very harsh with punishments, and since I had no proof of my freedom, he milked me for every ounce of energy I had. The father did nothing but sit in the town counsel at his elaborate dinner parties with the other aristocrats. Oh, how master would despise this.

It was now Friday, two days before my judgement day. Today I had a break from work and chores since Sabinus is on a trip today. For today's excursion, I chose to stay downtown and find some friends.

My way downtown was quite a walk, Marcus Erastus had built his house far from the forum, for the same reason many others hated the city: homeless. Passing many of the smaller homes and shops was quite interesting, seeing the hustle-bustle lifestyle of many of the citizens was inspiring in a way. By the time I made it to the forum, it was already noon and the sun was in full affect. The sweat flowed like the Tiber river, slowly draining my energy. Making to the steps was a relief for the town slaves set up the cloth canopies. Not sure what to do, I sat down and hung my head in my hands.

For a while, I sat feeling overwhelmed by all of this chaos. The fact that my ticket of freedom was almost over and the man who secured it was in recovery. And with the anxiety came guilt, mainly because I had failed to tell mistress Ophelia that Artorius had not died. It made me feel selfish; why should I bear such hopeful news when they suffer? Some minute thought, however, drew me away from my daydreaming and led me to a peculiar idea. Getting up from my folded position, I made my way to the fountain. Reaching my head towards the water, I quickly took a drink and gave my face a wash.

I ran all the way to the medicus, hopeful to see master. At first I couldn't find them, but after some questioning someone was willing to help. It was now noon and the air in the city was getting quite humid. Walking felt like a herculean task, but once there I stood at the front entrance. Staring at the door, I felt something different than normal. Instead of the invigorating feeling of wanting to be free and on my own volition, I felt a sort of sad depressing feeling of fear. I felt that it might be a bad idea to be free. But then I slapped myself, for I had realized how defeating that would be and how my real family would've wanted this for me. So, step by step, I entered the stone building. Walking down the halls, I dragged my hands against the rough clay and concrete walls.

As the slave stopped in front of the doorway, I took a deep breath and head in.

"Brutus! I was wondering when you might show. Where are the others?" His smile went from full to half mast in a matter of seconds.

"Well, they aren't allowed to come this far across town, they live on the west side, near the harbor... " He cut me off forcefully.

"Nonsense, who is in charge? I thought I left my brother in command of the house?" He seemed quite displeased with my news.

"Well I'm afraid he has grown weak and gluttonous, always attending the parties of the candidates. Rather your cousin Sabinus is now in charge." I looked down at the floor.

"The boy!?" He nearly choked on his words, eyes bulging with surprise.

"Yes, but he won't recognize my freedom either, he wants proof. He dismissed our scribe." I began to get angry, talking about Sabinus fueled the hatred I had towards him.

Getting up off the bed, master Artorius rose to his booming height and straightened himself out. He beat his chest with his closed fist until he grunted.

Looking as serious as ever, he turned to me and said,

"Come now Brutus, it's time to take back what's ours."

Altered Perspective

The grass was soaked with dew on that cool, spring morning. I scanned the quiet yard, mesmerized by the light that bounced off the droplets. The heat of that soon to be warm day crept into the atmosphere. It had been so comfortable, but now, as the sun beat down on me, I knew that was about to change.

Soon, it was no longer pleasant in the morning and as the days passed, I realized I was growing up. Every day as I was allowed to explore a little more, I noticed different things about my lovely yard. How the trees were bent toward the sunlight, how at night, the moon would wash over the half of the yard where the raspberry bushes were planted, creating a hazy, purple glow. I cherished these days. The days before my life would permanently change.

***

On one hot summer day when spring had bid a farewell, I noticed the flowers were closer to the ground, nearly touching it. During that stretch of warm days, the rain didn't visit and the wind didn't whisper. The fatigue from the heat made me feel like mush. What felt like almost every morning, a man would come into my neighbor's yard sitting on a loud moving object. A woman always followed the path of torn up grass using a pointy object to collect it all. The object must have had as many points on it as the blades of grass in the lawn. She would always follow behind him, moving her tool back and forth against the ground. Each time she did this, the pile of grass grew a little bigger. Then, after they were done with the neighbor's yard, they would stroll over to mine.

I was horrified. My siblings and I didn't know what to do. The woman seemed so nice in her yard and yet, when she came over to mine, the clawed object was much bigger than I had expected and I thought it would surely kill us all. I watched her as she moved the object back and forth against the parched ground. She was wearing something on her head, blocking the view of her face. I wished I could have caught her eye and glared at her for a long time. Maybe that would have made her understand; coming over with that pointy thing was very rude. It scared us.

***

Life was fast-paced for me. It whizzed by as if I had no conception of time. One day the air was cool, the next it was sweltering. One particularly sunny day, there was not a cloud in the sky. I would remember that day very vividly. My mother had a lesson to teach my brothers and sisters and me. She was solemn, which confused me. How could she be upset when the sun was out above us? At the time, I thought there was no way she would turn that day around for me. My mom didn't seem to care, delving into a deep conversation to which there was no way out.

"Summer is upon us. I feel that as your mother, it is my duty to teach you about the world we live in."

I was afraid.

Hoping she was about to retell her famous winter story, I tried so hard to turn the situation around. This story was told to me when I was born. A heroic tale of how she endured the cold. She described weather called snow as, "white and fluffy like a cloud coming down from the sky to say hello." She explained how pretty it was, how it would blanket the landscape and change the color of the yard. It was a scary, yet beautiful, time; I liked that, the contrast.

I drifted back into reality as soon as I realized she was continuing.

"For starters, as you all have noticed, it is gradually getting warmer out. Just feel the warm sun!" she was animated as she tried her best to engage us.

"I...I'm sorry. I shouldn't delay my message. It will only make it harder." Make what harder? Okay. So not the snow story, I thought. "... you may not know everything that will happen in your lifetime, " she continued.

I felt like I had hit the ground. I was immediately running through a million possible outcomes for the ultimate fall of our species. This was it. We would all be wiped out by some killer monster.

"It is my duty to teach you that...one day...we will all be gone. What I mean is, we can't live forever. There comes a time where we have to die. Please don't worry," she continued, "it must happen to everyone." She was wary of continuing as if she wanted to make sure we could cope with the news. I had never seen her like that before. Shaking as she told us this. Terrified.

My sister couldn't keep quiet any longer. "What? This doesn't make sense. It just...I mean...I thought you wouldn't let anything happen to us!" she rustled with all the willpower she could muster.

"This is a joke, right?" my brother echoed my sister's concerns. "Nope. No. It's not a joke. I see. Mom is letting us down. She was never going to protect us."

My sister continued to be struck with disbelief, "You can't do anything? We just have to accept this?"

Shortly after, all of my siblings would be yelling and looking around at one another in doubt. I was deeply saddened. The news wasn't easy to handle. I knew that they were just lashing out and that they would get over it soon enough, but at the time, it was so difficult to understand.

"It is plain and simple," my mother tried to calm us down in her trembling voice. "There is no escaping it. This is what I want you to know. It is a fact. But it is not what should be taken away from this conversation. Knowing this, every one of you should appreciate life more. There is no telling how many days we have left at any given moment in our lives. I love all my children and this is why this cannot be kept from you all anymore. Everyone has to learn it at some point." She finished by making sure we knew there was no escaping this lesson. She'd have to teach us at some time.

That night, the air cooled from the earlier heat that encased the yard. I assessed the lawn, paying attention to the moonlight that reflected off the pine tree. The lighting cast over the yard always intrigued me, but that night, my mother's words blared repeatedly.

I was crushed. I agreed with my sister and brother. I always thought my mother would protect our family from harm, no matter what. I thought I would be able to live a life void of fear. Now, things had changed. My perspective had been altered. I didn't like change. I never did. I never would.

The weeks passed and summer trudged on, the heat rising up, creating swirls against the hard, jet black ground in the distance. My sisters and brothers and I played outside nearly every day; my face radiated happiness as we danced under the sun. Some days it was so hot, I felt like my skin was wrinkling up. The raspberry bush exuded a sense of sorrow, half of the fruit scrunched, the other half littered on the ground below. It hadn't rained in days and the grass had changed color from a soft green to a prickly yellow. I thought the heat would never break. Now, in retrospect, I shouldn't have hoped the weather would change. Once it did, I wished it would switch back.

***

Soon, the colors of my yard would gradually shift; the earth couldn't decide whether to stay warm or not. Waking up that fall morning, light illuminated what was left of the flowers. As the day progressed, clouds rolled in and ate the sun. I couldn't comprehend what was going on. As the wind whipped past my face I glared up at the sky, angry at what it was doing to that perfect day.

No sooner had a few moments passed, then the rain came, torrential and unrelenting. At first, I was relieved and optimistic. The raspberry bush would be happy again, the grass back and prettier than ever. I couldn't wait until the storm passed so the yard could return to it former vibrancy.

Smaller than all my brothers and sisters, I was taken by the wind and swung left, right, left again. I pleaded to my mom for help. There was no protection against the rain. If I could have hid from the storm I would have, but I was frozen by panic and there was nowhere to hide.

"Help!" my sister was spinning around to find anyone available for assistance. I knew she was behind me but as soon as I turned around, she was gone.

"Where are you?" I pleaded. I couldn't project any louder, no sound would come out.

I thoroughly surveyed the dismal scene desperately searching, but couldn't find her. The wind was spinning me around as the world caved in on me. There was one place I hadn't looked. There. Below me. My sister lay on the ground battered by the wind.

I tried to scream, "No!" She was motionless. I didn't want to believe the simple truth that was slowly eating away at me, begging to be noticed.

"Wake up! Wake up. Please, please, wake up." I was competing against the pitter-patter of the rain and I knew it was no use. She wasn't coming back.

She was...gone. That lonely word was always so devoid of meaning to me until now. Now it meant something and I couldn't stop repeating it.

***

It had been awhile since the storm and I continued to mourn with my family. I remembered my mother's words that summer day, "...there is no telling how many days we have left..." That was true; my sister never expected to die that day.

My body drooped toward the ground. I didn't know how to cope with the pain. I had never felt this way before, like a withered up pile of nothing.

All too quickly the sun would peak into the lawn and slide down the edge of the house, engulfing it in gray. The days felt shorter than ever. Maybe it was because of the greif. Maybe the sun was playing hide and seek with the sky, I couldn't tell either way.

Come to think of it, I didn't feel good altogether. I thought I could push it aside but soon, it became too apparently obvious. I knew it from the day the dew on the grass stopped appearing, these would be my last days. My mother was quieter than usual, distraught. She had lost her daughter to the storm and now I had fallen ill. The deep admiration she had for me poured out into the open air, filling me with hope. My mom wouldn't let me die.

***

As that days came and went I settled into the idea that I would not let my mom save me. I would let myself go. My skin shriveled up...I wasn't like that before. Every passing day, I was feeling myself die; I couldn't live like that.

In tears, my mom was right by my side. Even if she wanted to save me, she could never do anything to help. It all came down to me.

One day, I couldn't hang on any longer. I felt like I was falling. I fell so far and so fast that I thought my skin would burn clean off. I was leaving the world, just like my mother told me would happen.

***

Lying in my yard, white snow floats from the light gray sky, lately, it hasn't been sunny. It is as quiet as that first morning in spring. It's come full circle. I guess life is like that.

My life has been grand, though I wish it was longer. I wish the days would return when my sisters and brothers and I would play outside, when the sun shined down and warmed us.

The snow is encasing me now and I'm looking up at my mom. She is weeping, the last time I will ever witness her express an emotion. Before falling, I was shaking from the cold, now, even though the snow is covering me that has stopped. It's odd to me because I know it's cold, but now, it's like I'm numb.

The memories of my brothers and sisters and I dancing in the wind come rushing back now. Waves of misery blanket over me like the falling snow. My memories won't cease to remind me of my young self, running through scenes of my life back then. The dangers that life would bring were insignificant at the time, a mere blade of grass in a large yard. I was innocent. Free. And right in this moment, as fast as a day going from light to dark, a realization comes to me: I had to learn about things I didn't want to. I had to experience loss. I had to...grow up.

The sky is a soft ashy grey like the bunnies that would hop across my yard when the air was warm. What a time that was. Today there is a great contrast; the clouds look sad, their tears crystallized by the cold air. I remember my mom's heroic snow story now. The snow does look beautiful, yet as I'm slowly drifting away from reality, it is making me grow sadder with every landing snowflake. They float down in waves of varying intensity mocking my newfound disdain. I shake on the ground as the wind pushes me this way and that. Even with sadness toward the white fluff, it has actually come to protect me from the force of the wind. As the last snowflake is silently gliding above, a sense of peace overcomes me. I hope that one day I will return to this earth, but what do I know, I'm just a leaf.